LOVE

A Novel of Grief and Desire

Jefferson R. Blackburn-Smith

Black Rose Writing | Texas

©2022 by Jefferson R. Blackburn-Smith
All rights reserved. No part of this book may be reproduced, stored in a retrieval system or transmitted in any form or by any means without the prior written permission of the publishers, except by a reviewer who may quote brief passages in a review to be printed in a newspaper, magazine or journal.

The author grants the final approval for this literary material.

First printing

This is a work of fiction. Names, characters, businesses, places, events, and incidents are either the products of the author's imagination or used in a fictitious manner. Any resemblance to actual persons, living or dead, or actual events is purely coincidental.

ISBN: 978-1-68513-085-5
PUBLISHED BY BLACK ROSE WRITING
www.blackrosewriting.com

Printed in the United States of America
Suggested Retail Price (SRP) $21.95

Love is printed in Garamond Premier Pro

Cover design by Zach Tyler

*As a planet-friendly publisher, Black Rose Writing does its best to eliminate unnecessary waste to reduce paper usage and energy costs, while never compromising the reading experience. As a result, the final word count vs. page count may not meet common expectations.

For Denise, who taught me what it means to love someone
and to be loved by them.

ACKNOWLEDGEMENT

Thank you to my early readers, Denise, Richard Gilbert, and Joan Dempsey, for your insight and encouragement. Special thanks to Linda Langton and her team at Langton's International for seeing something in this story worth bringing into the light of day, and for their patience and willingness to work with me through draft after draft. I am truly grateful.

Also by Jefferson R. Blackburn-Smith

The Ogre Prince

Forgiveness

Retribution

www.jeffersonblackburnsmith.com

LOVE

CHAPTER ONE

At least the bitch is dead, now.

Or soon will be, Ed Gideon corrected himself as he pulled into the hospital parking lot. It could not be a coincidence that Andie Love tried to kill herself so close to the anniversary of the accident, but that did not make him feel any better. Nothing made him feel better.

Northwest Christian was a brightly lit blight upon the otherwise dark countryside. It was where they had brought him after the accident. Lisa, too. He was treated for a concussion and a compound fracture of his right leg. He had known the entire time the emergency room doctors had worked on him that Lisa was dead, without a moment of unconsciousness to forget.

His phone, visible from where it leaned in the cupholder on the console, read May 3, 2010. How did that happen? Only a heartbeat ago it was 1983 and he and Lisa were about to be married. They were the couple who had been destined for fifty, sixty, even seventy years of marriage until Andie Love had driven drunk and destroyed everything.

Ed sat in his pickup truck, his body aching, a weird echo of what he had felt in the days after the accident, Lisa's voice in his head. *She's only a kid,* Lisa was saying, *younger than our girls.* Ed sighed, turned off the truck, and got out.

Sergeant John Smith was standing outside the ER entrance, smoking a cigarette. He was twenty pounds overweight, with thinning brown hair, wearing a suit rather than his Highway Patrol uniform. The badge he wore on a cord around his neck looked like something you would see the cops wearing on an episode of *Dexter*. John Smith was one of the officers who had responded to the accident.

"Who the hell decided this was so important you woke me up in the middle of the night?" Ed demanded.

Smith shrugged. "That was me. Give her five minutes and you can go home."

"Wonderful." Ed hoped his sarcasm came through loud and clear.

They walked down a brightly lit, antiseptic hall, the TV from the ER lobby selling cleaning supplies loudly enough that Ed could hear the pitch until the elevator doors squeaked shut. The third floor was much quieter. Lights were off in most of the patient rooms. They went through a sliding glass door into the ICU. Smith stopped outside a room, then motioned Ed to go inside. A small fluorescent wall lamp lit the room. Andie Love lay on the bed, but no one else was in the room. A jacket dangled from the chair next to the bed.

Ed stared; the room suddenly too warm. Andie Love looked tiny in the hospital bed, hooked up to a heart monitor, IV, and other machinery, a translucent oxygen tube snaking across her face. Her eyes were deeply sunken, her pallid face skeletal. The limp blonde hair that framed her face needed to be washed. Her lips were colorless, blending in with her ashen features. There was no life about her, none of the arrogance he had felt watching her walk into the court room when he had seen news reports about the trial. Ed had skipped the trial. The first deputy on the scene had failed to properly mirandize her, so what had been the point of going to the trial? Andie Love had only been convicted of reckless operation.

Ed looked at Andie Love and tried to feel something: anger, rage, even satisfaction that she was dying. This woman had killed the love of his life. Two years later, he still dreamed of Lisa all the time, and frequently woke up in deep soul-emptying grief, but at this moment he did not feel a thing.

"Do you hate her?" a soft voice asked.

Ed started and turned. A young Black woman stood just inside the door to the room, her cinnamon face surrounded by a mass of dark tight curls, not quite an afro. She looked too young to be a nurse and was wearing jeans and a hoodie. Did hospitals still have candy stripers?

"Do you?" she asked again.

"No," Ed said, shaking his head, too confused to be polite. "Who are you?"

"I'm Bobbi," the teen said shyly. "I'm her daughter."

"Do what?" Ed asked.

"I know, I'm Black. It throws everyone off. I never met my dad, but I'm guessing he was the culprit."

The daughter was slight like her mom, a few inches over five foot tall. Her face was puffy from crying, and that reminded Ed of his daughters in the days after the accident and suddenly he did feel anger at the woman in the bed: how can you do this to your own daughter?

"I'd hate her," the girl said. "I do hate her." Her voice broke.

Ed took a step towards the girl, then stopped. He was not here to comfort her. "You wanted to see me?" he asked.

Bobbi nodded. "She left a note and asked me to... to talk to you. She wanted you to know that she knew she was at fault for what happened. It was part of her AA work, making amends to those she had hurt, and you were the one person she couldn't ever reach out to and apologize."

Ed shrugged. "Thanks. I'm sorry for your loss." He edged past the teen towards the hall.

"Wait."

Ed turned around. The girl stared at him. Her eyes were a startling shade of light blue that gave her gaze an intensity Ed found unsettling.

"I don't know how to say this," she said, "because it sounds awful. But because of what she did—the wreck—I got my mom back. She was a drunk for as long as I could remember. Growing up, I hated her: hated her drinking, hated the men she brought home, hated never having money for rent and always moving. She quit drinking after she killed your wife, and I got my mom back. We had to live with Gram for a while, but she was sober and got a job, and we got an apartment, and I had a real mom."

"I'm glad for you," Ed said. *Why is she telling me this?*

"But it only came because she killed your wife," the girl said. The tears were silent, running slowly down her face. She did not wipe them away. "I was happy for the first time in my life because your wife was dead. Mom was happy too, and I think that's why she killed herself. It was wrong for us to finally be happy because of what it cost you. I'm sorry."

"You have nothing to apologize for," Ed said, wishing he had not come. He did not need to know this. "Where is your grandmother?"

The girl shook her head. "She died in February. Pneumonia. She was right here in ICU for three days. We thought she was getting better. Mom sent me to school that morning and Gram died an hour later."

"What about the rest of your family?"

"Gram was it."

"So, what happens to you?"

"I guess I'll go back in foster care, like when mom was drinking. I've been placed before when she was really bad."

Ed nodded. "Look I've got to go..."

"She wanted me to ask you one other thing," the girl said.

"What?"

"She wanted me to ask you to come to her funeral. You can say something about how her drinking destroyed your life, or you can just sit outside in your car. She doesn't expect you to mourn her death, but she wants you to know she really is dead and won't be troubling you anymore."

"I'll think about it," Ed said.

"No, you won't," the teen said with a sad smile, "I wouldn't either." She went and sat in her chair, near her mother's bed.

"What's your name again?" Ed asked.

The girl looked up at him, her eyes piercing. "Bobbi."

"Bobbi?"

"Yeah. Bobbi and Andie. She and Gram loved boys' names. God only knows why."

"I'm sorry for your loss, Bobbi."

"Thank you."

Ed turned to leave. Sergeant Smith was leaning against the wall a few feet away, watching the two of them, a tight smile on his face. Ed resisted a sudden urge to punch the man. Knowing the girl was hurting was too much like being with his own girls after the accident. He left the ICU and headed for the bank of elevators, Smith trailing behind him.

Ed pushed the button for the elevator. "What happens to the girl?"

"Children's Services will come get her sometime today."

"After her mom dies?"

"Depends," Smith said. "If Love dies soon, but I'd guess they'll be out here by mid-morning."

"You'd take the girl away before her mom dies?"

"Once we put the call in, they get here when they get here."

"Well don't put the call in until after Andie Love dies."

"I didn't think you'd care," Smith said.

The elevator opened. Ed stepped in, waving the officer away. "Just because that woman destroyed my life," he said, "don't make me out to be a monster. I don't want revenge. It doesn't bring Lisa back. And I don't want her kid to suffer needlessly. She's going to lose her mom. Don't make it worse for her just because you can." The doors slid shut.

• • •

Back in his truck, Ed glanced at his watch. 5:30 am. Not worth going home, but too early for the office. He pulled out of the parking lot and jumped on the freeway to go down a couple of exits. He could stop at Bob Evans for breakfast and still get to the office early.

Bob Evans opened at six, but when he pulled into a parking spot outside the restaurant, a young man was sweeping the walk and beckoned him to come in.

"Good morning, hon," a matronly hostess said much too cheerfully as he walked in the door. Lisa would have said the woman's hair was a shade too-red. She sat him at a table near the window where he would see the sun coming up and was back a minute later with a metal coffee urn.

"Becca will be your server, hon," the hostess said. His oldest daughter was a Becca, named Rebecca for her grandmother but shortened by her friends. Ed preferred Rebecca, but he'd never tell his daughter that.

Ed opened the menu but did not read it. Lisa had always teased him about having favorites, and she was right. He only ordered one breakfast at Bob Evans, the western omelet with wheat toast and hash browns and a side of sausage. Why experiment if you knew what you enjoyed?

Becca showed up at the table with a second pot of coffee, blushing prettily as she set it down. Her dark hair was pulled back in a ponytail that swished wildly with each shake of the head. She grinned, lighting up her green eyes.

"I'll take that back," she said with a giggle. She took his order efficiently, but Ed cursed silently when he caught her looking down at his left hand as she picked up the extra coffee carafe. He had taken to removing his wedding ring when he went to bed, a first step towards leaving it off altogether. He was surprised he left the ring on his nightstand, but he had been a little disoriented when his phone rang at three in the morning. Of course, he noticed someone like Becca. She was very beautiful, and her eyes sparkled with intelligence, but it was unlikely she would go out with an older man.

His girls, Becca and Sandy, were all over him about the ring and dating in general. Ed had no desire to spend the rest of his life alone. He was only forty-eight, but the idea of dating again, after being married for twenty-five years, just seemed overwhelming. How do you even ask someone out these days?

Ed was on his second cup of coffee when Becca brought his omelet. He ate mechanically, caught up in his thoughts. Although it was only Monday morning, the week had already been going badly before Smith called. Ed had been working on a quote for months, for a remodel job he thought would be perfect for his company. William Sanderson, who owned one of the biggest ad agencies in Columbus, wanted to build a two-story addition, with a new kitchen, master bath suite and sunroom. Ed had come in at $67,000 for a beautiful addition, slightly smaller than what Sanderson wanted, but with all the details he had requested, and within his budget. Ed had pitched the final quote last Wednesday, sure from the excited response of Sanderson's wife, Jane, that he would get the job, but Sanderson had said in an email late Saturday that he was going with a competitor.

Ed hated losing any job he bid, but he respected it when a client felt someone else better met their needs. Sanderson was going with Parkhurst to save five thousand dollars. If Sanderson had wanted cheap crap, he should have said so.

"Is everything okay with your meal?" Becca asked, breaking his reverie. She was a little too close to the table, and had crouched down on one knee, giving him a perfect view of her cleavage. Ed looked up at her face and she smiled, her cheeks flushed, clearly gratified that she had caught his attention. Ed blushed at being caught and nodded. He pointed at her name tag as cover. "I have a daughter named Becca," he said.

Becca laughed and shook her head, making her ponytail swish. "I'll let you in on a secret," she said. "I prefer Rebecca. They had the name tag in the back when I started, and it was so close that it seemed silly to order a new one. So here I'm Becca, but to the rest of the world I'm Rebecca."

"I'd be delighted to call you Rebecca," Ed said, embarrassed. Lisa would have called him out for his wandering eye.

"I'd like that. Can I get you anything else?"

Ed shook his head, looking away as she stood, fighting the urge to look at her breasts again. He watched as she walked away, surprised to feel his heart beating a little too fast.

"Whenever you're ready," Rebecca said a minute later, a broad grin on her face, leaving his check face down on the table. She had written *Rebecca* on the back of the check and drawn a smiley face. Ed ate at this Bob Evans every few weeks. He had seen Rebecca before but could not remember talking to her. She was behind the counter now, picking up someone else's order, but she kept glancing back at Ed's table. She was beautiful. Is that how you pick a date these days? In truth, Lisa's beauty had stopped Ed in his tracks the moment he saw her. He had seen her registering new students for orientation, and watched her until it was his turn to sign in. She was tall and lively, and he could not get her from his mind. He had approached her a week after move-in.

"Hey," he had said nervously, standing behind her in the cafeteria line, his heart pounding like a steam hammer. "Would you like to get a bite to eat sometime?"

Lisa had laughed, waving her arm to encompass the cafeteria. "Sorry, beat you to it."

Ed looked around quickly to see if anyone else had heard, furious with himself for being so awkward. He asked her out again, a few days later, but she said no again. She had sat with him while they ate, however.

"Look, I'm pre-med," she said. "My focus is school, not dating."

"Sure," Ed had said, but he was so happy she was sitting with him he did not consider it a rejection. They began to sit together at lunch several times a week. After a month, she finally agreed to go out with him. He was so nervous on their first date that he had not tried to hold her hand, let alone kiss her. On their second date, he still was not sure if she liked him or not, but their conversation was so easy that it felt natural to hold her hand on the way home from the movie. He still did not kiss her, though. That happened after a couple more dates, and she had kissed him.

Lisa had kissed him on the Oval, under a curtain of branches from a weeping willow tree. The kiss had gone on forever. When they finally broke apart to head back to the dorm, Ed had looked at Lisa and blurted out "I think I could marry you." She had laughed, but from that moment they were on a path that had seemed to rush them towards marriage. He had given up his plans to be an architect, dropping out of school after his junior year. Lisa had given up med school. She had been smart enough and had scored high enough on the MCAT to get in, but they had gotten married instead. His first job had been for a small remodeling firm. He had done design work and sales, and then started doing his own jobs on the side and within five years, about the time Becca was born, he went solo. Lisa had ended up as an administrator at a hospital, right there at Northwest Christian.

Ed lifted the little coffee pot, but it was empty. He turned to look for Rebecca. She was on a stool, behind the counter, reaching up to get something off a shelf, standing on her toes. Her calves, the back of her thighs and her ass were all taut and in sharp relief and Ed had a moment of longing he had not felt in two years. My God, he wanted to be with a woman again. Not just for sex, but that too. Ed missed the little things: the smell of Lisa's hair when she cuddled against him, the warmth of her body next to his when they spooned, just waking up next to her.

He felt Lisa's absence the most at moments like this. It was like having a black hole in his life where she should have been.

"I saw you holding your pot," a voice said, interrupting his thoughts. It was the hostess with the too-red hair. Her name badge said *Peggy*, so much of a cliché Ed almost laughed. He was about to ask Rebecca what she did for lunch, but Peggy had intervened.

"Thanks," Ed said after she refilled his cup. He turned his thoughts away from women and back to work. It was close to six thirty now, and Ed could be in the office in ten minutes. His breakfast had settled heavily in his stomach. He supposed it was because of the hospital. He should not have gone. The girl, Bobbi, was so brittle, just like his daughters had been at that age. He always thought his girls had been robbed of their final moments with Lisa, but how much more would it have hurt to sit with her and know she was dying?

Ed took his bill to the register, looking around for Rebecca, but she was not in sight. God's will, he thought as Peggy cashed him out, knowing he would not have really asked Rebecca out. A minute later he was in his truck and back on the outerbelt. He got off at the next exit, crossed the bridge and made an immediate left into his parking lot. He had been at this location for a decade. It had been a car dealership before he purchased it at auction for pennies on the dollar. He appreciated the glass front of the showroom, which was visible from the freeway, and the service department made a great staging area for his crews. It had been a great find.

A giant American flag was spotlighted at the top of a hundred-foot flagpole in front of the showroom. It was the one conceit Ed had kept from the dealership. The flags cost a couple grand each and he went through at least two a year, but it made Ed smile every time he saw it. What was he going to do with a giant flagpole anyway, but fly giant flags?

Several kitchen and bath displays were arranged in a wandering path through the showroom, ending at a replica of the rear of a two-story home with a deck and stone patio. Ed's office was inside the fake house and down a short hallway, away from the distraction of customers. It was a contradiction of success: the more successful the firm was, the less time he had to spend doing what he liked most, which was helping people change their homes into something that worked better for them.

• • •

Becca slipped in her earbuds and hit play on her iPod mini. Cathy, her roommate, teased her about being a farm girl who got up to milk the cows before sunrise every day, but Becca was like her father in more ways than one. She had been getting up at five thirty for as long as she could remember. She stopped on the porch long enough to redo her ponytail so it would not come loose during her run.

The sweet aroma of freshly cooked dough enveloped her as she trotted down her front steps and headed towards High Street. The Buckeye Donuts sign from next door gave the morning light more of a pink glow than the rising sun behind her. She started her run at a slow jog, crossing High Street against the light, preferring to warm up while running and stretch when she was done. Becca loved the apartment she and Cathy shared, but her dad hated it. He thought the landlord did not keep the building up and that her neighborhood was not safe. He did not like her running alone, either, but it was just too nice this morning to go work out in the gym, and she would have to walk through the neighborhood to get to the gym anyway, so what was the point in worrying? She found an early rhythm, her feet hitting the pavement lightly. She increased her speed, setting a pace she could keep up for forty minutes. She ran past the football stadium to the path by the river. Sandy was asleep in the tower dorm closest to the stadium. Dad had wanted Sandy to share the apartment with Becca and Cathy, but Becca had talked him out of it. Sandy was a Daddy's Girl, and no detail of Becca's life would be private.

Becca ran past the hospital complex, along the Olentangy River. Two giant construction cranes were silhouetted against the rising sun. The hospital had been a construction zone all three years Becca had been at school. Becca wondered if it would have made a difference if her mom had been brought to OSU Medical Center rather than Northwest Christian; OSU was a regional trauma center and had some of the best surgeons in the world. She had been living on campus, in the same building Sandy lived in now, when she had gotten the call. She could see it was her Uncle Jack calling, something unusual enough for her adrenaline to kick in, and then his soft voice revealed a horrible truth: Dad was in surgery and her mom was gone.

Becca still felt the strange weightlessness of that moment. "What do you mean, 'gone'?" she had asked.

"She's gone, honey," he repeated, his voice a whirlpool of agony and grief. "She didn't survive the accident."

Becca almost stopped running from the heaviness in her chest. Stop, she thought, trying to redirect her thoughts. She was thinking about her mom all the time recently. Dad had never really talked with her or Sandy about what had happened. He just said nothing could be done to save Mom, and that he was with her, holding her hand, when she died. Holding her damn hand, like it was a date, or she had cancer for years, or some other bullshit thing. Mom had not died, she been killed, murdered as surely as if that bitch had gotten out a gun and shot her.

Becca shook her head, trying to clear her mind, letting the run and the music do what it was intended to do. Increasing her pace again, she let the ache in her legs and chest consume her and burn away the sadness that seemed like a cocoon so many days. Dr. Merritt—Sylvia, as she insisted Becca call her—kept reminding her the grief was temporary, brought back into sharp relief because of the anniversary of her mom's death. Last year had been worse but knowing it would go away didn't make it any better when you were lost in it.

Actually, it did, and that was the point Sylvia kept making. Her dad had forced her to see a counselor and she had gone, grudgingly. Sylvia Merritt was in her late twenties, just a few years older than Becca. She sat next to Becca on a sofa in her office as Becca tried to explain her anguish.

"It's been four months," she had said, "but it just feels like yesterday."

"Four months isn't that different than yesterday when you're dealing with the death of a parent," Dr. Merritt had said. "You need to give yourself time."

"But I can't..."

"Can't what?"

"I can't stand feeling like this. Some days, I feel like I'm lost. I can't do anything."

"That's certainly not a good place to be. Let's plan to meet weekly, so we can talk through your feelings. Can we do that?"

Becca nodded. "Is there something you can prescribe? Something to make me feel better?"

Dr. Merritt had reached out to touch Becca gently on the arm. "You don't need pills to mask the way you feel, Becca. This is grief. As bad as it is, you're supposed to feel this way. What we need to work on is how to deal with these feelings, not how to cover them up."

Becca had left unsure if Sylvia knew what she was talking about, but of course, she had. She wondered if her dad realized she was still seeing Sylvia two years later. Some of her friends thought she should be over it by now, but it wasn't like she just talked about her mom. She had been having dreams recently, one in which she was little and lost Sandy at the fair, more in which she failed out of school, but in all of them she had to face her dad hating her for what she had done. Sylvia had pressed her at their last appointment—*why do you think he's going to reject you?*— and Becca had lied and said she did not know. Just knowing Sylvia was likely to ask again was making her anxiety worse.

High Street was busier as she returned home. CNN was visible on the TV through the porch window when she got back to her duplex. CNN meant Cathy was up; Cathy was a nursing major and a news junkie who got too emotionally involved in politics and whatever case of the week was being followed on *Nancy Grace*. She and Becca had lived together for three years, randomly assigned as roommates their freshman year. Cathy had saved her life as far as Becca was concerned. From her bed on the other side of the dorm room, Cathy had somehow heard Uncle Jack's call and had called her mom at six in the morning to come to campus and take Becca home. Cathy and her mom had come to the funeral. The other kids in her suite had acted weird when she came back to school after the funeral; only Cathy had been comfortable just hanging out with her. Life without Cathy was unimaginable.

Becca went to get a glass of juice from the fridge. A Labrador puppy adorned the 2010 calendar held to the front of the fridge with four big magnets. Four weeks until Memorial Day. Dad would want Becca and Sandy to come home for the three-day weekend. Her friend Leah had invited them to spend the weekend down in Hocking Hills. She really thought that would be more fun but was not sure how to talk to her dad about it. Another topic of conversation for Dr. Merritt later in the day.

• • •

Ed had just finished up with a client when his intercom buzzed. "Yes?"

"Ed, darling," Marjorie said. Marjorie was his executive assistant and had been his first employee. "Mr. Sanderson called while you were on the other line. Says he's rethought your proposal and wants you to call him around ten."

Ed shook his head. He would call Sanderson, but at this point he was not willing to negotiate. He had given him a good quote on the addition and if Sanderson wanted a quality job, he would take it. At a quarter of ten, he pulled the Sanderson file and reviewed the project. Ed felt irritated the minute he saw the floor plan and perspectives. He had put together a beautiful plan for an addition that would look like it had been part of the original house. A two-story addition was a difficult job, and one that included a new kitchen and master bath suite was just going to cost money if you wanted to do it right. He had already cut a significant amount of exterior work, including a stone patio and garden improvements to hit Sanderson's budget and there was just no way to cut anything else and have a job worth doing.

Ed dialed Sanderson's office number.

"This is Bill," Sanderson said, picking up on the second ring.

"Ed Gideon."

"I wanted to talk about our addition," Sanderson said. "I've been having second thoughts about Parkhurst."

"I understand. What can I do for you?"

"Getting down to brass tacks," Sanderson said. "I like that. I've been a businessman for over forty years, and I realize that sometimes the Sanderson Agency isn't the most competitive when it comes to pricing, and I've never wanted to let that keep me from serving a client, you know? So, what I was thinking..."

"Let me stop you right there. I think I know what you're looking for." Ed had been working on this quote since February and recognized Sanderson's habits, one of which was to tell a long story to prove a self-serving point.

"Great!"

"I can't do it. I gave you a quality bid at sixty-seven. I'd say that at this point, I wouldn't take the job unless we went back to the original specs and included the patio and garden work as well. That's another twelve grand."

"Really." Sanderson sounded stunned.

"Bill, I've made a commitment that I won't do a job that doesn't leave a customer with what they really want. When I spoke with you and Jane, it was clear you wanted an outdoor entertainment area as well as the addition. It's an investment not just in your home, but in your business, remember? You said that to me. So, if we're going to do it, let's do it right. If you sign a contract today, I can have you entertaining on your patio by the end of September, weather permitting."

"What were the terms again?"

"Twenty-five percent at signing, twenty-five when we start, twenty-five with drywall, and the balance on completion."

"So that's fifteen down?"

"Nineteen, with the patio."

"Jane will be thrilled," Sanderson said. "When can I sign the contract?"

"I'd be happy to drop by your office," Ed said. "Let me know what time."

"Four?"

"See you then," Ed said. Sanderson hung up.

Ed smiled. He had thought Jane had been sold on the job, and he had been right. He buzzed Marjorie on the intercom and asked her to print out a new copy of the original Sanderson contract and plans.

• • •

Ed drove downtown and parked in the garage underneath the Statehouse and then walked up two flights of stairs to the street. Ed found the Statehouse fascinating. An excellent example of the Greek Revival architectural style popular mid-19th century, the white marble building, with its unique, almost flat-topped rotunda, sat on a ten-acre, park-like setting that covered an entire city block. Finished during the Civil War, in part by Confederate prisoners-of-war, the Statehouse was a beautiful piece of history surrounded by steel and glass towers.

Ed hurried across High Street with a crowd of people. Sanderson Communications occupied an entire floor of the Huntington Center, on the corner of High and Broad streets, across from the Statehouse. He waited a few minutes at a bank of elevators before being whisked to the lobby of the twenty-ninth floor. Ed stepped off the elevator, surprised to find Bill's wife, Jane, sitting in one of the overstuffed lobby chairs.

"Mrs. Sanderson," he said, "I'm delighted to see you again. I thought I was just meeting with Bill."

"Call me Jane," she replied as she stood. Jane was tall and slender, with a smile that made Ed feel like it was just for him. She was reserved while her husband was brash and aggressive.

"When Bill said he had picked Parkhurst for the addition, I said no. I told him if it wasn't your company, we wouldn't do the addition at all. We had a pretty big row about it. When he said you were coming by at four, I knew I needed to be here making sure he didn't screw things up." She laughed gently, just enough to take the sting from her words.

"I thought you were sold last week," Ed said.

"I was. Bill too, but he negotiates to win, so when you didn't drop your price to get him to sign, he had to show you he was still in control." Jane leaned forward conspiratorially. "Can I share something with you?"

"Of course."

"I..."

"Mr. Sanderson will see you now," the receptionist interrupted. "Please follow me."

Jane sighed and nodded for him to follow the receptionist.

"Just a second," Ed said, turning back to Jane. "Please finish."

"I..., I'm delighted you're doing the addition." She linked arms with Ed and walked him past the receptionist to her husband's office.

Bill Sanderson met them at the door to his office and frowned at Jane. He was a squat, powerfully built man, wearing a tailored blue suit to fit over his broad shoulders. It was rumored that he spent a couple hours a day lifting weights at Gold's Gym. Ed thought the bulky muscles made Sanderson look more like an overdressed bouncer than an executive. Fifteen years older than Ed, Sanderson's tight curls of silver blond hair and dark tan signaled a man desperately trying to hold on to his youth. Jane, his second wife, was Ed's age.

"Ed, thanks for coming down," Sanderson said, shaking his hand enthusiastically. "You're going to make Jane very happy."

"Not you?" Ed asked, laying his papers on the conference table in the large office. Bill sat at the head of the table. Jane slipped around the table to sit next to her husband.

Sanderson grinned. "Coming in with a bid ten thousand less would have made me happy. But Jane knew what she wanted. I admit, I really expected you to come back with a counteroffer when I told you I was going with the competition. I thought you wanted this job."

"I do want this job," Ed said, "but only if I can do it right. I gave you the best bid I could right up front. I want this to be a job we can both be proud of, and I won't take on a job to lose money or do shoddy work."

Ed took several minutes to review the contract with the couple, showing them the elevations and floor plans, and reviewing the specs of the job and terms of the contract.

"You're sure about the end of September?" Sanderson asked.

"Barring acts of God or unforeseen problems, yes."

"The project takes five months, start to finish?"

"More like four," Ed said. "We allow for a cushion, just to be safe."

"If you start now, you could be done by..."

"Bill," Jane interrupted. "We have to respect the schedule."

Sanderson glared at his wife. "I'm giving him a lot of money today. I'd feel better about this if we started the job next week."

"Bill, I've got other clients in line to start next week," Ed said. "We're already booked through May, so we'll start after Memorial Day."

"Maybe you're too busy for a job like this. I expect..."

"You want me to do this job in part because we are so busy. That's the best reference I can give you. I promise you we will give this job the attention it deserves. We will do a tremendous amount of work behind the scenes the next three weeks, ordering materials and pulling permits, so that once we start, we can work straight through until the job is finished."

Sanderson sat back in his seat, scowling. "Your crews are all your own people, no subcontractors?"

"We use subcontractors for the excavation and foundation work, the drywall, painting, and the exterior masonry work. They're all people I've worked with for years, and I guarantee the quality of the entire job, regardless of who does the work."

"But they come in for a set price and do the work and then you bill me a mark-up."

"I'm in business to make a profit, just like you."

"Why don't I pay the subcontractors directly? I'll save a little money and you'll still get the job."

Ed rolled up the blueprints without a word and stood up. "Thanks for your time, Bill," he said, extending his hand. Jane shook her head angrily.

"Sit down," Sanderson said, raising his hands in mock surrender. "You can't blame me for trying."

"Bill!" Jane snapped. She looked at Ed and shook her head. "Let me apologize for my husband's poor manners. We did not ask you here to renegotiate the contract. We accept the project as you've designed it, and at that cost, don't we?"

"Okay," Sanderson said, clearly irritated. "Let's sign."

"One other condition,' Ed said. "Jane is the contact." She gave him a big grin.

"Jane?"

"She wants the project; you want to negotiate every detail. I can't do a job like that."

Sanderson nodded. "Here's my condition: I approve all change orders costing money."

"No," Jane said. Sanderson frowned deeply, looking like he was going to erupt. Ed felt the sale slipping away. It wouldn't be the first time he lost a sale because a couple got into an argument over the details.

"What if Bill approves all change orders over five hundred dollars and everything if the total changes reach twenty-five hundred?" Ed suggested.

"I can live with that,' Sanderson said. "Where do I sign?" Jane nodded her agreement.

Ed sat back down and pulled out the contract. He was surprised Sanderson had agreed to let Jane be the primary contact on the job. She was smart but comfortable to be around. She might even make up for how difficult Sanderson could be. Sanderson signed the contract quickly and handed it back to Ed. Jane shook her head again and held out her hand for the contract. She signed above her husband's name.

Ed left the office at four-thirty with the signed contract and a check for nineteen thousand dollars. He had been waiting on the call from John Smith to tell him Andie Love had died, but he had heard nothing. He felt bad for Bobbi, sitting alone by the side of her mom's bed, but what could he do? The thought was crowded out by Lisa's voice. *You know what you should do.* If things had been different, if he had died and Lisa had lived, she would be at the hospital now, making sure someone was taking care of Bobbi. He knew she would be disappointed knowing he had walked away this morning, but Lisa did not understand. Her compassion might have been unlimited, but not Ed's.

CHAPTER TWO

The Bob Evans parking lot was half full when Ed parked. For ten days the image of Rebecca kneeling next to his table had been seared into his mind. She had smiled when she caught him staring. Could she be interested?

He got out of the truck slowly, his heart hammering in his chest, feeling like a fourteen-year-old asking a girl to the school dance. It was silly; he didn't even know if Rebecca was working. He looked down at his left hand, his wedding band in the ring holder on his dresser, and whispered an apology to Lisa, telling himself he was not abandoning her but feeling like he was, the yearning to be in love again overwhelming.

Once inside, Ed could see Rebecca on the far side of the restaurant, chatting with an older couple as she took their order. She glanced at the waiting area, smiling. On her way to enter the order, she stopped Peggy, the brassy-haired hostess, and whispered something to her, then laughed.

Peggy came to seat him a few minutes later.

"If it's not too much trouble," Ed asked, afraid he was making a fool of himself, "could you sit me in Rebecca's section?"

Peggy harrumphed and shook her head, walking him past a couple of empty booths to a table and left without a word. Ed sat down, wishing he could slip away before Rebecca noticed. He was too old to be here, too old to think about asking someone out, at least someone as young and beautiful as Rebecca.

"Hi," Rebecca said, standing next to his table. She smiled, and her whole face lit up, right to her beautiful green eyes. "I hope you don't mind that I asked Peggy to seat you in my section," she said.

Ed laughed, feeling like a kid caught passing notes in class. Rebecca blushed, taking a half-step back, her eyes hurt.

"I asked her for the same thing," Ed said quickly. "Peggy shook her head at me, but now I know why. Looks like we've started a rumor."

Rebecca smiled again, and Ed was in love. He ordered his usual breakfast, and then ate slowly when it arrived. He tried not to stare at Rebecca as she worked but could not help himself. Their eyes locked several times, and Ed alternated feeling embarrassed and determined. He was sure Lisa was cheering him on, even as she laughed at his fear and awkwardness. He kept asking for more coffee until he realized the restaurant was full and they needed his table. He glanced at his watch, shocked that it was already seven-thirty.

Rebecca brought the check. Ed, afraid he was going to miss the moment, blurted out, "Would you have dinner with me?" His heart had not slowed the slightest bit since he pulled into the parking lot.

"Yes," Rebecca said. "When?"

"Saturday night?"

Rebecca nodded. Ed felt a wave of relief wash through him.

"Now for full disclosure," Rebecca said, taking a deep breath. Her direct look dared Ed to look away. "Saturday works because my ex-husband gets the kids this weekend. Does that change anything?"

"Should it?"

Rebecca beamed. "They're great kids. Greg junior is ten and has always been a bookworm, but to his dad's delight has just discovered sports. Lily is my princess. She's six."

"They sound wonderful."

"They're the best thing in my life," she said, "outside of Bob Evans."

Peggy seated an older couple in the next booth, tapping on her watch as she walked past.

Rebecca glanced around the dining room, frowning. "I should get back on station."

"Where do I pick you up?"

After adding her address to his phone, Ed watched Rebecca as he waited to be cashed out. She kept glancing over her shoulder to look at him, smiling when she realized he was watching her.

Once in his truck, Ed took a deep breath, his heart still pounding, and closed his eyes for a minute, trying to calm down. Bobbi's face floated up at him out of the darkness, her piercing blue eyes staring at him intently. He had never heard from John Smith, so he started checking the *Dispatch* every morning, but there was no information on Andie Love anywhere. He wondered how Bobbi was getting along since her mom had died and felt guilty that he had done nothing.

Ed pulled out his cell phone. He scrolled through his contacts until he found Smith's name and pushed the call button.

"John Smith."

"Sergeant Smith, this is Ed Gideon. I was just calling to follow up. I expected a phone call from you when Andie Love died."

There was a long moment of silence. "She almost died not long after you left," Smith said. "She coded and they had to put her on a ventilator, but then she stabilized. They took her off the ventilator last Friday."

"She's going to live?"

Smith laughed uncomfortably. "I wouldn't call it living. My understanding is she's a vegetable."

"You're kidding."

"I wish I was. It feels like she's hanging around just to haunt you."

"What happens now?"

"They're going to move her to a long-term care facility later in the week. Rosemont, out towards Plain City, off Post Road."

Rosemont Senior Care was just a few miles from Ed's home.

"What about Bobbi?"

"Bobbi?"

"Her daughter."

"Oh…, foster care. They'll pick her up tomorrow or Friday, whenever Andie Love gets moved. She'll go down to the youth facility in Groveport."

Groveport? It had to be forty miles one-way from Groveport to Rosemont. "How is she supposed to see her mom?"

"She won't. Unless they find a family willing to foster her that lives up by Rosemont."

"How likely is that?'

"Honestly? Not likely at all."

"Children's Services will pick Bobbi up tomorrow?"

"Yeah, or Friday. I listened to you and gave her as much time with her mom as I could."

Fifteen minutes later Ed was sitting in the parking lot at Northwest Christian. He did not know why he was there, but he felt like he needed to say something to Bobbi. He got out of the truck and hesitated, contemplating leaving. Bobbi was not his to worry about. He could hear Lisa's voice, though, sharp with anger. *She's only fifteen.* A minute later he was standing in front of the information desk in the lobby.

Andie's room faced southeast towards the interstate, the morning sun flooding the room. Bobbi had pulled a chair over next to the bed and was sitting with her back to him. There were no monitors, just a single IV on a stand. Andie Love was on her side, curled up as if she were taking a nap. An unopened Geometry book lay on the tray table, next to an empty snack pack of Cheetos and a can of Coke. Bobbi was curled up in the chair, curled tighter than her mom, holding Andie's hand, swinging one leg idly while looking out the window, an iPod balanced on the arm of the chair, earbuds snaking into her unruly mass of dark curls, her head moving in time to her music.

Ed stood frozen, hating being trapped between what he knew was right and the desire he felt to run away. After several minutes, Ed knocked softly on the door. Bobbi startled. Her blue eyes widened when she saw Ed. She pulled the earbuds loose from her head and Ed could hear the tinny strains of Katy Perry's *California Gurls*.

"Checking up on the funeral announcement?" she asked. "Sorry to disappoint."

Ed was suddenly more unsure than ever why he was there.

A nurse assistant came in, smiling brightly when she saw Ed. "It's time for her bath," she said. "I just need fifteen minutes."

Ed immediately backed out of the room, but not before he saw Bobbi lean down and kiss her mother's hand as she got up from the chair. She stopped in the doorway to the room, the view behind her cut off as the assistant slid the curtain partition along its track.

"Have you had breakfast yet?" Ed asked.

Bobbi shrugged.

"Look," Ed said, feeling the Bob Evans heavy inside him, "How 'bout we go to the cafeteria to talk, and I'll buy breakfast?"

She shrugged again.

Ed knew enough from his own girls that was as close to a yes as he was going to get, so he turned and headed back to the elevator. When they got to the cafeteria, Ed picked up two trays and handed her one.

"You get whatever you want," he said, pulling out his cell phone. "I need to make a quick call." He watched as she walked down the line in front of him and realized she may not have eaten a full meal in days. She got a breakfast sandwich, two orders of hash browns, and an apple. Ed poured himself a cup of coffee and met her at the register. Her eyes went wide again when she saw the coffee, but Ed just nodded and fished out his wallet.

"I thought you said you were hungry?" she asked accusingly when he sat down opposite her.

Ed shrugged. "It's okay, you eat."

"Why are you here?"

"I talked to John Smith today..."

She looked puzzled at the name.

"Sergeant Smith. He was the one who called me when your mom was brought in. Anyway, he told me what was going on, and I wasn't far away, so I thought I'd stop by."

Bobbi ate the sandwich first, and then alternated bites of the apple with her hash browns. Ed watched her eat, seeing the distrust on her face, and wondered if teenage girls weren't all the same at the very core. So fierce and fragile.

"Look," he said, "I understand your mom is going to be put in a nursing home..."

"Just till she dies," Bobbi interrupted. "They're just sending her there 'cause she didn't die fast enough here."

Ed hated hearing her speak so matter-of-factly. Should a kid be so resigned to the death of her parent? "And you go back to the county?"

Bobbi nodded. "I've been to the center before, a few times, actually."

"Is there any way you'll get to see your mom while you're there?"

"No," Bobbi said. "They don't have time to take kids all over the place."

"The only way for you to see your mom is if you don't end up stuck with Children's Services?"

She shrugged. "I guess. It doesn't matter. She's not getting better."

Ed nodded. "Knowing that, would you still want to visit her?"

"Only every day."

"You don't find it depressing to sit with her when she's like that?"

Bobbi offered a shy smile. "I cry every day, but that doesn't matter to me. I feel like I'm doing something for her when I sit with her and hold her hand. I know you can't understand, but when she's not drinking, she's a good person. She was so sad about your wife. She used to say she wished she'd been the one to die instead of your wife. It got worse after Gram died."

"You said your grandma died over the winter."

"In February. Mom got really depressed. She thought that was her fault too; Gram was living with us before she died. Right after the accident Mom moved up here and then Gram got cancer and moved in with us."

Lisa's voice flooded his mind, urgent. *You know it's the right thing.* Ed closed his eyes for a minute, wondering if this was the reason he was here. His life had been put on hold since Lisa died. Was it possible that helping Bobbi might help him move forward?

"I understand they're sending your mom to Rosemont."

"That's what the social worker told me," Bobbi said. "It's not too far from here. It must suck."

"Why?"

"To be cheap enough for someone like Mom? I'm worried they won't take care of her. More than anything, I wish I could help take care of her. I'd give her a bath every day, change the bed, whatever, just to be sure she was being looked after."

"And hold her hand?" He felt the weight of Lisa's lifeless hand in his, his heart racing for an instant.

Bobbi blushed. "Yeah. And I'd talk to her. That's what I do now. I tell her about my day, what's on the news. I'll tell her what I had for breakfast. When I tell her who bought, she'd fall out of bed if she could."

Ed sighed, knowing he was in trouble. "I'm not sure if I can do this, so don't get excited, but if I could get you a foster family up near Rosemont so you could see your mom every day, would you want that?"

"How?"

"I live near Rosemont. I'd be willing to let you stay while your mom is there." Ed knew it was a bad idea. The cafeteria was suddenly claustrophobic, and he couldn't breathe.

"Are you trying to sex on me or something?"

Ed laughed so hard he spit coffee all over the table. Teenage girls *are* all the same. He grabbed his napkin and started wiping the table clean. "No, I'm not," he said, secretly relieved, "but since you're worried about that, never mind. I just thought..."

"Yes."

"I don't know if the county will let you."

"Why wouldn't they? No one else wants me."

"For the same reason you brought up. They'll think I want to take advantage of you."

"Oh. What do we do now?"

Ed shrugged. "I need to talk with someone to find out. It may take a day or two."

• • •

"Are you fucking out of your mind?" Becca asked, her voice rising hysterically. "I don't want that little bitch living in my house."

"Becca! She's just a kid who needs help," Ed said, wishing he hadn't answered the phone.

"Whatever," Becca said. "They killed Mom. How could you even think of letting her live with us?"

"She had nothing to do with what happened to Mom, and you know it," Ed said, his anger rising. "And you're off at college..."

"I hate you for doing this. You have no right."

"Listen..."

"What about Sandy? What is she supposed to do all summer? Drive her around?"

Ed groaned. He hadn't even thought of the fact that Sandy would come home in a month. "I don't know," he said. "It's not likely to happen, anyway. I doubt Children's Services will agree, but if they did, she'd be spending her days mostly at the nursing home."

"Why didn't you tell us what was happening?"

"I didn't volunteer to get involved," Ed said. "Meeting Bobbi was the right thing to do."

"Oh great. She's some chubby little wanna-be-boy..."

"No, she's not, so knock it off. She's just a girl whose mom is terribly sick, probably dying."

"What happens if Andie Love dies?"

Ed thought for a moment. "I don't know."

"You'll adopt her. I know you will."

"It's not like that..."

"If you adopt her, I will never forgive you."

Ed suppressed the urge to snap at her for being so disrespectful. "Why did you call?"

"Memorial Day weekend I want to go down to Hocking Hills. Leah's parents own a cabin down there. Leah invited me, Cathy and Sandy."

Ed felt a pang of disappointment. "Your sister would go, too?"

"Yeah."

"What if I say no?"

"Then you'll get to spend the weekend with two bitchy girls."

"I'd rather you both came home."

"We were just home for Easter."

"For part of the day. I was looking forward to spending a long weekend with you. With both of you."

"But we can go?"

"Who is driving?"

"Me. I wouldn't let Leah drive us down, especially since we're going to go Thursday evening and it will be dark when we get down there."

"Okay, be safe. And remember, no drinking if you're going to drive anywhere."

"Dad..."

"Love you, darling." The phone was suddenly dead in his hand as she disconnected.

Ed scrolled through the contacts on his phone. He had a client who worked as a court appointed advocate when kids had been abused or abandoned. She might know what to do. He left a message asking for a call back. He did not feel like he could say what he was thinking on the voice mail.

Maggie returned his call twenty minutes later. Ed explained the situation and Maggie told him she would get back with him tomorrow. He was surprised when she called back in the early afternoon.

"Listen, Ed, this is very simple. In a case with a kid who is almost in her majority, Children's Services often lets the kid stay with a family member..."

"She's got no living family."

"Or a family friend. The key is she needs to be situated before Children's Services gets her, because once they do put her in the Youth Facility, then it's almost impossible to get her out without court approval and your case is too weird and everyone will say no."

"But they won't care if it's me before she's officially in the system?"

"Well, they'll know she is staying with friends of the family, without knowing exactly how you know the family. As long as she is safe, in school and being cared for, they won't pursue a case. There are just too many other kids that need help."

"Okay."

"But I have to ask you Ed – should you be doing this?"

"The circumstances *are* weird, aren't they? No one will..."

"That's not what I mean. Have you thought about what it means to have her living in your home? About how that will make you feel?"

"All I've really thought about is my girls not being able to say goodbye to Lisa before she died. I don't want Bobbi to go through that."

"You should know something else. Andie Love had a Living Will. Bobbi showed it to a nurse a couple of days ago. They won't do anything for her but palliative care. No extraordinary measures. She will die, eventually."

"All the more reason for me to do this."

"I wish you had more time to think about this..."

"It's not just the girls, but Lisa too. She would have done it in an instant. I feel like I need to honor that."

"Ed, this can't be about Lisa. *You* need to be sure you want to do this, but we have to act now."

"What's going on?"

"The social worker at the hospital said Andie Love is being transferred this evening, so she had already called Children's Services to pick up Bobbi. They'll be there sometime later today."

"I'll go get her now," Ed said. "What happens if they get there first?"

"I had the social worker transfer me to her mother's room. Bobbi seems like a nice kid. After she told me she really wanted to do this, I told her to gather up her stuff and go wait outside near the ER entrance."

"Won't they come looking for her?"

"I called the social worker back and explained we had a placement with a family friend. I had to pull your home and work addresses, email, everything I could find. I did the same with the County. That way, everything is documented, and they can contact her if they want, it doesn't look like she's running away, and the County should be satisfied."

"Thanks."

"Call me if anything comes up," Maggie said.

Ed headed back to the hospital. The heavy traffic was irritating. He gripped the steering wheel as tightly in his hands as a drowning man holding a life preserver. He worried he was going to let Bobbi down like he had his girls. He took a deep breath when he saw her standing on the walk outside the hospital, relaxing for the first time since Maggie's call. He pulled to the curb, and Bobbi climbed in.

"I've got an appointment at the office in an hour," he said, "so you'll have to come along. Tomorrow, you need to be back in school."

"Sure," she said. "Can we go by the apartment tonight, so I can get my things?"

Ed nodded, feeling strangely buoyant as he drove away. He glanced at the receding hospital in his rearview mirror. I'm finally taking something away from you, he thought, after all those years of you taking Lisa from me.

• • •

The apartment was a two-bedroom unit in a dilapidated brick row house just off the highway, crammed in behind a gas station, an Arby's and a Taco Bell. The carport across the parking lot housed several vehicles in various state of repair, including a battered station wagon, with no tires, on concrete blocks. Two old freezers, the doors littered with bullet holes, leaned against one end of the carport, surrounded by junk. An old man sat on a lawn chair in front of one of the apartments, smoking a cigarette, the sound of a blaring TV coming from the open door behind him.

"We're on the end," Bobbi said, pointing to the only unit with a storm door. Ed nosed the truck into an open spot several doors down from where she had pointed.

"Were you and your mom on a lease here?" Ed asked, wondering if there was some obligation to keep paying the rent.

"Month-to-month," Bobbi said. "Mom paid the last month's rent in advance, so we're paid for through June. The landlord already knows what happened." It took Bobbi ten minutes to throw some clothes into a couple of duffle bags and then raid the bathroom for her personal care items and she was back in the truck.

"Do you like dogs?" he asked.

Bobbi shrugged. "I've never had one. You have a dog?"

"Two. A black lab and a Doberman. Both rescues. They seem ferocious 'cause they're so big, but they're both just big babies. They've been sad all year since Sandy went to college, so they'll mob you for attention. Just ignore them if they get to be too much."

"You have a kid?"

"Two. Becca is twenty-one and Sandy is nineteen. Both at Ohio State."

"Mom never said anything about you having any kids."

"They weren't in the car the night of the accident. She probably didn't know."

Bobbi shook her head. "She knew. She made it a point to learn as much as she could about your family. She must not have wanted me to know."

"Why?"

"'Cause she was fucked up."

Ed winced. "Can you get on the right bus after school to get dropped off at Rosemont?"

"Sure."

"I can pick you up on my way home from work." He turned off the two-lane highway onto a smaller road that twisted and turned through a couple of miles of farmland before reaching his home. He and Lisa had bought the property fifteen years ago. It was a small farm, twenty acres, and Ed leased most of the land to a farmer down the road who put in a crop every year. This year was corn.

The brick house had originally been built in the early nineteenth century, when the county was just being settled. An addition had been added on almost one hundred years ago. Ed and Lisa had restored the house and had always been very proud of it. They had added a porch and stone patio in the back, so it was just lovely on summer nights. A big barn sat behind the house. He parked the truck in back, near the barn.

"Oh my God, you must be rich," Bobbi said.

Ed laughed. "Not at all. We got a great deal when we were younger."

"Where are the dogs?"

"Inside. Are you ready to meet them?"

"I guess." She sounded uncertain.

"Why don't you sit on the patio, and I'll let them out to meet you."

The patio had several chairs and a couple of small tables on it. Bobbi sat in the chair farthest from the house. She sat straight, her hands folded in her lap, looking lost. Ed unlocked the door. Both dogs sat patiently on the other side of the door, visible through the sheer curtain on the glass pane. Lisa had taught them that, working for months to get them to behave when she came home. Ed opened the door. The dogs looked at him expectantly. He turned to Bobbi.

"The lab is called Blackie and the Doberman is King." He turned back to the dogs. "Okay," he said.

They bolted from the kitchen, across the deck and patio, not even noticing the girl sitting there. King noticed first, cocking his head to one side as he lifted his leg against a tree in the back yard. As soon as he finished, he trotted back to the patio, stopping a few feet from the girl.

King moved slowly, his legs stiff. He sniffed her once, looked over at Ed and then pushed his big head into her lap. Bobbi giggled and tentatively petted him as he sniffed her chest, his stump tail wiggling back and forth. Blackie raced back towards the house from the barn, realizing he was missing out on the action. He barreled right into King, knocking him aside and unceremoniously jumped halfway into Bobbi's lap. The girl gave a startled whoop and turned her head from side to side trying to avoid him as he licked at her face.

"I guess they like you," Ed said. They followed Bobbi into the house, bumping against each other trying to get close.

Ed showed Bobbi the guest room on the first floor, and the full bath down the hall and told her to put her things away while he worked on dinner.

They ate spaghetti and a salad in the kitchen, in an awkward silence. Ed knew how to make teens comfortable; the problem was that it seemed inane to ask about school or what bands she liked when her mother was dying. He was sure she would talk about her mom if he asked, but he had no desire to hear anything more about Andie Love. The feeling he had at the hospital, that he was doing something good, something that was making a difference in Bobbi's life and in his, was gone.

When she was done eating, Bobbi cleared the plates from the table and started on the dishes.

"I have to go meet some clients," he told her after glancing at the clock.

"I'll be done here in a few minutes."

"You can watch TV or study," Ed said. "If the dogs want out, let them. They'll stay in the yard." She had turned her head to look at him over her shoulder, a surprised look on her face.

"If you're going to live here, I have to trust you," Ed said. "If you're going to run away, now's as good a time as any. There's fifty dollars in the sugar canister on the counter. It won't get you far, but it's a start."

He grabbed his keys and left before she could say anything. Ed got to his showroom half an hour before his appointment. He parked on the side of the building, taking up two spaces. He liked having open spaces on either side of his truck. Lisa had always teased him about it, and he had to admit her car never had more dings than his. It was a trait picked up from his dad, and now he did it as a sign of respect, just like he wore his dad's forty-year AA sobriety token on a chain around his neck.

• • •

Bobbi walked through the house after Ed left, the dogs trailing her. The main staircase in the front hall, with an ornate R carved into each of the balustrades, was straight out of the movie of *Titanic*. It was amazing. She knew she was one of the poor kids at school, but she had never imagined the other kids lived in houses like this.

Bobbi wanted to sit down with her drawing pad and sketch the stairs. All the angles and lines of the risers would create a hundred little problems with perspective that she wanted to solve, and the idea of making the stairs feel real, not like an architectural drawing, inspired her. She started up the stairs but stopped after several steps; going upstairs felt like snooping.

There were several family portraits hanging on one wall in the living room. Bobbi stared at the largest, picking out Ed's wife. In the portrait she was standing next to Ed, behind two sitting teen girls. Lisa was tall compared to Bobbi's mom, as tall as Ed, with long brown hair that curled gently on her breast. She looked like what a mom should look like, one hand on the shoulder of the teen in front of her, her other arm wrapped around Ed's waist. She was smiling, and you got a feeling that this was what made her happy, being with her family.

And she was dead because Andie Love was a drunk. Bobbi wondered if her mom had ever seen a picture of them. No wonder she killed herself. The two teens offset their mother nicely, their smiles as forced as Lisa's was natural. It was clear they had not wanted to have the portrait done.

Bobbi did not blame them. Gram had loved Olan Mills, getting pictures with Bobbi and her mom every year, even when they were living out of a car. Bobbi had hated it, her mom too, and you could see it on their faces, just like with Ed's girls. The family portrait was the biggest lie, the place where you shouted to the world *look at us, we're normal*, and the more fucked up you were, the louder you shouted. Bobbi wondered if the girls were fighting before the picture was taken, either with themselves, or with their mom. Ed would have stayed above it, too distant to care, because that was how men were.

When she looked at the portrait again, from the other side of the room, her cynicism gave way to sadness. It did not matter that the girls hated having to sit for the the portrait, from here you could see how they were a family. Bobbi felt their accusations now—Lisa's most of all—like they had expected Bobbi to control Andie's drinking to save them. The guilt Bobbi felt, discovered long before the accident, settled heavily around her. Bobbi had always known something terrible was going to happen. One time, when she was twelve, the year before the accident, her mom had passed out in her truck right in front of their apartment, some guy with her, both too stoned to move, and Bobbi had thought about calling the cops on them. Instead, she went to bed, too afraid to call. Would calling have saved Lisa's life?

She couldn't sit in the living room to watch TV.

The kitchen felt as big as the entire first floor of her apartment. She sat at the table, sketching pictures of the dogs in a new sketchbook, trying to relax. After several minutes she got up and rummaged through the fridge. She wrinkled her nose at the cans of diet Coke, finally settling on orange juice, and then had to look through the cupboards to find a cup. After pouring a glass and putting the juice away, she sat back at the table, trying to sketch. She wished she had someone to call to take her to Rosemont to visit her mom, but she did not have friends like that. She half expected that when she got back to school tomorrow none of the kids would even realize she had been gone. Her teachers would, but only because Mrs. Williams, her art teacher, had brought her school assignments to the hospital.

Pete would come if she called him, but he would not take her to Rosemont. He would want to make out or something first, and she was not entirely sure he would drive her later.

After an hour she decided to catch up on her reading for school. She had fallen behind in AP Euro History and wanted to be prepared if there was a pop quiz tomorrow. Bobbi took the money from the canister, just in case. The house did not feel like a place she could stay.

• • •

Lights were on in the kitchen and the guest room when Ed got home. Inside, both dogs were waiting for him in the kitchen. He walked over to the counter and looked in the sugar canister. The money was gone.

I tried, he thought, knowing he was lying to himself. He would call Maggie in the morning and find out how to report it.

Ed headed down the hall to the guest room. Bobbi opened the door before he got there, as if she were waiting for him. She was wearing a hoodie against the cooling evening. Blackie, who had followed Ed down the hall, pushed past the girl into her room and settled on the floor near the bed.

"I just wanted you to know I was back," Ed said, trying to keep the surprise from his voice.

"I heard your truck," Bobbi said.

Ed nodded to the dog. "You're welcome to let him sleep in here. King, too. They always sleep with the girls when they're home."

"Okay."

"Well, goodnight. I'll be upstairs if you need anything." Ed turned and left. He stopped in the kitchen to set up the coffee maker for morning and grab a glass of water. *Should I say something about the money?* Lisa would have. He did not want a confrontation; the arrangement felt too fragile as it was. He left the light over the stove on and went upstairs. He turned on the television, flipping to the hockey playoffs for noise as he checked email on his phone one last time.

Was it a mistake—did it dishonor Lisa—to have Andie Love's kid living in his house? Becca had certainly thought so. Was Sandy going to act the same way? He needed to call Sandy but put it off until tomorrow.

It felt weird having a stranger in the house. He felt so unsettled, he thought about heading down to the high school for a run. His schedule was off, and that was never a good thing. He had not gone for a run since John Smith had woken him in the middle of the night ten days ago. He decided against it, worried leaving again would encourage Bobbi to run away.

King slipped into the bedroom, bumped his head against Ed's hip and nosed around the room for a minute before going back down. Even the dogs had abandoned him. Ed shook his head wryly at the thought. *I am so pathetic.*

CHAPTER THREE

Twin lights shredded the darkness into brilliant pain, illuminating, for an instant, Lisa's peaceful face before the pickup truck hit their car. Ed jolted awake at that moment, disoriented, the room dark. The chatter of birds outside his window brought him back to the moment. He hated the dream; some nights it came as often as three or four times. He rolled to his side after a minute and flipped on the bed stand lamp. No dogs. Ed started to call out and then he remembered the girl. He pulled on sweatpants and a t-shirt, shuffling his feet into a pair of worn slippers next to the door and headed down to the kitchen. The aroma of freshly brewed coffee filled the kitchen. Ed grinned; he loved the timer on his coffee maker. He pulled a cup from the cupboard and reached into the canister on the counter for a couple of packets of sweetener. The money was back in the canister, along with a torn piece of notebook paper.

I owe you $10, Bobbi Love.

One step in the right direction, Ed thought. He poured his coffee and added creamer, and then went out on the deck to watch the sunrise. A handful of stars were still visible in the west as the sky grew lighter in the east. The chatter of the birds did not slow at his presence. He sat down in a padded chair and sipped his coffee, the caffeine slowly worming its way into his brain. He ran through his prayer list, an almost incoherent mix of saying thank you for and sending blessings to his girls, workers and friends. It was all he had left of his faith, other than church on the holidays because the girls expected it. He knew Lisa would be disappointed with him stepping away from church, but he did not need to listen to a minister who swore the wreck was all part of God's great plan for him.

Ed wondered if he could ever still his mind enough to stop thinking about Lisa's absence every morning. He closed his eyes and concentrated on the birds' morning chorus. A few minutes later the door creaked open and both dogs bounded out past him. Bobbi was slower, still yawning, in a tank top and shorts.

He lifted his cup to Bobbi. "There's coffee, and juice in the fridge."

"Thanks." She went inside and returned a few minutes later with a glass of orange juice. She had put on a hoodie and sweats but was still barefoot. She sat in a chair next to Ed.

"I wasn't sure you were going to be here this morning," Ed said.

"Yeah," Bobbi agreed. "I thought about leaving, but who would look after Mom?"

"You must love your mom a lot."

"Hardly."

Ed gave the girl a sharp look.

Bobbi shrugged. "It's complicated. I do love her, I guess, I mean she's my mom, but I spent so much of my life mad at her for fucking everything up..."—she shook her head after Ed winced—"Sorry. It's just I hated her for not being a real mom for so long. I mean look at you; you don't know me, but you're willing to take a chance on me and give me a place to stay.

"So, after all those years she finally gets sober, and guess what? She doesn't really change. Instead of being happy that she's finally being a good mom, she goes and kills herself. I'm not like her, and that's why I'm taking care of her. I want to prove to her, and everyone else, that I'm not like her."

"Okay," Ed said. "What do you eat for breakfast? There's some cereal in the cupboard..."

"Do you have any yogurt?"

"I can get some tonight. We've got apples and bananas..."

"Toast?"

"Yep."

"That's enough."

"What time do you need to be at school?"

"7:30."

"Okay. Can you check on getting the bus to pick you up? I'm usually in the office by seven."

Bobbi turned to stare at him. "What job do you have? You were out late last night, and you start at 7 in the morning? Do you sell drugs or something?"

Ed laughed. "Some days it feels like it." He got up to go feed the dogs. Bobbi sat on the deck and wrapped herself around her juice. Ed thought she might be crying.

• • •

Sandy wondered again why she had scheduled an 8am class this quarter. She was the late sleeper in the family, the one who had to be dragged from her bed kicking and screaming all through high school. Her mom used to bring a cold washcloth into her room and put it at the base of her neck to make Sandy get up. She would even put it in the freezer for a couple of minutes making it as awful as possible. Becca, of course, got up without even using an alarm.

She hated it when her parents compared her to Becca. Dad was better than her mom had been, but even he could not help himself sometimes. Was it her fault they only had two kids? Or that Becca had always known what she wanted, was naturally organized and was good at just about everything?

The only thing Sandy felt better at than Becca was dealing with their mom's death, and that just made her feel guilty. Sandy missed her mom, and still had moments when she thought of something and could not stop herself from crying, but she did not obsess on it all the time like Becca. *It is what it is.* Sandy shook her head even as she thought the words. They sounded so heartless, especially when she said them to Becca, but it was her truth. Feeling bad did not help. She would rather remember her mom for all the good times they had than dwell on her not being around now.

Sandy grabbed her bookbag and headed out the door. She had time to grab a coffee and call Dad on her way to class. She was thinking about staying on campus for a second year. She and Linda, from the suite next to hers, were planning on moving into a double together. Dad expected her to live with Becca next year, but Becca would never allow it, not when Cathy was there. She needed to tell him soon, but not today. Today was about the kid. Sandy did not understand why Becca was so pissed about it. She had been a little chafed when she heard, but mostly she was curious. Not that she would ask, but what was it like to know your mom was a killer? That was way worse than knowing your mom wished you were a little more like your older sister.

She called as soon as she was out the cafeteria door, a muffin balanced on the lid of her to-go coffee. It rang once and then he picked up.

"I hear you're not coming home for Memorial Day," he said.

"What?"

"Becca said that the two of you are going down to Hocking Hills for the holiday."

"Yeah..." Sandy could hear the smile on his face. She hated the way he tried making something he was upset about into a joke.

"When were you going to say something?'

"Yesterday, when you called to say you were adopting a kid."

"Ouch!" Ed said. "That stings."

"It was meant to, just like your comment. Seriously Dad?"

"I'm not adopting anyone. Bobbi needs a place to stay..."

"Becca is totally pissed with you. She could barely talk when she called. Did you even think about how we would feel?"

"I kept thinking about you and your sister not having a chance to say goodbye to Mom. I didn't want Bobbi to go through the same thing."

Of course, he was. "You still should have asked us."

"Look, it was really sudden, and Bobbi needed..."

"I get it! She had nowhere to go. It's not about her. We're upset you didn't care enough to ask what we felt about it."

"You're right, I didn't. I'm sorry."

Sandy was surprised to hear him apologize. "She'd better not be sleeping in my room."

"She's in the guest room. King and Blackie slept with her last night."

"Oh my God, the dogs like her?"

"Sucks, doesn't it?"

Sandy laughed. "Is it too weird that I feel sorry for her?"

"Do what?"

"I know Becca's pissed and everything, but what about her? Isn't it weird for her to have to stay at our place, too? Kind of a slap in the face, I'd guess."

"I never even thought of that."

"Of course, not. You never think about how something impacts everyone else."

"Really?" She could hear a note of hurt in his voice.

"It doesn't mean you should be doing something different. You just need to learn to ask people how they feel about stuff, just so they know you care about what they feel."

"I'd like to get dinner with you and your sister soon. We could talk about what's going on."

"I'll check our calendars. I'm not sure about Becca. She's really pissed. I'll let you know."

"Okay."

"I love you, Dad."

"Love you too."

Sandy thumbed her phone off and slid it into the back pocket of her jeans. Her eight am class was Art History, which she'd taken to get a requirement out of the way, but Sandy was surprised by how much she liked it. She was a Marketing major, but now she wanted to do something related to art and non-profit management. Dad wanted one of them to take over the business, and Becca wanted it to be Sandy, so they were both going to be disappointed.

Sandy took a long sip of her too-hot coffee, shaking her head as she forced it down. Sometimes family was more trouble than they were worth.

• • •

Beside a rural two-lane highway in the middle of nowhere, Rosemont Senior Care was a single-story sprawling relic of late fifties block construction, looking more like a cheap motel than nursing home. The front wing and parking lot were crowded against the road, reinforcing the feeling of fifties roadside attraction. Ed inched his truck into a too-narrow space.

He stopped at the front desk to get the room number and then walked down the front hall to get to the right-hand wing. Ed turned down the second hall and followed it nearly to the end, not surprised that they wanted Andie Love as far away from the other patients as possible. Bobbi held her mom's hand, an open textbook on the bed. Other than the hospital bed and an IV, no medical equipment was in the room: no monitors, or oxygen, or anything to help her recover.

Ed knocked softly on the metal door frame. Bobbi looked up and smiled, her blue eyes still surprising him, and motioned for him to come in. He felt a nagging sense of worry that she was going to think he had promised to take care of her. *Had he?*

"How's your mom?"

Bobbi shrugged. "The same. I thought I felt her squeeze my hand a couple of times, but the nurse said it was just a muscle spasm."

"I thought there would be more equipment here."

"Why? She came here to die."

"You can't lose hope," Ed said, hoping the lie didn't show on his face. He wanted Andie Love to die.

"They didn't put in a feeding tube," Bobbi said.

"Do what?"

"That's why she got transferred early. They were supposed to put in a feeding tube, but they didn't do it."

"So how..."

Bobbi pointed to the IV "That's it. When that runs out, she starves to death."

"I'm sure..."

"She signed something. No extraordinary measures. I never thought food was special. I don't understand how it's legal, but it is." Bobbi dropped the hand she had been holding back on the bed. "And the whole time her hand is squeezing mine like she's trying to say something. It's shitty." She looked up at Ed. "Can we go?"

"Sure," Ed said.

Bobbi picked up her book bag from beside the bed, stuffed the textbook she was reading inside, and then squeezed past Ed through the doorway. Ed watched her walking away, staring straight, not looking at anything as she went down the hall, the stiffness in her gait betraying the illusion of composure. He turned back to the room. Andie Love lay on her side in a fetal position, her knees drawn up towards her head as if she were trying to disappear into herself. She was a small woman and looked smaller in the bed.

Ed felt empty. He missed the rage that had occupied him for months after the accident; he had found comfort in the sharpness of his anger, but today he could not find it. Even his wish for her to die felt empty, more obligation than truth. In a few days, Andie Love would be dead, and it would not change a thing. Would not bring back Lisa, would not make their anniversary a day he could ever feel good about again. Andie Love was just going to hurt another person by dying and Ed could not take any pleasure in that. He headed for the truck, wondering what would happen to Bobbi once her mother died. The girls thought he was going to adopt her. There was an appeal to it, the redemption of turning tragedy into triumph, but of course it was all bullshit. Adopting Bobbi would just cost him Becca. He did not think he could survive another loss like that.

• • •

"What the hell is Dad thinking?" Becca asked as she slid into the booth across from Sandy, her burrito bowl on a round metal tray.

Sandy shrugged. "He should have asked before he let her live in our house."

"I don't understand how he could think this is okay. Especially so close to the day Mom died. It feels like he's trying to rub our faces in it."

"Don't you think he's doing this because of Mom?"

"Of course, Mom would have taken her in. That's what she did. She was always convincing him to do stuff for people."

"Do you remember the summer Leslie came and stayed with us while her parents were getting divorced? Or the guy from church who had his house repossessed?" Sandy asked.

"That's what they did, help people." Becca said. "But why this kid?"

"Because she needs help." Sandy unwrapped her burrito and took a big bite.

Becca shook her head. "It's still wrong for him to do this to us."

"Totally, but Dad can't help himself. He wants to make Mom proud."

Becca snapped the cover off her bowl and stirred the rice and veggies with a plastic fork.

"Did you go veggie again?" Sandy asked, pointing at the burrito bowl.

Becca grinned and shrugged. "For this week, anyway. He said yes to Hocking Hills."

"I know. I called him. He wants to go to dinner before we go."

"Is she going to be there?"

"That's the whole point."

"I don't want to go."

"I get it, but..."

"You want to have dinner with her?" Becca's tone made it a challenge, not a question. Sandy knew this was when she would usually back down, but she was tired of Becca controlling everything. "I don't know. Part of me wants to meet her."

"Why would you want that? That's the most fucked up thing you've ever said."

"Fuck you," Sandy said with a grin. "I hate you."

"Hate you too."

"Will you go?"

Becca was quiet for a minute, and then shrugged. "I can't go this week, but I could go next week."

"I'll tell him. How come Cathy didn't come to dinner?"

"Clinicals. She's got two nights a week this quarter. I know nurses work at night, but I hate when she gets home so late. How do you plan dinner or an evening when your… roommate doesn't get home until midnight?"

"Can I be honest?" Sandy asked, her heart pounding wildly in her chest. She wasn't sure when she would get another opening to ask Becca and keep things low key.

"Sure, Babe, what's up?"

"You don't have to pretend in front of me," Sandy said. She tried to smile, hoping it looked calm and reassuring, but sure she looked unhinged. "I know about you and Cathy."

"What?" Becca stared at her sister, a look of panic washing across her face.

"Look, I'm cool with it," Sandy said, taking a deep breath.

"I don't know what you're talking about..."

"Don't lie to me," Sandy said. "I'm not stupid and you suck at lying. It's clear you and Cathy are together. You're always touching each other and whispering and... it's just obvious."

Becca sank against the back of the booth, her shoulders sagging. She seemed to shrink, as if she were collapsing in upon herself. She was quiet for so long, staring at her hands, that Sandy wanted to comfort her, but did not know how. *I should've kept my big mouth shut.*

Sandy reached across the table and squeezed Becca's wrist. "I think it's great: you're happy again. I didn't think I'd ever see you happy after Mom died. I don't care if you're gay, just don't pretend around me anymore."

"How long have you known?" Becca asked, looking up, wiping her eyes with the back of her hands.

"I wasn't sure at first. I mean, when Cathy came to visit last year during Spring break, and I caught you guys napping in the barn? I thought nothing of it. I've fallen asleep in weird places with friends, so it wasn't a big deal. But once I got to school and started seeing you together all the time, it just seemed like you cared too much about each other to be just friends. And then one day before Christmas break, when I came over to your place, I saw you kissing through the front window before I rang the doorbell."

"Why didn't you say anything?" Becca asked, a look of irritation on her face.

"Don't get bitchy with me. You're the one keeping a big secret. I didn't know how to ask."

"Did you tell Dad?"

"Hell, no. You'll have to tell him some time, though."

Becca stirred her food. "I don't know how to tell him. I wish Mom were still here. It would be easier to tell them together."

"Yeah," Sandy said, nodding. "It would."

• • •

Rebecca lived in an apartment complex off West Broad Street at least thirty minutes from the Bob Evans. The apartments were two-story townhomes, four to a building, with small, fenced patios that backed up to each other. Ed drove past several cul-de-sacs, each made up of four buildings stacked almost on top of each other. A playground and pool in the center of the complex created some space for kids to play, but everything felt cramped and dingy.

Rebecca opened the door of her apartment before Ed was out of his truck. She was wearing a yellow sundress with matching pumps. He hurried around the truck to open the door for her.

"I saw you pull in," she said, giving him a nervous smile. She seemed fragile, almost ready to snap. Ed, his heart pounding in his chest, nodded to her, trying to think of something to say, suddenly feeling stupid for taking her out to dinner in his work truck but he had never replaced Lisa's car after the accident. The first few minutes of the drive were spent in an uncomfortable silence.

"Listen," Ed said, "I haven't been out on a date since Lisa died. I feel like I've forgotten how to talk with a woman. It's been two years."

Rebecca glanced at him shyly. "I know what you mean. I wasn't even talking to Greg for the last six months before our divorce, so I have no idea what to say."

"Do you like Asian food?"

"Other than pancakes or McDonalds, anything will be fine."

Ed glanced at Rebecca out of the corner of his eye. *How did I end up on a date with such a beautiful woman?* "I didn't think you were dressed for McDonalds."

Rebecca laughed, clear and loud, and Ed decided that might just be her best feature. He wanted to keep her laughing all night.

Dinner was at an upscale Asian fusion restaurant at Tuttle mall. The bar was loud and boisterous, but it was separated from the dining room enough to allow them to talk over dinner. Rebecca swirled her wine nervously, glancing away shyly, and Ed thought he might be in love. It turned out Rebecca had waited on him, Lisa and the girls several times before the accident, but he had only been seated in her section once or twice in the last two years, until the other day. They talked about his business and the girls.

"What about you?" Ed asked after their second round of drinks arrived.

Rebecca smiled hesitantly before beginning a distracted summary of her marriage. She had met Greg at Otterbein, a small university on the outskirts of Columbus. Greg was an athlete, two years ahead of her, and she had fallen for him hard. People thought they were a magical couple, but Greg was insanely jealous, and they argued a lot. She had been thinking about breaking up with him when she turned up pregnant. They married the week after his graduation. Greg had gotten a great job in corporate banking, and they bought a home right away. He insisted she be a stay-at-home mom, and Rebecca had agreed, on the condition that once the baby started kindergarten, she would go to work. Greg junior had been a blessing.

Things had seemed wonderful until about a year after Lily was born. Rebecca was shocked to find out Greg was having an affair with a young woman on his team. She felt caught between divorcing Greg or trying to save her marriage. She thought things were getting better, but then his girlfriend, whom he had told her he dropped, had turned up pregnant.

When she confronted Greg, he shoved her against the wall and told her to mind her own business.

"What a bastard," Ed said.

"It's fine," Rebecca said, waving his concern away, "it was more Greg brushing past me than shoving me. It meant nothing, not compared to the news he'd knocked up his girlfriend.

"That was the deepest betrayal, and it hurt worse than his cheating. Greg was willing to leave for a new woman and a new baby." She shook her head and picked up her wine, draining her glass. "I felt so bad for Greg junior and Lily. Like I'd let them down somehow."

"I'm sorry," Ed said. "That must have been awful..."

"Don't you dare feel sorry for me," Rebecca said. "I didn't tell you this for sympathy. I know your story and I wanted you to know mine. I was too young when I married Greg and it was a mistake. My life is much better now."

When dinner was over, they walked through the mall, chatting and window shopping. The stores were all closed by the time they made their way to the exit. He took Rebecca's hand in his as they left, stopping her on the sidewalk outside.

"I had a lovely time this evening," Ed said. "I hope I can see you again?"

Rebecca blushed, a shy grin on her face. "I'd love that. I'm only available on the weekends, when the kids are with their dad. I hope you understand, but I don't want to introduce them to you until I know you a little better."

Ed nodded. "I do."

"Greg picks them up at six on Friday."

"Friday it is..., unless you'd be available for lunch tomorrow?" Ed grinned anxiously.

"I'd love it."

"What time can I pick you up?"

"I get off at two and could get home and changed by two thirty. The kids come home at six."

They drove back to Rebecca's apartment in a comfortable silence. When he parked in front of her place, she leaned over and gave him a light kiss on the cheek. "I can't invite you in," she said. "That's not who I am." She slid out of the truck and walked to her apartment. She turned and waved after she got inside and stayed in the open doorway as he drove away.

Ed had not considered she might invite him in, but now that she had raised the question, it lingered in his mind. The sudden longing was so intense that Ed shook his head, embarrassed. He drove home in silence, the faint scent of her perfume filled with possibilities.

Bobbi was on the back deck with the dogs when Ed parked the truck. She was sitting with her knees pulled up to her chin and her arms wrapped around her legs as if warding off a deep chill, staring off past the barn, looking at nothing.

Ed sat next to her, feeling a moment's irritation that she was there. He wanted nothing to intrude upon his feelings for Rebecca. King got up and nosed his head into Ed's lap, his stump of a tail moving slowly back and forth. Ed fondled the dog's ears absently.

"How are things?' he finally asked.

"She's really going to die," Bobbi said, her voice so soft Ed could barely understand her.

Ed did not know what to say. *Why did I think offering a room was going to be enough?*

"It could take a week or two, but she's going to starve to death."

"Shouldn't they do a brain scan or something?" Ed asked. "To be sure she won't recover?"

"They did one in the hospital," Bobbi said. "The doctor couldn't say one way or the other."

"Can't you ask them to feed her?"

"I did. She put it in that thing she wrote: no food or water."

"I'm sorry."

"Don't be. She deserves to die, and it's what she wanted, but it's so hard to watch. She seems to get smaller all the time."

"That must be hard," Ed said. He remembered his girls' grief after Lisa died and suddenly realized he was going to go through it again. He had been powerless to make things hurt less for them. He would do anything to avoid feeling that way again.

"It wouldn't be so bad if she wasn't so active," Bobbi said. "She squeezes my hand all day. They say she's just spazzing and it means nothing."

Ed did not respond. He was caught in a memory: Lisa staring at him, her eyes flicking up and down as if she were checking that he was okay. He had thought it meant she was still there. A doctor told him later that it had all been involuntary muscle response. Lisa had died instantly. She had already been dead, but her body did not know it yet. He had not really held her or comforted her.

But he had.

"It probably reassures her to feel your hand in hers," Ed said.

"She squeezes the most when I talk about staying here. She likes that I'm here somehow. I don't get it. It's just another thing my family has done to yours."

"You have done nothing to my family," Ed said.

"Tell that to Becca."

"You spoke with her?"

"The phone rang. Someone called three times in a row without leaving a message. I was afraid it was important."

That was Becca, Ed thought. A habit she learned from Lisa, just in case you were walking a little too slowly to pick up the phone.

"What did she say?"

"Nothing we need to talk about," Bobbi said. "Although I spilled the beans about your date."

"Damn." Ed had been planning on telling the girls at dinner next week.

"Yeah. That didn't go over well. She thought I set it up or something. I didn't say anything else."

"Thanks."

"I'm sorry. I didn't realize she didn't know about the date until she started cussing at me."

When Becca started cursing, it meant things were bad. Another trait of Lisa's. Ed shook his head. Both girls were growing up to be versions of their mom; it meant Lisa lived on in some way. But it was a pain in the ass as well.

"It's not your fault I didn't get around to telling them," Ed said.

"I know. She apologized after a couple of minutes. She also said Thursday was good for dinner."

"Thanks. Does Thursday work for you?"

"I'm not horning in on dinner with your daughters. I'll eat here."

"You have to meet them sometime," Ed said. "Thursday is as good a day as any. Did she say where?"

"The Mexican place at Lennox."

Bobbi turned and looked at Ed. "Do you go to church?"

"We used to," Ed said. "Lisa and I went to a church not too far from the hospital. She liked the minister. He was a volunteer Chaplain at the hospital. Now we only go for special occasions."

"Could you take me tomorrow?"

"Sure."

Bobbi turned away and Ed could see she was starting to cry. He gave her shoulder a squeeze and stood up and went inside. The dogs watched him go, not straying from Bobbi's side.

CHAPTER FOUR

The church had been built over one hundred years ago, from limestone quarried near the Scioto River. The choir sang from a balcony above the pulpit, filling the three-story nave with their harmonies. Ed loved sacred music, but he hated the choir. One woman's voice seemed an echo of Lisa's, making him even more aware of her absence.

Bobbi leaned forward and listened intently as the minister gave his sermon, but Ed let his mind drift. He did not need people telling him how to live his life, or their awkward assurances that Lisa's death was part of God's plan. Ed refused to blame God. God was eternal and only focused on eternal things, not on the bullshit that humans did to each other. If a woman got drunk and climbed into her pickup truck and drove home in the dark without turning on her headlights until it was too late and missed a stop sign and killed a woman celebrating her twenty-fifth wedding anniversary, well, that was just tough luck. Long live free will.

They left as soon as the service was over. This church had been so important to Lisa, but it was empty without her. He had no desire to go back.

"Can you come in for a minute?" Bobbi asked when he pulled into the Rosemont parking lot. "I want to show you something."

"I can stay a couple of minutes," Ed said. They walked the long hall slowly, waves of irritation battering him. What did she want now?

When they got to the room, the door was partially closed. Ed, a wall of discomfort settling around his chest, realized Andie Love might have already passed. He was relieved to find Andie in her bed, curled on her side. She was pale, her eyes sunken, her breath rasping wetly in her throat. Ed made a mental note to talk to the staff about calling him when Andie died. He did not want Bobbi to find out alone.

Bobbi pulled a chair up to her mom's bed. "Hi," she said, taking her mom's hand in her own. "Ed brought me." Bobbi motioned for Ed to come closer to the bed. "Take her hand," Bobbi said. "I want you to feel this."

Ed shook his head, but Bobbi grabbed his left hand and pulled him close. She put her mother's hand in his. Andie's small hand felt warm, alive, not like someone who was dying.

"Ed's still here," Bobbi said. The pressure on his hand was unmistakable. "That's his hand you're holding," Bobbi said.

The hand in his squeezed so tightly that Ed pulled away in shock. *What was this?* Andie clung to him, and Ed had to snap his wrist sharply to break her grip. Bobbi grabbed her mom's hand out of the air before it hit the bed. "See what I mean?" she asked, looking at Ed over her shoulder. "They say it just happens, but she heard what I said."

Ed nodded. It had seemed real, as if there was some intention behind it, but Andie was brain dead. "What time should I pick you up?" he asked.

"I have to finish a paper for AP Euro History," Bobbi said. "It's due tomorrow. How about five?"

"How about six? I'm going to be busy at five."

Bobbi turned away from her mom to look at Ed. "You're going out again already? Wow."

Ed felt his blush rise. "It's just lunch," he said, irritated with himself for feeling a need to explain.

He walked down the hall, adrift. It was not fair that Bobbi was getting something from him he had not been able to give his girls when Lisa died. He felt like he was betraying them, but he could not just walk away and leave Bobbi to deal with this alone. He could only hope for Andie Love to die quickly so his life could go back to what it had been.

The showroom was closed on Sundays. Ed parked on the side, slipping inside through one of the converted service bays. He sat at his desk and pulled out a stack of invoices to review but could not get Andie Love out of his mind. When she squeezed his hand, it seemed intentional. They had promised him she was brain-dead and that's what he needed her to be.

His body ached again, the wreck-echo he felt whenever he got too deep into his feelings about Lisa. What if Andie was not brain-dead, but they were killing her? He made the call before he had time to think it through.

The phone answered on the first ring. "John Smith."

"John, this is Ed Gideon. I hope I'm not bothering you."

"I'm at a Clipper's game with the family. Sunday matinee and Dime-a-dog day."

"Let me call back tomorrow."

"No, go ahead. They're down six runs in the top of the fourth. Game over, brother."

"I'm calling about Bobbi Love. About Andie, really."

"Oh, did she die?"

"No, not yet. She... the thing is..." Ed paused, unsure what he wanted to say.

"Yeah?"

"Well, Bobbi's worried her mom isn't brain-dead. That they're killing her by withholding food."

"I bet she is, especially if she's sitting there every day watching it happen."

"Her mom responds to her, John. She squeezes her hand when Bobbi talks. Hell, she squeezes her hand whenever I'm in the room."

"So?"

"I need you to order a test or something."

"Me? No can do, brother. I see this all the time. Accident victims, other suicide attempts. It's hard on the family."

"But the family can order a test. Bobbi can't."

"Have you spoken to anyone at the nursing home?"

"Me? No."

"Try the Head of Nursing or the social worker. That's the best I can offer."

"Jesus, I'm an idiot. Sorry for bothering you."

Smith laughed. "You owe me for this. A free addition or something."

"I'll be happy to rescreen your storm door," Ed said with a laugh.

"That would be par for the course."

"Enjoy the game."

"The game sucks, but I've got my twenty-ounce Yuengling." The phone went dead.

• • •

Lunch came from Wendy's, and they ate in the showroom because Rebecca wanted to see it. They were sitting in one of the display kitchens, at an island with tall chairs, their fries pooled between them on top of the empty food bag. Rebecca asked about the history of the shop, how often he changed displays and what it was like to run his own business.

Ed was smitten. She was intelligent and beautiful. He had not been this close to a woman, physically and emotionally, since Lisa had died. He did not know the rules anymore. *How do you say I'm getting lost in you?*

"Did you see your daughters today?" Rebecca asked.

Ed shook his head. "I'll see them for dinner Thursday."

"So, you'll have to eat dinner all alone. That's so sad."

Ed laughed. "To tell the truth, we didn't eat that many meals together when they were in high school. They were always busy with something. You raise them up to become independent and then they do, and in a way, it kills you."

"I'm not sure either of my kids will ever be independent," Rebecca said. "Most days they can't keep track of their shoes, let alone manage their lives."

"You'll be surprised at how quickly that changes," Ed said. "With the girls, it wasn't the gradual thing I expected. One day Sandy was asking us to make her lunch and do her laundry and the next she was volunteering at Faith Mission and planning a coat drive."

"Your girls sound like nice people."

"Don't let them fool you," Ed said, smiling. "Teenagers aren't nice people, at least not to their parents. The girls were hell on Lisa. I know it was about growing up and claiming their independence, but it was rough. They've both become nice again and seem to get nicer by the day."

"Who was the tough one?"

Ed thought for a minute. "They're so different, it's hard to say. Becca needed more space and wanted approval, even when she was pushing us away. She wasn't ever going to stay out after midnight, but she hated having a midnight curfew. Sandy is much more the free spirit, lives in the moment, so she missed curfew all the time because she couldn't plan ahead to save her life."

Rebecca laughed. "I've apologized to my parents so many times for how I acted when I was a kid," she said. "You know, once your kids do something and you remember doing it? I imagine it will be twice as bad once the kids are teenagers."

"Lisa used to say the same thing," Ed said. He winced as soon as he heard the words come out of his mouth. "I'm sorry. I don't mean to keep bringing her up..."

"Ed," Rebecca said, taking his hand, "Your memories of Lisa will always be part of your life. Don't worry about when she pops up in conversation. I'm sure I'll have plenty of questions about her if we keep going out."

"If?"

Rebecca grinned and took a bite of her sandwich. She stared at Ed, studying his face. "If some other woman doesn't capture your attention. Someone prettier than me." Ed could feel his face flush.

"You must notice when they flirt with you."

"Women don't flirt with me."

Rebecca laughed. "You are the sweetest, most clueless man," she said, shaking her head. "It's really touching. Now take me around and show me everything."

Ed gave her the big tour, showing off all the parts of the store that the public never saw, and they ended up back in the showroom an hour later, having made the full rounds.

"I'd like to invite you to dinner," Rebecca said, "but I don't think it's time for the kids to meet you yet."

"That's wonderful," Ed said, "I get it about your kids. I feel the same way about the girls. If we're going to date, they should meet you, but I need a little more time for us first."

'I just feel bad about you eating dinner all alone."

"Don't feel bad," Ed said. "I have a dinner date."

Rebecca's eyes narrowed, making Ed laugh. "It's not like that," he said, feeling a need to share. He told her everything that was going on with Bobbi and her mom.

"Oh my God," Rebecca said, her brow wrinkled deeply. "They're letting you keep her kid?"

"Why wouldn't they? No one else wants to take her in."

"I don't know, Ed. It doesn't sound right." She glanced at her wristwatch. "I should head back," she said. "I've a couple of errands to run before Greg drops off the kids."

They rode back to Rebecca's apartment in a comfortable silence. Rebecca gave him a quick peck on the cheek. "I'll call you?" she asked, looking at him hesitantly.

"Please," Ed said. She slipped out of the truck and disappeared inside her apartment without looking back.

Ed went home and took the dogs for a walk in the field behind his house. The dogs ranged ahead of him, running from spot to spot, happy to be outside on a nice afternoon. Ed wanted to call Rebecca, just to talk, but she had to be busy with her kids coming home. She had gotten quiet on the ride home. Had something about Bobbi upset her?

He had hoped he could repair the hurt his girls had suffered when Lisa died by helping Bobbi, but he wasn't saving Bobbi from anything. Her mom was going to die, and she was going to end up with Children's Services.

He pulled out his cell phone.

Becca answered on the first ring. "Yeah, Dad."

Ed winced at the anger in her voice. "I thought we should talk."

"Why? You're just going to do what you want."

"I heard you talked to Bobbi yesterday."

"Yeah. She told me about your date."

"I know. We went out again today."

"Really?"

Ed noticed the faint tone of interest and smiled. "Her name's Rebecca, like you."

"That's awkward," Becca said. "When will we meet her?"

"I don't know. Let's see if this thing has legs."

They were quiet for a minute. "So why did you call?" Becca finally asked.

"To apologize. I realize I should have asked you and Sandy how you'd feel about my helping Bobbi. I'm sorry I didn't. I thought you would understand what she's going through."

Becca was quiet. "Maybe I should," she finally said. "But I can't think about her sleeping in our house and pretend nothing happened. You can't expect that of me."

"I don't. I understand you're upset. You don't have to like her."

Another long pause. "We'll meet her at dinner Thursday?"

"No," Ed said. "She thinks you and Sandy don't want her around."

"I don't. Sandy wants to meet her."

"Do what?"

"She thought we should just drop over last night and surprise you. I told her about your date. She seemed happy for you."

"I'll ask Bobbi again, but I'm still not sure she'll come."

"Let me," Becca said. "I owe her an apology."

"She said you apologized."

Becca laughed. "Looks like she's not perfect. She told you a bold-faced lie."

• • •

Monday morning, Ed left a message at Rosemont. He left a second message at ten, his irritation growing. At 11:45, Marjorie buzzed him. "There's an Annie Watkins from Rosemont on line two." Ed answered immediately.

"Good morning," Watkins said. "I'm returning your call."

"Are you the Head Nurse?" he asked.

"I'm the social worker. I liaison with families about their patients, so the nursing staff can focus on care. How are you related to Ms. Love?"

Ed sighed. He was tiring of being called Andie Love's family. He explained the situation with Bobbi and her concern about Andie.

"There's not a lot we can do in situations like this," Watkins said. "There's a directive in place that is a legal document that we can't violate."

"I understand," Ed said. "Bobbi's not asking that you feed her mom, she just wants to be sure Andie isn't suffering. Can you order a brain scan or something?"

"Only a Neurologist can do that, and we need a referral from a physician..."

"Get one."

"Ms. Love doesn't have a primary care doctor."

"You're telling me you're a skilled care facility, but you can't find a doctor to look at one of your patients?"

"She's not really a patient. We're providing a bed until she dies."

"And her fifteen-year-old daughter thinks you're killing her."

Watkins sighed. "I'll tell you what I can do. We have a Family Nurse Practitioner that does rounds. I'll ask her to check in on Andie. If she sees something, she can order a test."

"She'll look at her today?"

"No. Emily is here twice a week. I'll put Andie on the list."

"Thank you." Ed did not know if Watkins' promise would change anything, but at least it meant he tried. The rest of the day passed quickly. Ed was distracted, thoughts of Rebecca intruding at work and home. He missed the way her smile lit up her entire being, the way she laughed, the touch of her hand on his arm. He called her twice, hanging up before the first ring, because although he wanted to hear her voice, he didn't want to be pushy. She said she would call.

Ed was prepping to close a kitchen remodel Tuesday morning when Marjorie buzzed his intercom. "Jane Sanderson on line one," she said. "Do you want me to take a message?"

He glanced at his watch. 11:50. The Robinsons were scheduled for noon. "No, put her through."

"Ed, I hope this isn't a bad time?" Jane asked.

"I've an appointment in ten minutes, but right now I'm free."

"Oh. I'll call another time then."

"Not at all. Unless you want to redesign the job?"

"That's Bill's job."

"Believe me, he knows."

"Is he pestering you?"

"No, that's what I'm here for. He does call every day."

"Jesus Christ," Jane said with a heavy sigh. "I'll talk to him."

"What can I do for you?"

Jane was quiet for several seconds. "Nothing really," she finally said. "I guess I wanted to apologize for Bill's behavior after you gave us the bid. I know you're the right man to do our job and Bill..."

"Doesn't agree? Maybe we should reconsider."

"No! That's not what I was going to say. I think when I tell him how glad I am that you're handling the project it makes him insecure."

"Bill?"

"I know. He's forceful, but all bluster. That's what's driven his success, more than any special talent at marketing or advertising. He can sell people on anything from the force of his personality. When he feels like he doesn't know what he's doing, he gets belligerent."

"He's not the first client who's acted that way, so don't worry about it. And I want to know what's on your mind. I'm sure you didn't call just to apologize for Bill. What's up?"

Marjorie buzzed on the intercom. "The Robinsons are here."

"Oh," Jane said, sounding relieved. "I'll let you go."

"They can wait for a couple of minutes."

"No. We can talk later. Bye." Jane disconnected. Ed wished he knew what was bothering her.

Wednesday was Ed and Lisa's anniversary. He filled his schedule with sales calls, but it did not help. He picked Bobbi up at Rosemont a little after six. He texted her from the truck, so he would not have to see Andie Love. Bobbi came out several minutes later, listening to her iPod, her afro shaking gently as she moved to the music.

"Is everything okay?" Ed asked, not sure if he was asking her about school or her mom. She gave him a look, but just shrugged. Once they got home, she dug in the fridge for an apple, and then took the dogs out back for a walk. "I don't need dinner," she said as she slipped out the door.

Ed heard her come back an hour later, while he was watching CNN. He went in the kitchen to check up on her, but she was already in her room with the dogs, door closed. He grabbed a glass and a bottle of scotch and went out back to sit on the patio and watch the stars come out. Lisa was hardest to find on days like today. The memories were there, but her voice, which seemed so real and alive much of the time, was silent. Was she mourning today as well? Or was she truly gone, and birthdays, holidays and their anniversary were the times he felt it most? As the stars bloomed above him, Ed sipped his scotch and felt nothing. It turned out to be a better evening than last year, for which he was grateful.

• • •

Lennox shopping center sat on the site of an abandoned Lennox air conditioner plant, across the river and freeway from Ohio State, a mix of big box stores, small restaurants and a movie theater complex. El Domingo's was housed in a stand-alone building on the north end of the grounds.

The girls were sitting on a green leather couch in the waiting area. Seeing them, you immediately knew they were sisters, but it was as much the way they carried themselves as how they looked. Becca was a couple inches shorter than her sister, with a more athletic build and darker hair. Sandy had light brown hair that was almost blonde in the summer. Ed could see their mother imprinted on them, but differently, somehow molded to their personalities. Sandy waved as they entered. Ed's cell phone rang before he reached the girls. He held it up, a look of irritation flashing across Sandy's face. She knew it was probably a client with a problem and he could be gone for hours. Bobbi walked forward shyly as Ed turned away.

"Ed Gideon," he said, stepping back outside into the early evening beauty.

"Hi," a woman said hesitantly, "it's Rebecca."

"Hi," Ed said, caught off guard.

"Do you have time to talk?"

"I'm at dinner with the girls."

"I won't keep you," she said, her voice soft.

"We're still waiting on our table. What can I do for you?"

"Oh, great, now you're being all professional and treating me like a client. You hate me."

"No, I ..."

"Yeah, you do. I can hear it in your voice. I don't blame you. Goodbye..."

"Wait! Don't hang up."

"Are you sure?"

"Of course. What's up?"

"I called to apologize."

"You have nothing to apologize for. I can't wait to see you again."

"I know I screwed things up by not calling," Rebecca said. "I want to see you again. I don't have time to explain right now, but I want to make it up to you. Greg's picking up the kids tomorrow at six. Can you come over after? I'd like to cook dinner for you."

"I'd love to."

There was a long moment of quiet before Rebecca spoke again. "Are you going to tell your girls about me?"

"I can't," Ed said.

"Oh."

"Bobbi already told them. They're curious as hell to meet you."

"Call me tomorrow?"

The scent of her perfume surrounded him, bringing with it the memory of her quick kiss from Saturday, and he desperately needed to see her again. "Yes," he said, the word inadequate to convey his desire to talk with her. He hung up, wishing they were having dinner, and went back inside.

The girls were sitting in a booth along the back wall. Ed was surprised to see Sandy and Bobbi sitting on one side, with Becca across from them. The two girls were talking intently, heads bent together over a notebook, Bobbi's darker skin and afro a stark contrast to Sandy's pale skin and straight hair. Becca waved and got out of the booth. She met Ed a few feet away.

"What's going on?"

"Sandy knows her from school," Becca said, disgusted. "They're looking at her sketchbook."

"You know each other?" Ed asked as he slid into the booth.

"We both had Mrs. Williams for art. Bobbi's great. Show him your sketches."

Bobbi shook her head.

"Show him," Sandy repeated.

"Okay," Bobbi said. She slid a wire bound 8 x 10 sketch pad towards Ed. The first picture was the barn behind Ed's house.

"I just started this pad the night I moved in," Bobbi said. The next page held several small sketches of Blackie and King. Ed was impressed. He had designers on staff who didn't sketch anywhere nearly as well as this.

The next drawing was a woman, sleeping. She had the bed covers drawn up over the bottom half of her face, so you could only see her eyes and hair. Her brow was wrinkled as if she wore a ferocious frown on her face. You could really see the frown even though you couldn't see her mouth. The next was the same woman, you could tell from the hair. She had thrown the covers off and was wearing a thin gown that showed off the fullness of her breasts.

The next sketch was Andie's face, pressed tightly against a thin pillow. The next revealed the hospital bed.

"What the fuck are these?" Becca demanded.

"My mom," Bobbi said. She said it quietly, no emotion in her voice, but Ed was sure if she wasn't on the inside of the booth, she would have grabbed the pad and bolted.

"Becca," Sandy said, "who did you think she was going to be sketching? Seriously?"

"She's my mom," Bobbi said. "She always refused to model for me, said she was ugly. She's not, at least not on the outside. I wanted something to remember her with."

"Put it away," Becca snapped. "I don't need to see that shit."

"I'd like one of Blackie and King," Sandy said, glaring at her sister. "If you take requests."

"Sure," Bobbi said, hesitantly. Becca shook her head. Ed could not tell if she was angrier with her sister or Bobbi. She spent the entire dinner sitting rigidly beside him, not talking. Sandy told a funny story about a date gone awry. She had Bobbi and Ed laughing as she imitated her date trying to convince her to let him order her something from the bar.

"What about you?" Ed asked Becca. "Are you dating someone?" Becca gave him an odd look and did not respond. She excused herself to use the washroom, walking quickly away as soon as Ed stood and let her out. Ed looked at Sandy who just shrugged and turned back to Bobbi to continue their conversation. When Becca returned, she was composed, but distant. Ten minutes later, Ed was paying the bill. He agreed to drop Sandy off at her dorm on his way home.

He walked Becca to her car, giving her a kiss on the top of her head. Becca grabbed him by the arm and shook her head.

"I can't do this again," she said. "I don't want to be around her. I don't understand Sandy, acting like nothing happened..."

"Becca..."

"You're not listening to me," Becca interrupted. "I don't care if she didn't kill Mom herself. She's part of it. I don't want to be around her. I don't want to be around you, if it means being around her. It's not fair that you'd put her above me."

"I'm not."

"Yes, you are. You and Sandy both." She turned and climbed into her car.

Sandy and Bobbi chatted during the short drive to campus. Sandy slid out of the truck and disappeared into her dorm, giving a quick wave before the door closed behind her. Sandy was okay, and that was good. Becca was another issue. Was it all Bobbi? She would not accept Bobbi living at the house, at least not quickly. *She'll come around eventually.* She was a compassionate girl.

Could anything else be bothering her? She had gotten even more distant when Sandy had been talking about her date. Was Becca having a problem with her boyfriend? Ed was embarrassed that he did not know her boyfriend's name. Becca had had a boyfriend her first quarter, and he vaguely remembered Lisa telling him that was over. He could not remember a big break up story, just that Becca had moved on. Was she so serious about school she was not dating at all? She never talked about it, and Ed did not feel comfortable asking. If something traumatic had happened, Sandy would break a confidence and let him know, wouldn't she?

The sun had disappeared behind the horizon leaving the clouds a deep, angry red. "That wasn't so bad, was it?" he asked Bobbi as he flipped on his headlights.

She shook her head and looked out the window.

"Everything okay?"

"I'm just thinking about Mom." Bobbi sat in silence for several minutes. "She seems to be getting more and more uncomfortable."

"How so?"

"She's not supposed to feel anything. It's been a week since they removed the IV and she's getting agitated. Every time I ask about it, they just say it's normal."

"Is she still squeezing your hand?"

"All the time now. The more she does it, the more the nurses say it's nothing. And she's moving now."

"Moving?"

"Yeah. She rolls over from one side to another."

"I've heard that people in a coma can do that, sometimes."

"Yeah, me too, but being in a coma differs from being brain-dead. I looked it up on the web and she's not acting like she's supposed to."

"Have they said when..."

"Maybe another week. Maybe two at the outside. I don't want her to suffer. She's not supposed to feel it." Bobbi was quiet for a few minutes. "I read all these stories on the web about people that woke up after being in a coma for a long time. I wonder if that's what's happening."

"But she's not in a coma, right?"

"Right."

They drove the rest of the way in silence.

CHAPTER FIVE

Ed pulled into the complex where Rebecca lived ten minutes early, resisting the urge to angle his truck into two spaces when he parked. His glanced at his phone and saw her text. *Had to work over, don't rush.* Rebecca pulled up twenty minutes later, driving an older Ford Fiesta, an embarrassed blush on her face when she saw him.

"Oh my God," she said, "I'm so sorry!" Her dark hair was pulled back in a ponytail that just brushed the top of her white blouse. The brown jumper she wore had a dark stain on the shoulder. She handed Ed a six pack of Sam Adams through the open window, rolling her eyes dramatically as she told him about having to work a double shift and then a tour bus coming in just as she was supposed to get off. Greg had been angry about picking the kids up from their afterschool program rather than her apartment. When she got out of the car, she grabbed a sack from KFC. "Dinner," she said over her shoulder as she unlocked her door. "I was hoping to cook for you, but not after today."

The door opened onto a small dining room dominated by a row of white fiberboard bookcases that ran along one wall. The shelves were filled with upright books, with more books crammed in sideways on top of them. A small desk with a computer was on the other wall. The center of the room was taken by an oval table, covered with a light green tablecloth and surrounded by four chairs.

A small galley kitchen, too narrow for a table, was directly behind the dining room with a bar top pass-through to the living room. A couch, loveseat and chair were crowded together, arms touching as they surrounded a coffee table. A TV sat on a wheeled stand against the wall, leaving just enough room for a person to walk past the coffee table.

Ed put the food on the kitchen counter and turned around. Rebecca was standing in the open doorway, wiping her eyes with one hand.

"What's wrong?"

Rebecca shook her head, fighting the tears. "I had something nice planned. I even bought an outfit. I just feel like I can't do anything right."

"Go change. I want to see this outfit. I'll dish out dinner."

"Really?"

Ed nodded. Rebecca stepped forward and gave him a kiss on the cheek. Ed dished out the food, poured two of the Sam Adams into tall glasses, and then looked for a place to sit together. Ed looked past the crowded living room to the patio. A patio table and chairs sat under an open umbrella. Ed took everything outside. He was coming back for the beer when Rebecca appeared at the top of the stairs. She was wearing a sleeveless casual dress, pastel pink, which clung to her body like a glove until it reached her hips and then loosened. The skirt fell a few inches above the knee. The scoop top was a wonderful effect; Lisa would have worn nothing so low-cut. As Rebecca walked down the steps, smiling nervously, Ed stared. How long had it been since a woman had put on something special just for him?

"You're beautiful," Ed said when Rebecca reached the bottom step.

She blushed at the compliment and Ed felt that love thing tugging on him again. How could she move him so quickly? Love was not the right word, he knew, but what was?

Rebecca followed Ed out to the patio. The sun was still high enough to shine over the tall patio fence, bathing everything in a golden hue. Ed pulled a chair out for Rebecca, angling it so they were sitting more side-by-side than across from each other. As she sat, he leaned in to kiss the back of her neck, below her ponytail, but stopped, afraid that was too intimate. He let his fingers brush gently across her shoulder before he sat and was delighted to see Rebecca offer him a dazzling smile in response.

"Tell me about this special dinner you were planning," Ed said after taking his first bite of chicken.

Rebecca blushed. "It probably wouldn't have turned out as good as the KFC," she said with a light laugh. "My grandmother used to make this pasta in lemon sauce, with chicken and peppers. It was always a favorite. I was going to throw in a salad and some garlic rolls."

"Sounds like I should have brought a bottle of wine," Ed said.

Rebecca nodded, a wide smile on her face. "No wine ruins everything."

Dinner was a blur as they chatted about their day, finishing off the chicken and a second beer each. The temperature cooled quickly after the sun set, so they moved inside. They sat in the living room, on the love seat, in the gathering darkness, the only light spilling in from over the kitchen sink.

"I want to apologize again," Rebecca said.

"Please, don't," Ed said, "dinner was wonderful."

"Not about dinner, about not calling you this week."

"You already did," Ed said. "There's nothing else to say."

"Yes, there is," Rebecca said. "I want you to know who I am. It's scary, and makes me really uncomfortable, but I'm trying to learn to be up front with myself."

Ed nodded. "Okay. Why didn't you call?"

"I got scared..."

"Scared?"

"You're so busy, running your own business and everything, and I'm just a waitress. I don't know why you like me..."

"You're beautiful, you're funny, you care about other people..."

"And then you tell me about Bobbi and her mom. I didn't know what to think. I wouldn't do that."

"It's not like I planned it," Ed responded. "Believe it or not, I'm helping myself more than I'm helping her."

"You are the only man in the world who would see it that way. Greg would keep a running tally of everything she was eating."

"How do you know I'm not doing that too?"

Rebecca stared at him, her eyes wide, shaking her head in amusement. She leaned forward and kissed him. A small kiss. Ed was enveloped by her scent, a musky, sweaty note hiding below her perfume. The surprise contact of her kiss sent an electric jolt to his groin. She pulled back, eyes searching. He pulled her close and she melted into his arms. The second kiss seemed to go on forever, all of her concentrated into the heat of the kiss and the warmth of her body in his arms.

Rebecca sank back into the love seat, pulling Ed with her. He was kissing her neck, where it met her jaw, tasting the slight saltiness of her skin, her thigh pressed between his legs. His hand was on her hip. She had a hand on his face and was making soft sounds, until she pulled his mouth back to hers.

Her tongue slipped into his mouth and Ed almost cried. He had forgotten that sweet intimacy. Not forgotten but given away so he wouldn't be tormented by the knowledge that it was lost to him forever. His hand was on her naked thigh, just above the knee, near the hem of her dress. She shuddered when he touched her, raising her knee in an invitation to explore. Ed stopped, some part of him afraid to go on, but then he felt her hand brushing the front of his pants, feeling him. He let his fingers slowly caress their way down her thigh, feeling the tension under her skin. Her breathing was ragged, her kisses hungry.

Rebecca rolled from underneath him, pulling herself away. Ed caught his breath, drinking in her beauty. She stood, grabbed his hand and pulled him from the couch and then led him to the stairs. As she started up the steps, Ed stopped. Rebecca turned to look at him, a question on her face.

"You don't have to do this," Ed said, his voice low and deep.

Rebecca smiled, her green eyes studying him frankly. "I know. I want to do this."

"Are you sure?"

Her laugh was deep and clear. "No," she said with a smile. "I haven't risked getting naked in front of someone I really care about since my divorce. I'm scared to death you won't think I'm attractive and will run from my bedroom, so please shut up and take me to bed."

Ed wrapped his arms around her, bringing her close. He kissed her, letting the warmth of her body dull his own fear. When he finally broke the kiss, he nodded up the stairs with his chin.

She kissed him again, briefly, and then turned, pulling him behind her.

• • •

Ed drove home reliving the wonder of their lovemaking. They had made love twice, the first time urgent and breathless and soul wracking. The second time had been slower and sweeter, an exploration, and even more emotional. Ed could not deny the deep attraction he felt for Rebecca or the fear he was abandoning Lisa.

That's bullshit, he thought, but the idea did not temper his guilt.

When he pulled into his drive and parked, all the lights in the house off except for the front porch, he was overcome with a rush of emotions. He missed Lisa so much. He never thought he would make love again. His tears surprised him, draining the sense of elation he had felt on the drive home, leaving him feeling weak and melodramatic. Ed took several minutes to catch his breath and calm down. He dried his face on the sleeve of his jacket and went inside.

King wandered into the kitchen to give him an accusatory stare and then went back to Bobbi's room without going out. Ed groaned. He had not told Bobbi he was going to be out so late. Nothing like having your dog make you feel guiltier than you already did. The digital clock on the stove top read 1:37. He slipped soundlessly through the dark house and up to his room.

Ed lay on his bed, staring at the ceiling. He and Rebecca were going out tomorrow and he was already thinking about exploring her body again. Did tonight give him any right to expect to make love to her again? When he had been pursuing Lisa, he had already told her he wanted to marry her before their second kiss. In his mind, they had made a promise to each other, although he had been too young to understand what that promise meant. Now he did, and he was unsure about making that kind of promise again, but he wanted Rebecca in his life. Did it need to lead to marriage?

Stop. It was one evening.

He got out of bed and walked through the dark house to the bathroom between the girls' empty bedrooms. A nightlight illuminated the room, casting small shadows around the medicine cabinet. Inside the cabinet, Ed found the unopened box of condoms he and Lisa had put there years ago and replaced every year. The box had never been touched, but Lisa had seen it as a reminder. Ed took the box and dropped it in the top drawer of his dresser. Rebecca had thought it was sweet he had been unprepared tonight and had condoms in her nightstand. He didn't want to make that mistake again.

• • •

Ed dropped Bobbi off at the nursing home just after ten on Saturday, telling her he would pick her up at two-thirty. Bobbi was getting distant as her worry for her mom consumed her. The social worker had never called him back after promising to have the FNP examine Andie.

He wished Andie Love would die already and leave him alone. But that did not really solve anything. Lisa would come back and haunt him if he let Bobbi go into the county system. Becca was afraid he was going to adopt Bobbi. Would she be okay if he became Bobbi's legal guardian?

The sky darkened gradually all morning, the heavy thunderclouds building ominously. By the time he left Bobbi at the house to head to Rebecca's, fat raindrops were splattering against the truck, whipped into an occasional frenzy by wind gusts.

Rebecca was waiting for him, in jeans and a tee, her door open. She ran out to the truck in the rain, holding a newspaper over her head to shield herself, climbing into his truck breathless from laughing. They spent the afternoon at the Franklin Park Conservatory, wandering through the different climate zones to look at the plants, holding hands the entire time. Ed did not give a damn about any of the plants, but Rebecca's hand in his was a wonder. There was a whole level of communication in their hands that he spent the afternoon trying to learn.

Standing in front of a fifteen-foot Saguaro cactus, the three upturned arms looking like a green candelabra, Rebecca dropped his hand, sidled closer and wrapped her arm around his waist. Ed copied her, feeling the heat of her body against his. Her fingers were tracing a lazy circle on his hip, a gesture so intimate that he wanted to make love to her right there.

Ed was just about to suggest dinner when Rebecca's cell phone buzzed. She glanced at the number and shook her head, mouthing "Greg" to Ed as she stepped away to take the call. He could see her talking animatedly as he walked away. She came back a minute later.

"I'm sorry, Ed," she said. "Lily got sick and threw up and now she wants to come home. I need to go get her."

Ed took her hand in his and started out towards the parking lot, feeling like a kid who had been promised Christmas and then told Santa had not come.

"You're not mad, are you?" Rebecca asked. "I could tell Greg he needs to deal with it..."

"Good God, no," Ed said, even though he wanted to say something else. "Lily needs her mom. She'll feel better at home with you."

The rain had stopped when they left the Conservatory, but the heavy clouds were still low in the sky. Twenty minutes later he dropped Rebecca at her apartment. She leaned over and gave him a quick kiss that was more promise than apology, and then she was gone, waving to him briefly as she drove away.

Lily made a full recovery by Sunday morning, but there was no opportunity for Ed and Rebecca to see each other. They spent an hour on the phone Sunday night, talking about nothing, Rebecca's voice low and flirty in his ear.

"I want to apologize again about yesterday," she said, after telling him goodbye twice.

"There's nothing to apologize for," Ed said, finally believing it. "Lily comes first."

"That's what I'm sorry about," Rebecca responded with a giggle. "You didn't come at all. Neither did I. And I was so looking forward to it. I don't know if I can wait a whole week."

Ed laughed, thrilled to hear the desire in her voice. His need to be wanted by her was so great he was afraid he might cry again. She hung up with a breathy kiss, and he lay in the dark of his bedroom, his cellphone in his hand, his heart pounding.

Monday evening, Ed picked Bobbi up after seven, grabbing dinner from a Chinese carryout. Bobbi took her dinner into her room to eat and do schoolwork. Ed did not ask her about Andie, and she volunteered nothing. He ate alone at the kitchen table, washing his dinner down with a scotch on the rocks, waiting impatiently for Rebecca to call.

He was on the patio when she called, clouds making the night sky even darker. "Ed Gideon," he said, picking up the call on the first ring.

Rebecca laughed. "Don't you look at who is calling when you answer the phone?" she asked.

"I try not to," Ed admitted. "Otherwise, I might not answer a client's call because I'm waiting on you."

"I don't see the problem with that," she said, laughing again. "I miss you so much. How can it only be Monday?"

"Maybe we should get a sitter to watch the kids one night..."

"Not yet," she said. "You don't know how much I want to do that, but they don't even know I'm dating anyone." They talked until it got too cool for Ed to sit outside. He set up the coffee maker with his cellphone pressed between his shoulder and ear, finally saying goodnight after ten.

They talked on the phone every night that week for hours at a time, telling each other goodbye over and over but still talking, until one of them couldn't stay awake any longer.

• • •

Thursday afternoon Ed was in his office, on the phone with William Sanderson, when his cell phone started vibrating. He ignored it, but it started again almost as soon as it had stopped, and again after that. He turned it over when it started vibrating for a fourth time, so he could see the number. He did not recognize it.

"I want the best quality materials..."

"I know you do," Ed interrupted. He wanted to get Sanderson off the line, so he could check out the other call. Sanderson had called every day this week to discuss some detail of the job. Ed was going to have to enforce the agreement that Jane was the only contact, or he would not get any other work done all summer.

"Bill, I've got a maniac trying to reach me on my cell phone, probably one of my girls, so I'm going to have to let you go. If you're not happy with the samples, we'll talk about a change order. I hate to cut you off, but I've really got to get to this other call."

"Listen, I've got a couple of other questions..."

"I've really got to go. I'll call Jane tomorrow." Ed disconnected. He grabbed his cell phone. Someone had called five times. He hit the redial button.

"This is Bobbi. Leave a message."

Great, Ed thought. What does she need? He scrolled to his messages to see if she had left him a voice mail. Only one, on the first call. Ed hit play.

"Ed, it's Bobbi," the message began, her voice soft. His heart immediately sank. "Call me when you can. Mom's gone."

Ed took a deep breath, a sense of relief flooding over him. Thank God that was over. He immediately felt guilty, knowing Bobbi's life had changed forever. *Shit.* He tried Bobbi's phone again but got her voice mail. *Why the fuck hadn't the nursing home called him?* That was what they were supposed to do, so he could be there with Bobbi when she found out. Unless Andie had died while Bobbi was there?

Ed stopped at Marjorie's desk on his way out. "Can you reschedule my six o'clock? Tell them I have a family emergency."

Ed climbed in his truck. The ache in his chest and shoulders was back. He should have called the social worker at Rosemont again and pushed harder for the nursing home to do something. He had been so caught up with Rebecca that he had not followed up. To be honest, he just wanted Andie Love to die. Ed chided himself for feeling guilty. Andie Love was always going to die. A doctor examining her would not have made a difference. She had killed herself. At least justice had been served. Finally.

Thinking about what Bobbi must be going through brought back one of his worst memories about Lisa's death: he hadn't been the one to tell either of the girls that Lisa had died. He'd known Lisa was dead, had felt her slip away before Andie Love had even finished the 911 call, but because of his own injuries they sent him into surgery before morning. He had called Jack from the ambulance, and like a true older brother, Jack had accepted the responsibility of telling the girls their mom was dead. The hurt he felt washing off the girls when they rushed into his hospital room had been the single most difficult part of the entire ordeal. It was even worse than knowing Lisa had died. And now he was going to feel it again, from Bobbi.

Ed parked in front of the nursing home. An attendant at the front desk tried to flag him down, but he ignored her, heading down the long hall to Andie's room. When he reached the room, he could see the empty bed, and Bobbi sitting in the chair next to the bed, talking quietly on her cell phone.

She looked up when he entered the room and smiled at him. "Gotta go," she said into her phone, then thumbed it dead. "Let's go," she said to Ed.

"Go where?"

"They took her down to OSU," Bobbi said, beaming. "I was right; she's not brain-dead."

"Do what?" Ed, gut-punched, could not breathe.

"She's going to recover," Bobbi said. Ed's heart skipped a beat at her words.

"She might recover," an older woman said from the doorway. "I'm Sue Cranston, Head of Nursing..."

"You never returned my call," Ed said venomously, heart pounding, as he spun to confront her.

"Because you spoke with Annie Watkins. She coordinated with me. A neurologist retested Ms. Love today and ordered her taken to the emergency room at OSU."

"She's going to recover," Bobbi said again.

"She's still very ill," Cranston said. "She had a high fever this morning. We're worried she might have pneumonia. And even if she recovers physically, there is still no guarantee she'll ever wake up from her coma."

"You just want her to die," Bobbi said. "You wouldn't listen to me!"

"The truck's out front," Ed said to Bobbi. He walked her into the hall. "I'll be out in a second." Once she was out of sight he turned back to

Cranston. She was standing uncomfortably, looking like a child caught in a lie. "How could you screw this up?" he snarled.

"We had a diagnosis," Cranston said. "And a living will."

Ed wanted to punch the bureaucratic smile off her smug face. "And you still fucked it up. Why isn't she dead already?"

"I'm sorry?" Cranston asked, her face as pale as Andie's had been yesterday.

Ed caught himself. He took a deep breath, exhaling the tenseness from his shoulders and chest, pulling on the veil of civility. He could pretend he was normal, that none of this hurt so badly that he wanted to hurt other people just to make them understand, even for a second, what his life had become. "Is she really going to recover?"

Cranston looked at him anxiously. She was quiet long enough Ed thought she would not answer. "The doctor was cautiously optimistic. If they knew she was responding to Bobbi, they would have never sent her here. Bobbi should have told someone sooner."

Ed felt his rage flicker again. "Don't you dare blame Bobbi for any of this." He spun on his heels and wandered down the hall, moving mechanically, his body operating on muscle memory to get him to the front door. Ed had never thought Andie Love might recover, or that he would play a part in it. He should have just told John Smith to go fuck himself. If he had never met Bobbi, she would not have manipulated him into doing this. He had betrayed Lisa and the girls by getting involved. Could he refuse to go? If he just stood here long enough, would Andie Love die? That was the only thing that would make what had happened to Ed and his girls bearable; Andie Love had to die.

Bobbi was leaning against the grill of his truck, smiling, when he came out the front door. Ed had not seen her smile before, nothing more than a quick grin when she was embarrassed. The smile highlighted her striking blue eyes, illuminating them somehow. Bobbi looked beautiful, like a fifteen-year-old on holiday, rather than the tired, wizened adult she frequently resembled. She was listening to music, moving her body in time to the beat, her curls shaking gently around her head. Her smile widened when she saw Ed. She launched herself from the truck with a laugh, wrapping her arms around him, her head resting on his chest. Ed froze, standing stiffly, wanting anything but this.

"Thank you, thank you, thank you," she chanted. "They told me you did this." She started shaking and pulled back, wiping away the tears that were falling freely. He could feel Lisa standing behind him, her hand resting gently on his back, her touch telling him to let go. If there was a heaven, she was happy right now. Ed did not understand, but he could feel it.

Bobbi suddenly stepped back, a look of horror on her face.

"You look happier when you smile," Ed said. "You should be smiling now. Your mom might recover."

"Oh my God! You've been waiting for her to die. You don't deserve this."

Ed could tell that she meant it. Her words were like a dagger to his soul. How could he want anyone to die? "Look, it's complicated, but your mom dying makes nothing better for me or the girls," Ed lied, trying to understand if that was true.

"It's closure."

Ed shook his head. "Not really. Lisa's dead, and nothing that happens to your mom changes that. It would be easy to hate your mom, and there are days that I do. Those are the days everything is fresh and agitated. Truth be told, I just had a moment like that, but its better now. Let's go."

"No."

"Do what?"

"I don't want to be the reason you keep thinking about your dead wife. I'll get someone else to take me to the hospital."

Ed shook his head. "Bobbi, everything makes me think of Lisa: seeing one of her favorites in the grocery store, hearing a story on NPR I think she'd like, talking with the girls. Sometimes I think 'I have to tell Lisa something' and then I have a moment of realization that I can't and it's like she just died all over again. Other times I just smile and feel blessed to have had twenty-five years."

They climbed in the truck. They were quiet until Ed was out of the parking lot and headed towards the freeway.

"I want my mom to get better," Bobbi said quietly, "but you won't like me anymore if she does."

"Nothing could be further from the truth," Ed said. "You should want your mom to get better. And I like you for who you are. I think I'm better for knowing you. On the drive over, I was feeling guilty because I thought Andie had died, and I felt like I'd let you down, not being with you when you heard the news."

Bobbi clapped her hand over her mouth, her eyes wide. "Fuck," she said. "I didn't think about what I said. I should have called you back as soon as I knew where she'd been moved."

"I tried to call you, but your phone went to voice mail."

"I was talking with Pete," she said softly.

"Pete?"

"My boyfriend."

"You have a boyfriend?" Shit, Ed thought. I know nothing about this kid.

"Kind of."

"You *kind of* have a boyfriend?"

"He said he wants to be my boyfriend, but we haven't gone out on a date yet."

"How old is Pete? Is he in your grade?"

"He's ahead of me."

"How old?"

"He's a senior."

"No."

"What?"

"He's not your boyfriend, and he's not going to be your boyfriend, at least not now."

"But he says he likes me."

"I'm sure he does. You're smart, funny, and pretty. But he's not your boyfriend."

"You're not my dad. You can't tell me what to do."

They were approaching the on ramp for the freeway. Ed pulled the truck over to the berm and put it in park. "You're right, I'm not, but you are living under my roof..."

"Are you kicking me out?"

"Do what?"

"Are you going to throw me out of your house?" Bobbi looked like a child again, petulant and scared.

"Why would I throw you out?"

"Because I'm disobeying you?"

"I haven't told you what to do, so you're not disobeying me. Even if you did..."

"You told me I can't go out with Pete."

"No," Ed said, shaking his head, "I told you he's not your boyfriend. At fifteen, you won't fit in with his friends, he doesn't fit in with yours, he'll be going off to college and you'll be here for two more years, so it's not a good idea. There are age differences between fifteen and eighteen that matter."

"You are telling me I can't go out with him."

"No. I'm telling you it's not a good idea. If he's the one, then he'll be around in a few years."

"He's a nice boy."

"I'm sure he is. It's still your choice, but..."

"And you won't kick me out?"

"Why do you keep asking that?"

"My mom would kick me out."

"No, she wouldn't."

"She'd say no."

"That's the first good decision I've heard her make."

Bobbi laughed. "So, what were you going to say?"

"I don't think it's a good idea. I would want you to know that you could call me at any time, and I would come pick you up and you wouldn't be in trouble. I'd need an agreement from you that you'd call at the first sign of any alcohol or drugs." Ed thought about the box of condoms he taken from the girls' bathroom. He'd move it downstairs to her bathroom. "You'd have to promise to use birth control if you were going to have sex..."

"Ewww!"

"But I wouldn't kick you out." He put the truck in gear and merged back into traffic and then onto the freeway.

"Okay."

"Okay?"

"I'll wait for a while."

Ed glanced at her out of the corner of his eye. He felt drained. Bobbi wanted a father. Needed one, but he couldn't be that person, even if the pull of it was so strong. Lisa's disapproval enfolded him, that nagging sense he was letting her down. But Andie Love was recovering, so he needed to say goodbye to Bobbi.

• • •

The OSU medical complex sat just south of the University, more than a dozen buildings spread across several blocks. Ed parked in a big garage on the south edge of the complex. Two ambulances, one with red lights flashing, were parked outside the emergency room entrance. Ed and Bobbi walked through the sliding glass doors, and then had to wait in line to go through a security checkpoint to get into the waiting area, only to learn that Andie was no longer in the emergency room. She had been admitted to ICU, on the second floor, away from the ER. They followed the directions of a volunteer, backtracking twice. It took ten minutes to find the right bank of elevators and make it upstairs.

Andie Love lie curled on her side, swaddled under several blankets, an oxygen tube under her nose, an IV line in her hand connected to four different bags on a stand. Her breathing was slow and labored and sweat glistened on her brow. A bank of machines glowed red and green with sharp, irregular lines, reminiscent of the night she tried to kill herself.

For the first time that afternoon, Bobbi faltered. She stopped inside the door and turned to Ed. "What's wrong with her? She looks like she's dying."

Ed did not want to stoke Bobbi's fears but could not ignore her point. "She is very sick," Ed said, "or she wouldn't be in ICU. You sit with her, and I'll find a doctor." He pulled a chair up for her next to the bed. Andie looked like she was on the edge of death. Her breathing, so labored and uncertain, reminded him of the day his father had died. As his father had slowly slipped away, there had been short pauses, five or ten seconds, between one breath and the next, that had made Ed think each breath was the last. He had dreaded the sound of the next breath as much as he feared not hearing it.

Ed had always hated that the girls had not had a chance to say goodbye to Lisa, but was this any better? Andie still had a chance to recover, but if she did not survive, would it have been better if she had died that first night?

Looking at Bobbi whispering earnestly to her mom, Ed could not say. Bobbi had gotten four weeks to say goodbye, to tell her mom how much she loved her and that she was going to miss her. Four weeks to prepare herself, but can you ever prepare yourself? When Ed's father had died, fourteen months after being diagnosed with lung cancer, it had been a smack in the face, something that knocked his breath away.

Maybe it was stupid to think that a few extra days ever mattered; when you lost a loved one it just hurt and was not fair and you never quite got over it.

• • •

"Hey, Sands," Cathy called from the passenger seat of Becca's car. Sandy waved and walked over to the car. She piled her duffel bag of clothing into the trunk and climbed into the backseat with her bookbag. Becca pulled away from the dock, then waited for a break in traffic to pull out. In thirty minutes, they were southeast of downtown and headed for Hocking Hills.

"What did you do for their anniversary?" Sandy asked.

"Sent him a card," Becca said.

"I didn't do anything."

"He doesn't expect us to do anything," Becca said.

"I know," Sandy said, "but this year must be a bitch, with what happened."

"He doesn't realize no one else in the whole damn world would have taken her in. Except you."

"Me? No way," Sandy said. "Why would you think that?"

"Cause you're the most like Dad. Once you get something in your head, you just dig your feet in and never let go of it."

"I'm too emotional to be like Dad. I'm more like Mom."

"You're spontaneous like Mom, but stubborn like Dad."

"What about you?"

"I'm smart, like both of them."

"Fuck you," Sandy said, playfully punching her sister on the arm.

"Admit it, you're not even upset she's living there. You like her."

Sandy shrugged. She did not need an argument with her sister to ruin the weekend. "What happened to Brian and Leah? Did they drive down separately?"

"They canceled," Cathy said. "Leah's parents wanted her to come home for the weekend to see her grandparents. She was pretty pissed."

"And we still get to go?"

Cathy dangled a key chain from her left hand. "Her mom didn't want to ruin our weekend, only Leah's."

"Wow, that's cool." She turned to Cathy. "Becca told you that I know, right?"

Cathy laughed. "She practically had a break down when I got home that night."

Sandy punched her sister in the shoulder, harder this time. "Why? I told you I was cool with it. I like Cathy."

"You know she's a worrier," Cathy said. "I didn't think you'd care."

"Are you out?"

"Kind of," Cathy said. "My mom knows. Brian and Leah know, and a few of our other friends."

Sandy settled back in her seat. "So, are you going to get married?"

"Slow down, Sands!" Becca said. "Let's graduate first, okay? It's not like we can get married anyway..."

"You can go to Canada..."

Cathy laughed. "We've talked about the future, but don't know. We always thought we'd meet guys and have kids."

"You're not gay?"

"I didn't say that," Cathy said. "I knew I was gay in middle school, but I still had this fantasy of having a big wedding and a lot of kids. If I still lived in Marietta, I'm pretty sure I would have ended up married. I'm not naive enough to think there aren't any lesbians back home, but they're invisible."

"That's awful!"

"Yeah."

"Remember when we used to pretend about having a double wedding?" Sandy asked her sister. "Then you just quit. Did you know?"

"I don't know," Becca said. "It took me a while to accept I was .... I even dated a couple of boys when I got here."

"Like make-out dated or just dinner?"

"Anyway," Becca continued, "I couldn't keep denying to myself that all my crushes were on girls..."

"What about Heath Ledger?"

"I was seventeen and he's dead. It's safe to have a crush on a guy you can never meet."

"True. When are you going to tell Dad?"

"I don't know. I don't want to let him down, you know?"

"Don't be stupid. You've always been his favorite. He won't care."

"I'm not his favorite."

"Bullshit. You should tell him."

"It's not like he needs to know right now. He's got too much on his plate anyway, what with the little bitch staying at the house."

They rode in silence for several minutes.

"So how did you meet?" Sandy asked, and then laughed. "That's a stupid question. How did you, uh, hook up?"

Becca shook her head. "Jeez, Sands..."

"You know what I mean."

"It was right after Mom's funeral. I was really depressed, just struggling with stuff, and Cathy was such a help..."

"Were you out to each other?"

"No," Cathy said, laughing. "I'd dated a couple of girls but wouldn't bring them back to the room because I wasn't ready for Becca to know. Becca seemed so prim and proper..."

"She can be the Ice Queen," Sandy said.

"Hey!"

Cathy laughed. "Anyway, Becca always had these guys coming around, trying to flirt and stuff. She never went out with any of them, but it never occurred to me she might be gay. One night after your mom died, she was lying in bed crying and it was just breaking my heart, so I climbed in with her and held her and we fell asleep like that."

"When I woke up," Becca interrupted, "and found myself in Cathy's arms, I freaked out. I thought I'd outed myself. Cathy thought she'd done the same thing."

"So, you made out?"

"No!" both girls said in unison.

"We talked for a long time, and again a couple of days later. It was a week before we kissed."

"Of course, it was. You better tell your kids you just fucked. That's more romantic."

CHAPTER SIX

The resident on call was a young Latino who didn't look any older than Becca. He was tall and lanky, with three-days growth of stubble, and a full head of curly, dark hair that seemed out of the seventies. "If your mom is alive tomorrow morning, then we've got this under control, or at least in retreat," he said.

"She could die tonight?" Bobbi asked, panicked.

"She could," the resident said, moving up to the bed. He pointed to the monitor. "But her heart rate is improving and her oxygen is up a couple percent, so she's better than when she arrived. The squad was worried she might die in transit. If she's a fighter, she can beat this."

"What about her brain?" Bobbi asked. "If she lives, will she be normal?"

"I'm not a neurologist," Dr. Rojas said, "so I can't answer that question. You'll have to talk with..." he consulted her file "... Dr. Bergeron. Please excuse me, I need to check on other patients." He left the room.

Dinner was eaten in shifts in the hospital cafeteria. Bobbi went first, leaving Ed on watch in the room. Ed sat against the far wall, the only noise in the room the hum of the equipment.

Andie Love was curled tightly on her side, her knees drawn up almost to her chest. Her skin was pale and translucent, like an old woman's, the dark blue veins in her arms and hands clearly visible. Her breathing seemed slower, less ragged than when he and Bobbi had first arrived, but Ed could not tell if that meant she was getting better or worse.

Ed stared at her, trying to see the woman who had killed Lisa, the drunk who had been so intoxicated she had walked around on a shattered ankle and not felt it. Where was his anger? Immediately after the wreck, rage had burned in him, a desire to get a gun and kill the woman who had killed Lisa, the feeling as sweet as a shot of booze to an alcoholic. He wanted to disappear into that rage and let it swallow him up, knowing it would dull his pain and grief and make things bearable. Then the girls had shown up at the hospital, and they needed him because their mother was dead, and he had to bury his anger. For two years he swallowed his anger, so he could be a father to his girls.

It had left a hole in him.

All Ed had left was his own guilt.

That night had started his war with God, and he was not winning that, either. Ed grinned and shook his head. What a romantic notion, with him the hero at the center of it all. He had no war with God. He had no time or energy to waste on trying to win a game that was rigged against him. You always died in the end.

His cell phone hummed in his pocket. He smiled when he saw the number.

"Hey," he said softly, looking around the room to be sure no one was close.

"Hi." He could hear the smile in Rebecca's voice. "Is this okay? I wasn't sure if you'd be with a client."

"No, it's okay. How are you?"

"I can't stop thinking about you," she said.

"Can I see you tomorrow?"

"Greg picks the kids up at six. I'm all yours at six-oh-one." She laughed.

"I'll be there."

"Better make it six-thirty. He's always late. Unless he sends his wife to get them."

"Ouch!"

"I know. He does it to make me angry, like he's still sixteen. You don't still act like a sixteen-year-old, do you?"

"I thought I did last week."

She laughed, long and low, so passionately that Ed felt himself twitch. He shook his head. He *was* acting like a sixteen-year-old.

"What are you doing tonight?"

"I'm at the hospital," Ed said.

"Oh my God, is something wrong with one of the girls?"

"No." Ed told her what was going on with Bobbi and her mom.

"You're too nice to that girl," Rebecca said.

"She needs someone nice in her life," Ed said. He told her about how when Bobbi met him, she had apologized.

"I know what she means," Rebecca said. "I'm happy right now, but only because you experienced this tragedy."

"You can't think that way. I worry that I made you a promise I can't fulfill."

"The only promise you made to me was to be loving and kind with me. And you were, and it was incredible and I'm so happy we did it."

"Me too."

"Besides, what makes you think it's going to happen again?"

Ed laughed. "So, that's what I should be worried about?"

"That's right, buster. At least until tomorrow night. Then I'm going to need some serious loving."

"The last time I did this, you know, started a relationship with someone, I was eighteen. I didn't understand the emotional impact of it, I was just so desperately stupid to be with her that I took all kinds of risks..."

"You're not desperately stupid for me?" Ed could hear the playful pout in her voice, and the undercurrent of truth as well.

"In ways I'll never be able to explain, but it is a little different."

"You're not walking around with a hardon all day?"

Ed busted out laughing.

"Hey, I was eighteen once, too," Rebecca said, her own laugh light and airy. "I remember how dangerous it was to slow dance at prom."

Bobbi came back from the cafeteria and sat in her chair next to her mom.

"My young ward has returned."

"I need to get dinner on the table, so I'll let you go. Let me know if anything happens."

"I will."

"Goodnight." She hung up, the phone going dead against his ear. *How long had it been since hanging up was so soul wrenching?*

"Was that your new girlfriend?" Bobbi asked over her shoulder.

"I'm gonna grab a bite. I'll be back in a few." Ed said, knowing he was blushing.

"Yeah, right."

He could tell from Bobbi's laugh as he walked out the door that she thought he was going to call Rebecca again. If she hadn't laughed, he probably would have.

• • •

The moonlight, seeping through a gap in the curtains, painted the bedroom in a faint, silvery glow, as if it were a Thomas Kincaid painting. The room was too stuffy, the heavy air suffocating. Becca pushed the covers off, unable to relax. The only sound was Cathy's slow, even breathing. The ethereal light illuminated Cathy's bare shoulder as she lay next to Becca, sleeping, having rolled away angrily when Becca didn't respond to her kisses.

How could she, with Sandy right next door? What irritated Becca most was that she knew if Sandy hadn't outed her, she would have snuck in here to be with Cathy as soon as Sandy went to bed. She pulled the sheet back up, and then kicked it off her right leg. Maybe she should just get up?

"Will you stop moving around?" Cathy asked, a note of irritation in her soft voice.

Becca startled. "I thought you were asleep."

"Can't sleep."

"Me neither. Not with Sandy..."

"Sandy's not the problem." Cathy rolled over. Her eyes were dark and intense in the faint light. "You are. You're wound up like a spring. What the hell is going on?"

"I don't know," Becca said. "I wish Sandy had brought a boy with her. Then I wouldn't feel so awkward."

"Bullshit. You wouldn't even be in this room with me."

Becca shook her head. "I need to practice."

Cathy frowned. "Practice?"

"Coming out. So, I can tell Dad." She ran her hand down Cathy's neck and across her shoulder.

"I think your dad will be fine when you're ready to tell him." Cathy said, shivering from the caress.

"I don't know. Before the accident, with Mom there, I think he'd adjust. But now his life is upside down and I don't want to take anything else away from him."

"Like what?"

"I don't know, grandkids?"

Cathy reached out and grabbed Becca's hip, pulling herself close, until their faces were almost touching. "You're gonna look so sexy, all fat and pregnant with our babies," Cathy said. "He's still gonna get grandkids."

"You want kids?"

"Fuck, yeah, I want kids. I'm gay, not antisocial. My mom would kill me if I didn't give her some grandbabies to play with."

"You never told me you wanted kids."

"Have you asked? Let's be serious, you haven't been ready to talk about the future, not seriously, have you?"

"No, I guess not," Becca said.

"We graduate in a year," Cathy said. "June thirteenth. I already marked it on the calendar."

"Yeah."

"After graduation, let's go to New York."

"New York?"

Cathy nodded, a hesitant smile on her face.

Becca shrugged. "Okay. Sounds like fun," she said.

"To get married," Cathy said, her smile blossoming. "Let's graduate and go to New York and get married. Officially start our lives together."

Becca nodded, her pulse racing. A spark of anger flared in her breast. "You want to get married?"

Cathy nodded. "It's legal there."

"Yeah, but..."

"I was looking at this magazine and they have all these wedding venues in Niagara Falls, but we could go to the city, or even somewhere along the Hudson River. There are so many places to get married, it's almost like Las Vegas."

"You want to elope?"

"No," Cathy said. "Mom would kill me. I want a real wedding. I want our families to be there. You know Sandy will be excited. She could be Maid of Honor."

"Sandy?" Becca felt like she was going to suffocate; Cathy was boxing her in. She took a deep breath, and then a second, but it didn't help. "You're asking me this now?"

"Yeah. Like I was saying, Sandy could be your Maid of Honor and Leah would be mine. Your dad could..."

"No," Becca said, shaking her head.

Cathy looked startled, her face falling as Becca's words became clear. "What?"

"No," Becca said again. "You can't just drop this on me without time to think about it. That's not fair. We need to..."

"It's called proposing," Cathy said, her voice getting tight. "People do it all the time."

"Normal people," Becca said. "We're not normal."

"Fuck you and your shame," Cathy had said. "You're the only one who thinks this isn't normal."

"What do you want from me?"

"I want a beautiful wedding, just like other people get. I want a dress and a big wedding cake and dancing."

"Well, I don't want a damn charade," Becca snapped. "We can get married in New York, but it doesn't even count here. That's just stupid."

"You're calling me stupid?"

"No. I said it's stupid to pretend we can ever be like other people."

Cathy shook her head, fighting back tears. She rolled over without a word. Becca listened to her soft crying for twenty minutes until Cathy fell asleep.

• • •

The twin lights shredded the darkness into searing brilliant pain, illuminating, for an instant, Lisa's peaceful expression, and then the world ended. The car rolled–how many times?–and somehow Lisa flew past Ed without him seeing her and out his open window, because when everything stopped, and Ed was hanging upside down by his seatbelt, Lisa wasn't there. There was not anywhere for her to be; her side of the car was accordioned down so completely that it ended next to Ed. His first thought: Lisa was crushed inside her seat. He needed to push out her side of the car to find her. Then he heard her. *Had he heard her?* He could remember seeing her mouth moving as she tried to speak but no words. What had he heard? Something, because he freed himself, fell from the ceiling and out the window to find her.

Was he upside down or just disoriented? Someone had hit him in the head with a baseball bat, he couldn't pull his thoughts together. Upside down? No, not upside down, not through the window, but pushing the car door open, the metal screaming in protest, wailing like a fucking banshee, and then spilling from his seat onto the asphalt road, his leg burning like a red-hot poker. He almost vomited when he saw the bone protruding from the gash in his lower leg, but then he saw Lisa. Had she moved? Something had caught his attention. Did she speak?

Ed hated that he could not remember what Lisa had said to him before she died.

Lisa was under the car, still alive, her eyes so big and afraid. She knew she was dying. The car had rolled across her at least once, maybe more. How had she gotten out past Ed? The physics of it seemed impossible, but there she was under the car, no way out from her crushed seat, so she had to have flown past him while the car rolled. Why hadn't he caught her? He always wanted to know what she had been saying to him. It was not fair, somehow, to lose that. He had grabbed her hand and squeezed, but she could not squeeze back, so he touched her cheek and held her while she died.

He could not remember what he had said either. He hoped it had comforted her, but how could it, when she knew she was dying? The crazy thing, as he looked around in a panic, trying to find someone to save his wife, was that one headlight from the truck was still on, illuminating the horror before him. His car was pancaked down to half its normal width, but the truck's left headlight had not shattered, shining crazily through the mist of steam from the broken radiator, illuminating Andie Love on her cell phone.

"I just killed someone."

Those were the words he could remember, but not Lisa's. Andie Love was calm: no panic, no urgency or request for help, just a matter-of-fact statement of her guilt. He had to admit she had been steadfast in accepting her guilt; had told everyone on the scene that she had done it.

Had Lisa's words been so fearful and haunting that he chose not to remember them?

Headlights shredding the darkness into brilliant searing pain. That moment was the one he relived every night when he fell asleep. That reminder that we are truly powerless, no matter what lies we tell ourselves. We do not control anything.

Ed shifted on his seat, swimming back into consciousness, glad to be free of the dream. Bobbi was sleeping, bent over awkwardly, her head resting on the hospital bed. Ed shook himself, stretching. He hated the dream. The only night he had escaped it recently was last week after making love with Rebecca.

The monitor was pinging incessantly. Ed looked at it, uncertain. All the lines were moving up and down, nothing flat. It wasn't the monitor; it was the IV machine. The little bag, the one with the medicine, was empty. After a minute, he struggled to his feet to look for a nurse, but she was there before he got to the door.

She nodded brusquely, crossed the room and turned off the alarm. Checked her notes on the chart and then started to leave without saying a word.

"How is she?" Ed asked, breaking the stillness of the night.

"Temp's down," the nurse said. "That's a good sign. You should go home."

"Can't," Ed said, pointing to Bobbi. "She'll never leave. The doctor said tonight's critical."

"I think she's passed that point," the nurse said. "Her respiration has improved, the fever is down, blood pressure is up. All good signs." She returned a few minutes later and moved past Ed to disconnect the empty IV bag and hook up another and left the room without saying another word.

Ed looked at his watch. Three forty-five. Not worth going back to sleep. He did not have any sales calls today, but since it was Friday, he had planned on stopping by several work sites. He tried to remember what jobs were on tap to finish, but his mind was not clear enough for him to visualize the work chart that hung on the wall next to his desk.

Ed slipped into the hall and called Marjorie's direct line, leaving her a message that he did not think he would make it in today and could she please email him the list of any jobs that were finishing and confirm that he had no appointments.

Another alarm started in the room, this one more insistent than the last. Ed stuck his head inside. Bobbi was stretching in her chair. She reached out and grabbed her phone from the bedside table and turned off her alarm. Bobbi stood, stretching again, looking over the monitors and then at her mom.

"Looks like she made it," she said softly. "Let's go."

"Go?"

"I've got a test in AP Euro History this morning. This bitch is not making me miss that. I'm working on a four-point-oh for the semester." She was out the door and headed down the hall before Ed could reply.

• • •

"What the hell are you doing here?" Marjorie growled as Ed walked past her desk a few minutes after eight.

"It's a long story," Ed said with a tired grin. He had driven home in silence, Bobbi on her headphones, moving in time to music Ed couldn't hear, irritating him with every smile and shake of her head. Ed could barely muster the enthusiasm required to eat a bowl of Corn Chex and drink his coffee. At seven-fifteen he was pulling out of the drive, travel mug in hand, to drop Bobbi off at school.

Ed sat down at his desk, looking over the list of jobs that were finishing. He was tired, but Fridays were all about cash flow and that was his responsibility.

His intercom buzzed. "Bill Sanderson is on line one," Marjorie said.

Ed picked up the phone. "Bill," he said, trying to sound fresh, "what can I do for you?"

"Just wanted to confirm that we're on target to start next week," Sanderson said.

"Tuesday morning. Be sure to leave a key in the lockbox we put on the back door."

"I've got the draw check for you," Sanderson said. "Can you come down to the office and pick it up? Say four o'clock?"

Ed hesitated. "Can't do it, Bill," he finally said. "I've got other obligations this afternoon. Just leave it at the house on Tuesday. I'll pick it up then."

"I'm going out of town next week," Sanderson said. "I'm not comfortable leaving the check on the fucking kitchen table. You need to come down and pick it up."

"I'm tied up this afternoon. I could send someone else..."

"I want to review the job with you. Four o'clock."

"Bill, I don't think we're communicating. I am not able to come downtown today. Not at four o'clock, not at two o'clock, not now. If you need to talk to me today, I can squeeze you in here at lunch time, but I can't come downtown."

"I'm a busy man, I want to talk with you, and under no circumstances am I going to leave a check at the house. I'm out of town for two weeks."

"Then we'll just need to delay the start of the job," Ed said, "if you really need me to come down to your office."

"What? You made a commitment to do this job on a schedule..."

"That doesn't include my coming downtown today on a whim. I got a kid staying at my house whose mom is in ICU and that's where I'm going to be this afternoon. So, you can come over to the office at lunch, leave a check on the table or delay the job. Your call."

"Maybe I made a mistake by going with your company."

"Maybe you did," Ed agreed, "if you're looking for someone to push around. We agreed that Jane was going to be the primary contact on this job, and I am going to have to insist on that. I respect you Bill, you clearly made your mark on the city, but I'm the expert in this situation and you don't know enough to do anything but screw up this job. Jane accepts that and is going to work with us. She has no ego in the game."

"Are you saying this is about my ego?" Sanderson fumed.

"You demanding I come downtown to pick up a check? Absolutely, that's an ego move, and I don't have time to play that game. If you want to cancel the job, now's the time to do so."

Sanderson was silent for several seconds. "No, I don't want to cancel the job," he said. "I really do have questions. If I stop by at twelve-thirty, can you see me?"

"Yes, but I want you to turn the job over to Jane, as we agreed. You don't like me," Ed said, "and you don't need to, but it doesn't serve this project. Jane knows what she wants, and I guarantee you that she will get it."

• • •

Jane Sanderson was dressed in a blue suit and a green silk blouse. Her light brown hair framed her face in a gentle bob that softened the sharpness of her features. She was genuine where her husband was blustery.

"Don't mind Bill," she said as she laid a check for twenty thousand dollars on Ed's desk. She laughed at his startled look. "He called me after you spoke. He's just so used to getting his own way that he doesn't respond well when he doesn't."

"Please sit down," Ed said.

"I don't want to take any of your time," Jane said. "I just wanted to apologize."

"Bill said he had questions?"

"Not about the addition. We can talk another time."

"No, please sit down. I'm available."

Jane settled into the chair across from his desk with a smile that lit up her face, making her look younger and more vibrant. "We're really excited about the patio," Jane said. "It will let us entertain outside during the summer when the weather cooperates. But it doesn't help much if it's cool or raining."

"We could do an arbor or something else to provide a little coverage..."

"But that would change the nature of the patio and I don't want to do that. Do you do party barns?"

There was an old barn on the Sanderson property, probably older than the house. He had never been inside.

"What condition is the barn in?"

Jane shrugged. "It's old. We don't use it, but Bill likes the look of it on the property. Keeps it looking like the country instead of a suburb."

"I can walk through it next week when we get started," Ed said. "How much of the original building do you want to keep?"

"From the outside, it needs to look like it does now. Bill won't even want to paint it. He likes the rustic look."

"This may require a specialist."

"I'd want you to be the general contractor on the job, no matter who does the work."

"Thank you," Ed said. "Depending on the condition of the barn, it could be a very expensive project."

"Bill and I have more money than we know what to do with," Jane said with a grin. "In addition to his business and my work, I inherited quite a bit from my parents when they passed. My father was a builder. Hospitals. Bill negotiates because he likes it, not because he's worried about the money. He wants to win. I told him he's not allowed to have any more conversations with you or the crew."

"Thank you."

"Bill said he almost fired you today. I blew a gasket."

Ed laughed. "I think the truth is that I was on the verge of dropping the job. I apologize. I have a lot going on right now..."

"Bill said something about a relative in ICU?" Jane said as she stood up to leave.

Ed shook his head. "Not a relative..., not even a friend. It's complicated and that's the problem. I'm in the middle of someone else's life and I don't want to be there, but I've got a fifteen-year-old who needs help, so what am I going to do?"

"A friend of your daughters?"

"No, she's just a kid whose mom was dying and now isn't, maybe."

"So, it's good news," Jane said, flashing the dazzling smile.

"It's just complicated," Ed said. "She's in intensive care at OSU."

Jane sat down again. "Go on," she said. "I've got a minute before I need to be back."

Ed studied the woman sitting across from him. Her eyes were frank and clear and just a little demanding. She seemed caring and genuine, but it made little sense to share anything with a client. He tried to think of a polite way to say no.

"Who is the attending?" Jane asked.

"Attending?"

Jane grinned, a faint blush on her cheeks. The mixture of confidence and shyness made Ed realize she was beautiful. "I'm sorry," she said. "Who is the doctor taking care of her?"

"The resident on call said Dr. Bergeron. We haven't met with him yet."

Jane frowned. "A neurologist?"

Ed was surprised that Jane knew who Dr. Bergeron was. He gave her a brief update on Bobbi and the last three weeks.

"Poor kid," Jane said. She dug in her purse for her cell phone and then punched in a number, ignoring Ed. "Linda? Hi, this is Jane... Can you pull a file for me? For..." Jane looked at Ed.

"Andie Love." Ed was mystified.

"Andie Love," Jane repeated. "I'll wait..." she put her phone on speaker and set it on Ed's desk, soft classical music filling the silence.

"Oh my God, this is her, isn't it?" Jane asked, the color draining from her face, her hand covering her mouth. "Andie Love? She's the one who killed Lisa?"

Ed nodded, feeling very disoriented. "How do you know about that?"

"Hospitals are small communities, Ed. We all know each other," Jane said. She looked like she was going to say something else, but then shook her head.

"Hello?" the phone said. Jane picked it up and flipped it off speaker, listening quietly, her eyes shiny.

"I understand Dr. Bergeron is the attending. Do me a favor, will you? Page Dr. McGregor and tell him I want him to take over the case. Tell him I need him to find time this afternoon to look in on her and review the file. And get a dietician in right now. She needs to be treated for starvation and hydration. Have McGregor call me once he's reviewed the case. He'll need to be available to talk with the family around..." She looked at Ed questioningly.

"Five thirty?" Ed said.

"Around five thirty. They haven't been consulted yet. Thank you, Linda." She hung up and gave Ed a sad smile.

"What just happened?" Ed asked, feeling lost.

"Leo Bergeron is a fine doctor, but it sounds like this case is a little exotic for him. Dr. McGregor will be a better fit. The suicide attempt and long period of deprivation makes this a trickier case."

"Who are you?"

"I'm ashamed of you, Ed," Jane said with a grin. "You didn't know I work at the hospital?"

Ed shook his head.

"I'm the senior vice president for community health," Jane said. "I oversee all of OSU's community health programs: the community clinics, mobile clinics and the regional health centers. That's how I met Lisa. We served on a regional emergency response committee together. I'm also a neurologist. I used to be chair of the Neurology department."

"How did I miss all of this?"

"I just like keeping that air of mystery," she said with a laugh. "Everyone assumes I'm the trophy wife, so they don't ask what I do. I guess they all think I work at Macy's or run a flower shop or something. I wouldn't mind the flower shop, to be honest."

Ed grinned, shaking his head at his mistake. "Thank you. Bobbi will be delighted to know her mom is getting the best care possible."

Jane stood up and offered Ed her hand. "I need to get back to the hospital," she said. "I'm glad we picked you to do the addition. You're one of the good guys."

"I'll let you know about the barn," he said. She was gone before he finished speaking.

CHAPTER SEVEN

She woke slowly, the room not dark enough to remain asleep, drifting towards awareness like a drowning woman under water who can see the sky but not quite reach it. The sun bore into her brain relentlessly, not letting her drift away, but her brain seemed absent her body. Her first thought, real thought, was that her daughter was gone, and it induced such panic that she knew she was crying, even if she didn't feel the tears on her face.

Where was she? She tried to look but could not move, her body deadweight. She knew her daughter was missing, that she should be here with her, but she could not remember if her daughter was an infant or an adult. If...

Bobbi.

Was Bobbi dead? Andie sucked in her breath, her heart spiking, and the tears came faster, but some part of her brain roiled in protest. She would remember if Bobbi were dead. Her breathing slowed as the panic ebbed. Maybe *she* was dead. Maybe that was why she was alone. Maybe the light was like in all those stories of people gone to heaven, but none of them said anything about it being so fucking annoying, more like a train bearing down on you than anything else.

Had she been hit by a train? Were the last two years just the dying embers of her consciousness, the fantasy that played out as she drifted towards nothingness? The train tracks had come out of nowhere, her stomach dropping as the pickup had lurched upward, the truck groaning in protest at the sudden disequilibrium. There must have been more than one set of rails because the truck bounced hard several times.

"Fuck," Andie muttered, suddenly aware she could not see a damn thing. The rain was very light now, so she rolled the window down and held her cigarette out the window like a torch, laughing as she raced down the road.

"Fuck," she repeated as the cig flew from fingers. Where the fuck were the headlights? She started feeling for the switch along the wall, laughing when her fingers ran across the air vent. This wasn't her fucking apartment, damn it.

She continued to search, feeling along the dash, until she accidentally flipped the turn signal. The blinking green arrow was mesmerizing, but suddenly she remembered. *Who the fuck decided you turn on your headlights with the turn signal?* She wanted a switch, as big around as a beer can, so she could not ever forget. She had forgotten, that was all. Who hasn't forgotten?

She flipped the lights on, delighted with herself, and looked up. Something hit her in the face, a fucking sledgehammer between the eyes and she could feel blood trickling down her face. Her left foot was jammed behind the brake petal, and she knew that her ankle was broken. Probably her nose, too.

There was a little blue car in front of her, rolling and rolling and rolling in the air, her headlights strobing off the chrome trim around the doors. Andie started laughing, so hard she was sure she was going to pee her pants. The car had gone up, flipping and flipping and flipping and then it came down, but did not go anywhere at all. Just up and down and around and around and around. She saw people in the little car; they were laughing too, because it had been so fucking funny, until it wasn't.

That was the light--their headlights--staring her down in the otherwise black night, eliminating any thought of running away.

The light was not welcoming, was not a path to heaven. It was like a fucking vacuum cleaner, sucking her up, sucking away her consciousness. Did hell have a light too? No one ever got away and wrote about hell. And hell would be her only refuge, after the car. Not hitting it, any fuck up could do that, but laughing so hard she peed her pants. But it had been so fucking funny, until it wasn't. She knew she had fucked up this time. That wasn't anything new; her entire life had been a giant fuck up. The panic was back. What will happen to Bobbi?

"Ms. Love? Andie?"

"Fuck you," she managed, although the words never came out.

Why was she even here? She *was* dead. She had waited for Bobbi to go to school, remembering too late Gram was gone and there was no one to take care of Bobbi. How the fuck do you forget your own fucking mother is dead? She still owed the funeral home four thousand dollars, and for what? Gram laid out in a rental casket in a threadbare blue dress, so much rouge crayoned on her cheeks that Gram had looked like a fucking whore. And then the minister had droned on about accepting Jesus and salvation. Jesus Christ! There had been no salvation in Gram. None at all.

How the fuck do you forget that? She hoped to God she had not killed Bobbi too. Had she turned the gas on? She remembered sitting in front of the stove, the door open, cussing as she looked at the electric heating element. *Why the fuck hadn't she turned her lights on?*

"Ms. Love." The fucking light again, boring down into her brain like a train running down a car stuck on the tracks. Had there been a train that night, further down the track, which had distracted her? She could not remember. Couldn't fucking remember who she'd been with or why she was so far away from home, or what the fuck she'd been doing but drinking and fucking. She could still feel his flotsam trickling out of her like an oil leak, and shuddered, wishing she had a tampon to keep her panties clean. She had blacked out twice in her life: the night she got pregnant and the night she killed someone. A life for a life, like they always fucking say. The rest of the fucking stuff she had done to herself she could remember: fifteen years of degradation and humiliation and trying to prove that she was as worthless as everyone treated her. Well, she finally fucking did it.

If she thought about it long enough, really dug into the twisted alleyways of her childhood, she could pinpoint the moment her life had changed. *That wasn't right.* The moment her awareness had changed, and she had become aware the game was rigged and she could never win. She was downstairs in a darkened living room with her mother, her father upstairs, both drunk.

They had been arguing. Fighting, really, but her mother would only call it arguing despite the black eye that would be visible by morning. Andie had been fighting too, tormented by her older sister, who was six and a half and would die at sixteen, driving into a bridge abutment at sixty miles an hour. In school, already known as Betty Blowjob, her death would lift her to celebrity status.

Andie could no longer remember what Betty had done to make her cry; it did not matter. She idolized Betty, loved her more than she loved her parents, and by morning she would have forgiven whatever petty thing Betty had done. But she was five and seeking justice.

Her mom poured Andie a little paper cup of wine, pouring it from her big glass. She drank wine from Highball glasses, twelve ounces at a time, three or four glasses every night. When she felt exotic, she poured her wine over ice and called it Sangria. She poured Andie a Dixie cup of wine, spilling all over her lap and not noticing, and then, holding a bag of frozen peas to her face, listened to Andie pour out her sense of injustice over whatever the fuck Betty had done.

When she was done, her mother reached out and ruffled her hair, and spoke, her voice soft and sibilant. "There's just one thing you need to do, darling, and Betty won't ever bother you again."

"What, mommy?" There was something so special about being taken into her mother's confidence, in the dead of night, to hear the secrets that made the universe work, to learn the esoteric code of adults. Andie leaned in closer, her chest pressing against her mother's legs and sipped her wine, wrinkling her nose against the bitter taste.

"Punch her in the fucking nose, as hard as you can. Make her bleed. Once for sure, but if you can get in two or three shots, do it. And don't wait for her to start something. Do it when she's unaware. You know, wake her up and punch her. Tell her you'll kill her if she ever touches you again. Can you do that for mommy?"

"Yes, mommy," Andie said, recoiling, her heart collapsing upon itself in pure horror. Hit Betty? Not on your fucking life. Betty was more God-like than God. Betty could beat her to death and Andie would not raise a finger to defend herself. Andie felt this sudden emptiness in her soul, burned there by the awful realization that this woman, beaten by her drunken husband, unable or unwilling to defend herself, would order Andie to do what she could not. She knew now, as an adult, that Gram was a fucking hypocrite. At five, all she knew was that sense of horror a hypocrite spawned. Her mother was full of shit. She would never be a place of refuge again because she was a liar, a drunk, and a bully.

And Andie had not called her mother out, had not said you're a bitch, you lie, or even how can you say this to me? Andie was just the same.

From that night on, it was game over. Andie was shit and she knew it. She had fucked up everything in her life since that night she was five. Except when she decided not to get an abortion. Bobbi had been the only good thing in her life, until she had fucked that up too.

"Andie."

She cried again, this time for real. She could feel the tears on her face now. The voice only meant one thing: she had even fucked up killing herself.

• • •

Dr. McGregor was in his late fifties, with a receding hair line and a neatly trimmed goatee. It was a little before six. Andie was asleep, not curled up, but on her back, the head of the bed raised slightly. Her knees were positioned awkwardly, a pillow underneath them. The oxygen line, IV, and monitors were still there. She was pale, but something was different. Better. Her face wasn't slack, like no one was inside, and her hands had some form to them again.

"Has mom been awake?" Bobbi asked as soon as Dr. McGregor introduced himself.

"No," he said with a brief shake of his head. "We've given her medicine to keep her asleep while her body recovers. Our testing this afternoon showed significant neural activity. We want the antibiotics to have time to work and the nutrition to make a difference and then we'll bring her out of the coma slowly."

"Will she be okay when she wakes up?" Bobbi asked.

"That's a hard question to answer today," McGregor said with a shrug. "The amount of activity suggests a high level of functioning, but it's not always the case. It's likely your mom will need PT and OT..."

"What?" Bobbi asked.

"Oh, sorry," Dr. McGregor said. "She'll need physical therapy because of the tightening of the tendons in her legs. It was part of the process of dying, but now that we've arrested that, we need to stretch the tendons out again and that will take some time."

"And the OT?"

"Occupational therapy. That helps with any life skills she might struggle with. We'll bring her out of the coma in four or five days, as long as her health keeps improving," he said. "Once that happens, she'll go to Dodd Hall for rehab. Her tendons are going to require significant PT. Maybe even surgery. She is going to need a lot of help," McGregor said. "She may need to go to the nursing home to recover."

"No," Bobbi said. "I'll help her."

"That might be a possibility," McGregor said. "The first thing is for your mom to keep responding to the medication and shake off the pneumonia. This is still a long-haul operation."

The sun was casting long shadows down the hall when Ed stepped out of Andie's room to call Rebecca. His cell phone said it was after six thirty. He shook his head as he dialed.

"Hello?" Rebecca said, a note of irritation in her voice.

"Hey, it's me," he said, feeling guilty. "I'm sorry, I'm running late."

"Did something go wrong on a job?"

"No," Ed said. "I'm at the hospital..."

"What?"

"They put a new doctor on Andie's case today. She seems to be doing better."

"Ed..."

"I cut into our time and I'm sorry. I just need to drop Bobbi off at the house and I'll be over. An hour, max."

"Is she taking advantage of you? Getting you to take her down there?"

"We needed to talk with Dr. McGregor about the long-term prognosis, so we can plan..."

"We?" Her voice was suddenly acidic.

"Look," Ed said, "If this wasn't something Lisa wanted me to do, I wouldn't even be involved..."

"You sound like Lisa still talks to you."

"Well," Ed said, suddenly embarrassed, "she does. Not literally, of course, it's just a feeling, but I know what she'd want."

"And what does she think about us?" Rebecca snapped and hung up.

His phone buzzed a minute later. "Yes?"

"Now you know Greg's side of the divorce," Rebecca said, her voice soft. "I'm a crazy bitch."

"No, you're not."

"I did just act like a crazy bitch. You probably want nothing to do with me, especially not while you're in the middle of this..."

"I'm gonna be at your place in an hour. We'll have dinner and we can talk."

Ed made it to Rebecca's apartment in forty-seven minutes. Rebecca greeted him stiffly at the door, with a little kiss on the cheek that conveyed more irritation than affection. They drove to a quiet Italian eatery a few blocks from her apartment without talking.

The waitress, sensing the tension between them, stayed away from their table after taking their order, other than a quick trip to bring more bread. It took two glasses of wine to get Rebecca to open up. She looked up from her plate of lasagna, candlelight from the table's centerpiece reflecting in her green eyes.

"I'll never measure up against Lisa or the perfect marriage you had," she said, toying with her dinner, "and now you're going to be focused on Andie Love all the time. It's kind of overwhelming."

Ed speared a piece of shrimp from a bowl of Cajun Pasta, not sure how to respond.

"I feel terrible for even saying anything," Rebecca continued. "I'm jealous of your dead wife and a woman in a coma. What kind of person am I?"

Ed laughed. He saw a look of pain flit across Rebecca's face, but quickly get replaced with a wry smile.

"It does sound ridiculous, doesn't it?" she said, grinning and shaking her head.

"You don't have to be jealous," Ed said. "Not of Lisa, and certainly not of Andie Love. As soon as she's out of the hospital I'm done with her and Bobbi."

Rebecca looked away with a small shake of her head. When she looked back at him, he was not sure if she was on the verge of tears or an outburst. "It's not just Andie Love. I'm not like Lisa. I'm just a single mom who dropped out of college because I got pregnant. I'm so worried that you'll grow bored with me."

"You have nothing to be worried about," Ed said. "I never thought I was going to date again, not really. Especially not such a beautiful, intelligent woman. You've changed my life."

"Have I?"

"Yes."

Rebecca wiped a tear away with the back of her hand. "I just look at Lisa and I'm sure I can't measure up."

"It's not like that," Ed said. "I love Lisa, and I always will. Our marriage was wonderful, but it was a marriage. We had our fights..."

"You don't have to tell me any of this," Rebecca said. "You were a nice family. I saw you at Bob Evans. You were in love."

"That's my point. We were in love. Deeply in love. But that didn't keep us from all the other crap that haunts a marriage."

Rebecca was playing with her wine glass, swirling the wine and making a miniature whirlpool inside the glass. She stared at the swirling liquid, then shook her head. "I don't know if we should be dating," she finally said. "Why do you like me? I'm just a waitress."

"Like I said, you're smart, funny and beautiful. You could finish college if you wanted to."

"Do you think so? Greg always laughed when I said I wanted to go back."

"Yeah. It wouldn't be easy, but I think you could do it."

She gave him a brilliant smile. "Thank you for saying that."

"I mean it."

"I know you do, that's why I'm grateful. I've got a bottle of wine back at my place. Would you like to sit on the patio with me and have a nightcap?"

"That would be lovely."

They rode back to Rebecca's place in silence, her hand in his whenever traffic allowed. They never made it to the patio or the wine but ended up making love on the couch in the darkened living room. He sent Bobbi a text after midnight, telling her he would not be home, and then followed Rebecca upstairs to her bed, to sleep next to someone for the first time in two years.

CHAPTER EIGHT

A discordant chorus of songbirds woke Becca before sunrise. Cathy was sleeping on her side in the dim light, facing away from the curtained window as if shielding herself from the faint but offending morning light, her short blonde hair a tousled mess. Becca did not move, studying Cathy's face. How was she going to tell her father she was in love with Cathy? *I wish Mom were still here.* It would be so much easier to come out to them together.

Becca had almost said something to her mom, right before she left for college. They had been at the Outlet Mall in Jeffersonville, shopping for her dorm room; Sandy was being bratty and had refused to come along. Becca noticed the women holding hands, a tiny infant in a sling across one woman's chest. Her heart raced when she saw them, as if she feared they were going to stop and accuse her of being gay, too. Why else did she even notice them? She tried to circle around them, but then her mom reached out and stopped her.

'What a beautiful baby," Lisa said to the couple.

The woman with the infant on her chest smiled broadly. "Thank you," she said. The second woman, who was tall, with blond hair, leaned down and kissed the baby on the head. "He's our blessing," she said to Lisa.

"How old is he?" Lisa asked.

"Almost eight weeks," the mother said.

Lisa turned to Becca, pulling her into the conversation. "It's hard to believe you were once that small and now you're going off to college."

Becca shrugged, uncertain what to say.

"How exciting!" the blond exclaimed. "Where are you going?"

"Ohio State," Becca said, feeling her blush rise.

"That's great," the blond said. The way she looked at Becca made her feel like the woman expected something else.

"What's his name?" Becca asked.

"Anderson," the mother said, "after my grandfather."

"But we call him "Coop" for Anderson Cooper," said the blond.

As they watched the women walk away, Becca felt a moment of courage. "Mom, what would you do..."

"Let's go to Victoria's Secret," her mom said at the same time, pointing out the store across the little square. "I saw a nighty in their flyer that would drive your dad wild." She raised her eyebrows and grinned.

"Geez, Mom," Becca said, blushing. She turned around and headed towards the lingerie store.

"What were you saying?" her mom had asked when she caught up to her.

"Nothing." Becca hadn't been able to say anything when her mom was being so blatantly hetero. Becca knew they had sex all the time, they were annoyingly affectionate, but for God's sake, had she had to bring it up right then?

Becca slipped out of bed, pulling on a pair of sleeper shorts and a t-shirt. She padded barefoot through the silent cabin to the small kitchen to put on coffee. As soon as the coffee had brewed, she poured a mug and headed out to the porch.

Sandy outing her had been a blessing. Becca should have known Sandy would figure it out. She and Sandy had been best friends since they were little, and how can you hide something like a being gay from your best friend?

But that did not solve her problem with Dad. *God, I wish Mom were still here.* He was not equipped; Mom would have helped him figure things out. He would be embarrassed by two wedding dresses, but that was who she and Cathy were. They both wanted to wear the dress, to walk down the aisle, to fulfill that storybook princess role. She knew coming out to him would change everything between them, but she had to tell him. Otherwise, she risked losing Cathy, and she could not bear the thought of that.

What would Cathy want? A wedding date would be good. Cathy wanted the year of planning and fretting and having fun; the showers and parties and things that all brides got. *Rings.* A pair of matching engagement rings would be just the thing to show Cathy that Becca was not afraid to let the world know they were together. She grinned, finally feeling like she figured it out. She could not go overboard, but she could afford two small solitaires. Cathy loved white gold.

Becca took her empty coffee cup back in the cabin for a refill. To her surprise, Sandy was standing at the counter, pouring a cup of coffee, wearing an oversized t-shirt and sweats as pajamas. She smiled when she turned and saw her sister in the doorway.

"Why don't you wake up your lazy ass girlfriend, so we can go for a hike? We only have two more days down here, so I don't want to waste any of today."

Becca nodded and put her empty coffee mug in the sink. The clock on the wall said 7:45. She thought about Cathy, naked under the covers, and grinned. She knew a way to wake Cathy.

• • •

"Go away."

King prodded his nose against her face again and whimpered. Bobbi groaned and pushed him away, trying to wipe the sleep out of her eyes with one hand. The sheets were wrapped so tightly she could not roll over. Blackie was on the bed next to her, his weight trapping the sheets. *Stupid dogs*. Then she remembered the late text from Ed and realized he had not been home to let them out or feed them. King whined again, insistently.

"Okay, okay," she said. "I'll let you out." King bounded away, headed for the back door, Blackie trailing him. Bobbi followed slowly, the floor cool on her bare feet. She felt stuck here, having no idea when Ed would be home, or if she would get to go to the hospital to see her mom.

She wondered if she could get Pete to take her down to the hospital. He was probably still mad she had not let him come over last night. Once he found out Ed was gone, he had gotten insistent, and Bobbi had almost said yes. She knew Pete wanted to make out. She was not against the idea, she was as curious as anyone, but she remembered the box of condoms that had shown up in her bathroom and could not say yes.

She did not want Ed to think of her like *that*.

Bobbi poured a glass of orange juice, wiping the counter clean after she dribbled a little outside the cup. She smiled, imaging the fight she would have had with her mom for not cleaning up after herself. She did not know how she was ever going to live with her mom again. She had not lied to Ed, the night all this began, when she said she had gotten her mom back, but that did not mean that everything was okay between them. How could it be? Andie had abandoned her too many times.

She wished she could stay here with Ed, but that would not happen, not if Andie was okay. Maybe if her mom ended up defective, but even that was farfetched. At some point, Ed was going to say he had done enough and let the county take her away.

She doubted she would still be here in two weeks when Sandy got home from OSU, unless her mom was a basket case. Sandy at least tried to be nice at dinner, unlike her bitchy older sister, but it was not like they were ever going to be friends.

The truth was Bobbi did not have friends. Not to hang out with. There were kids like John, a smart kid she studied with, and then Pete, who would pick her up if she asked, but made it clear that someday he expected something in return, but she had never had friends out of school, not even when she was little. How do you bring home a friend after school when you are afraid Mom will be lying on the couch in her underwear? Or worse, that the man Mom brought home from the bar last night will be next to her?

Only the wreck had changed anything. Killing Ed's wife had changed Andie. She stopped drinking, immediately. When she did not go to prison for killing Ed's wife, Bobbi had been thrilled, but Andie had been upset.

"God's just going to punish me later," Andie had said, trying not to cry. That just proved her mom was crazy, but it did not change the basic question. *How the hell was she going to live with that woman again?*

• • •

Ed woke slowly, the room darkened by pulled curtains. The ceiling fan came into focus, swirling gently, reminding him that this was not his room, not his house. He glanced to his left and saw Rebecca lying on her side, her head pillowed on her hands, her green eyes wide, a shy smile on her face. The sheet was pulled up over her hip, pooling around her waist, leaving her breasts bare. Ed's heart skipped a beat at the sight of her. He rolled on his side facing her.

"Good morning," she whispered, a radiant smile blooming across her face.

"Good morning," Ed replied. "How long have you been awake?"

She glanced down, shy again. "Maybe an hour," she said softly. "I didn't look at the clock."

"Why didn't you wake me?"

Rebecca raised her eyes to look at him, her smile luminous once again. "I didn't want to. It made me happy to see you sleeping there. I was afraid when I woke up that you would be gone..."

"Why would I be gone?"

The downward glance again, so vulnerable and afraid. "When you grow tired of me..."

Ed's hand was across her mouth, gently shushing her. "Tired of you? How could I ever tire of you?" He let his fingers trail down her chin and neck and down to her breast. He circled her nipple, smiling as it grew puffy and erect, before slipping his hand down her belly. She was wet for him and groaned at his touch. Her desire made him hard. She leaned in for a kiss, her fear forgotten, her lips soft and eager. She broke the kiss to roll away, opening the drawer on her side table. A second later she was back, a foil pack in her hand, a mischievous grin on her face.

"Last one, big boy," she said. "You'll have to buy more to prove how much you want me." Their lovemaking was as urgent as it had been on the couch last night.

Afterward, as he lay with his head on her hip and Rebecca toyed with his hair, Ed wondered how long he could keep this up. He and Lisa had been like this once, but over twenty-five years the edge had gone away, the urgency replaced with trust. They had still had moments that surprised them, but it was not like this, so overwhelming and out of control. When had they lost that sense of urgency? Lisa had known they had changed, she complained about it sometimes, but he had not quite understood. Could he have both: the easiness and the urgency and need?

"Don't you need to go to the hospital?" Rebecca asked, breaking his reverie. Ed raised his head to look at her. "Do what?"

"Don't you need to go to the hospital to check on Bobbi's mom?" Ed glanced at the clock on the bedside stand. It was almost eight.

"Damn, what about your work?"

"I traded shifts with someone. Now what about the hospital?"

"Are you kicking me out?"

"You can come back later. Go ahead, I understand."

"Why don't you come with us?"

"What? No, I don't belong. Not in any way."

"No, that's not what I mean. We could drop Bobbi off at the hospital and then go do something and pick her up when we're done."

Rebecca shook her head. "I don't think so."

"Why?"

"Didn't you tell me Bobbi said something about our first date to Becca and that's how your daughters found out about me?"

"Yeah."

"You want Bobbi to meet me before they do? You are not thinking clearly. I'll never have a good relationship with your girls if I meet Bobbi first. They'll blame me for it, and I can't let that happen."

Ed crawled up the bed even with Rebecca. "I guess you're right. Maybe we could all go to dinner sometime soon..."

"Ed, slow down."

"Do what?" He gave her a puzzled look.

"Don't be in such a rush. I want to meet your daughters, I really do, but I want to figure us out first. I need a little time. I don't want to introduce you to my kids and then have you disappear a week later."

"What does that mean? Do you need an engagement ring before you introduce me to your kids?"

Rebecca laughed. "No, silly. Who said I'd consider getting married again? I just need a better sense of who we are as a couple, and how we fit together. If it becomes apparent that we don't fit together, I can spare them going through another breakup. The divorce wasn't kind to them. Same with your girls. Once we decide who I am, whether it's girlfriend or partner or fuck buddy, then we can tell them."

"I never called you my..."

"Ed!" Rebecca rolled on top of him, her legs entwined with his. "I'd like it if you took a shower with me and took me to breakfast."

"Yes, ma'am."

"And I hope you plan on sleeping here again tonight."

"Yes, ma'am."

CHAPTER NINE

"Can she talk to me?" Bobbi asked Dr. McGregor in the hall outside Andie's room. Ed could see Andie in the bed. He had seen no difference in her appearance over the last four days.

Dr. McGregor shook his head. "She can wiggle her fingers and toes, and squeeze a hand, but she isn't fully conscious. We're going to move her to Dodd Hall and start physical therapy today. Early interventions pay off."

Bobbi went to sit with her mother.

"When do you normally do rounds if we have other questions?" Ed asked.

Dr. McGregor shook his head again. "At this point rehab takes precedence. I'll get called back in if any additional neurological issues are discovered during rehab."

"How is our patient this afternoon?" a woman behind Ed asked. Dr. McGregor looked up, his eyes widening. "Dr. Sanderson," he said. Ed turned, surprised to see Jane Sanderson standing behind him.

"Mrs., ...err..., Dr. ...," he mumbled.

Jane laughed. "Knock off the formalities. It's Jane to both of you. How is she?"

"Things are looking up," Dr. McGregor said. "Ms. Love is out of the coma."

"Great. May I go in?"

Ed nodded. "That's Bobbi, her daughter, with her."

"Your houseguest?"

Ed nodded. Jane went in the room.

"Your houseguest?" Dr. McGregor asked.

"It's complicated," Ed said. He spent the next ten minutes giving Dr. McGregor a brief narrative of how Bobbi had ended up staying with him.

"Now I understand why Jane got involved," McGregor said. "Leo Bergeron's a great doctor, but it was the right call. Things like immediate rehab probably wouldn't have happened." He left just as Jane came out of the room.

"Can I buy you a cup of coffee?" she asked.

Ed glanced towards the room.

Jane grinned. "They're engaged in quite an animated conversation. Totally one-sided of course. She's a remarkable young woman." Ed followed her to the cafeteria.

"So, what happens now?" Jane asked once they were settled in the cafeteria.

Ed shrugged. "You tell me. I just get used to Dr. McGregor and now he's done. I'm feeling kind of lost, myself."

Jane smiled. Her wide-set eyes were deep brown and seemed to both challenge and comfort him. "A hospital is an assembly of related, but separate, units, all working in the same general direction, but working independently. Dr. McGregor understands that the work they do in Dodd Hall differs from what he does and leaves it to the experts."

Ed nodded. "As an outsider, though, it's all just 'the hospital.' It's like what I do for you. I don't pour concrete, but to you, I'm your concrete guy. I hope you're not here to tell me the crew didn't show up today."

Jane laughed. "You know they did. I saw you out there at six forty-five this morning, when I was getting out of the shower. Thankfully, I might add. Bill called at five minutes after seven to see if the crews were at the house."

"I thought you and Bill were out of town this week?"

"Bill is out of town. He's in Atlanta today; then he's off to Los Angeles for a Pro-Am he sponsors and to see his grandkids. He wanted me to take the week off, but he didn't ask until the last minute. So, what happens for Bobbi, now that her mom is recovering?"

Ed shrugged. "I don't have a clue."

"Andie Love is going to need intensive physical therapy and that's best handled as an inpatient. That might get us through the summer."

Ed took a sip of his coffee. "I never thought Andie Love would recover. I'm not sure I would have signed on if I had known she might."

Jane nodded, her left hand in her right, as if she were holding it in place. "I understand. Did you look at the barn yet?"

Ed grimaced. "I'm sorry. I should really call someone..."

"I don't want anyone else doing it," Jane said.

Ed laughed and spread his hands in an apologetic manner. "Like I said, you think I'm your concrete guy."

"I'm too busy to deal with separate contractors, so you're the man."

"Okay."

"Could you stop by tonight and look at it?"

Ed glanced at his watch. "I've been summoned by my girls for dinner, and then I've got to get Bobbi home, so it would be late."

"When?"

"Eight? Maybe eight-thirty?"

Jane nodded. "That's not too late for me. Just knock on the back door when you get there." She got up from the table, gave him another brilliant smile and left the cafeteria.

• • •

The Sanderson's owned ten acres squeezed in between the Scioto River and Riverside Drive, an irregular plot of land that gradually descending to the river, where they had a boat house with a private dock. Ed pulled past the main house to the barn, his headlights illuminating Jane as she sat, beer bottle in hand, in a folding chair near the barn. Several split logs were burning inside a stone ring. Jane stood, dressed in jeans and a flannel shirt against the cooling evening, as Ed parked the truck. When he turned off the headlights, the small fire glowed brightly in the night.

"Wow, you look like a real farmer in that outfit," Ed said, climbing from the truck.

Jane raised her hands and did a slow spin. The flannel shirt was unbuttoned, hanging loosely over a tight-fitting white tank. With her long legs and slender waist, she looked more like a model than a farmer.

"I grew up in a farming community," Jane said. She kicked a wide metal bucket that sat on the ground next to the chair. "Would you like a beer?"

"Sure," Ed said. "I won't negotiate price when I'm drinking, though."

Jane grinned as she opened a bottle of Heineken and handed it to him. "You caught me," she said. "I want to get my contractor drunk and take advantage of him... in negotiations. Would you like to see the barn?"

Ed's cell buzzed. Rebecca. He felt a flash of irritation. Didn't he always call when he was done for the evening?

"Do you need to get that?" Jane asked. Ed shook his head. He hit ignore and turned the ringer to vibrate only.

The barn had a large sliding door, big enough to drive a tractor through, with a smaller door cut into it that Jane opened to let them inside. She disappeared into the darkness to their left, muttering, and a second later several naked incandescent bulbs cast a harsh light that revealed the wonder of the barn. The center gallery soared forty feet above their heads, flanked by a hay loft on each side. Eight posts, a foot square each, supported the roof and the lofts in the central gallery. Another eight posts, four on each side, rose from the main floor and through the lofts. Ed walked over to one of them and rapped gently on the hardwood. He could see the two-inch wooden pegs that had been pounded into the posts instead of nails, dating the barn to the civil war era, making it fifty years older than the Sanderson's house.

Jane held Ed's beer while he climbed down a wooden ladder to the lower level of the barn in darkness, searching the wall for the light switch Jane told him was to his left. More incandescent lights. The lower level had its own sliding door to the rear and a row of wooden stalls. Ed could see some settling had occurred to the stone foundation. Ed turned off the lights and climbed back up the ladder to where Jane was waiting.

"I'm hoping for small parties here," Jane said, "no more than thirty to forty people, fundraisers for the hospital or entertaining Bill's clients."

"It's a great space," Ed said. "I can see the potential. I would remove the loft on the right side and give a view to the roof, to create space for your guests. The stone foundation will need work, and some of the siding should be replaced. Then the electrical system, add steps to the basement and loft, and a bathroom. Do you think you need heating and cooling?"

"We won't use it in the dead of winter. I was thinking if we used it when it was cool, we could use portable gas heaters, like restaurants do. I never thought about air conditioning."

"The space has plenty of ventilation for portable heaters. Install ceiling fans instead of air conditioning. It keeps a certain vibe and saves money."

Jane nodded, taking a swig from her beer. "What does all that cost?"

"I can't give you a quote yet," Ed said. "It wouldn't be accurate."

"I'm not going to hold you to anything," Jane said, sounding a little irritated. "I need to know if it's worth pursuing at all. Are we talking twenty thousand or a hundred?"

"I'd guess thirty to forty thousand, depending on how much we have to do to level the foundation. Would you be using the lower level?"

"Not for entertaining, but we'd want it for storage. If I wanted a kitchen..."

"Don't do it," Ed said. "That could add another forty thousand. Just find a good caterer who would be comfortable working here. Plus, if you wanted to rent the space, you need to be ADA compliant, meet a whole different set of codes and have a commercial kitchen. Could run you two-fifty easy."

Jane nodded. "We'd never get the zoning variances to do anything commercial here. Bill looked into it when I first mentioned redoing the barn. He was all for it when he thought he could make a profit with it."

"Bill doesn't want to do the barn?"

"No," Jane said. "This is my project, my money. The house is too, to be honest. I own all this real estate, free and clear. It was my requirement before we bought it. I love this place. As far as Bill's concerned, he could sleep in a different hotel every night."

They had ended up back outside, in front of the fire pit. Jane pointed to the bucket. "I've got another couple of beers if you'd like to stay."

Ed shook his head, knowing Rebecca was waiting for his call. He had forgotten that feeling, like being newly married and on a tether, when you cannot stop with your friends for a few drinks because you will piss off your wife. It irritated him to feel Rebecca hovering in the background interfering with his ability to chat with a client. *Why shouldn't he stay and have another beer?*

"It's nice out here," he said, sitting next to her. "We ended up going twenty-five miles north of here to find the same atmosphere. We couldn't have afforded something down here. We got our place because the house was sound, and it was a great piece of land. We remodeled the house one room at a time."

"I love being able to sit outside at night and enjoy the sky and have a beer," Jane said.

"I would have guessed you for a wine drinker, not beer," Ed said as she handed him a second bottle.

Jane grinned. "Bill always tried to get me to switch. He doesn't think it's elegant for a woman to drink beer. I've been the lone woman at so many functions holding a beer bottle..."

"That's why Lisa always insisted on a glass," Ed said.

Jane looked away.

"Are you okay?" Ed asked.

Jane shook her head. When she looked back at Ed, he could see her eyes were wet. "I feel horrible," she said. "I haven't meant to keep a secret..."

"What?"

"Lisa and I were friends."

"Do what?"

"One of my first projects when I took over the Community Health program was to develop a stronger regional emergency response task force. Lisa was the lead for Northwest Christian. We got to know each other very well. We even went to a couple of conferences together..."

"You're that Jane? Jane from OSU?"

Jane nodded. "Bill and I were in Europe when the accident happened. I didn't find out until a couple of weeks later. Lisa was supposed to be at a regional task force meeting and didn't show. I was devastated. I sent a card..."

"I remember the card. You signed it Jane from OSU. It came late, compared to the others, that's probably why I remember. The ink was smeared, like you'd been crying."

"I'm sure I had been. Lisa and I clicked. I loved her. We had lunch regularly. We talked about going out with our husbands, but Bill wouldn't have been interested if it wasn't a business deal."

"Why didn't you say anything sooner?"

"Bill picked all the contractors who bid on the addition, and he wouldn't have known. Remember that first meeting, when I came in late?"

Ed nodded.

"When I saw the name on your truck, I thought it just couldn't be. I was going to say something, but Bill didn't even introduce me. It felt awkward, to interject something like that out of the blue. I planned to say something later, but then, when I realized I wanted you to do the job, I thought Bill would be... jealous, I guess, if he knew."

"Bill doesn't know you knew Lisa?"

Jane looked away and shook her head. "And I'm not going to tell him."

She was quiet for a minute before turning to look at him. There was a challenge in her gaze. "I almost said nothing tonight. I was going to tell you the day we signed the contract, that's the real reason I was there, but we got interrupted, and then I called you a few days later but you had clients, remember? Please understand how difficult this has been. First to learn that Andie Love was in my hospital, when I was so angry at her for killing my friend, and then to hear that you were trying to help her; it all just left me confused. I decided if you could help, then I could help. But I still didn't know how to tell you I loved Lisa."

"I never realized you were that close," Ed said.

"Maybe we weren't," Jane said, "from Lisa's point of view. She had you and the kids. But she was my best friend for two years. I could talk to her about work, and Bill, and she listened."

"And talked about me in return," Ed said.

"She loved you," Jane said.

"I know she did," Ed said, "when she wasn't completely pissed at me. I'm sure she vented."

Jane smiled. "She did. But she still loved you."

"I'm glad you knew her," Ed said after a minute. "She was a good lady to know."

"I was jealous of you..."

"Please don't say that," Ed said.

"It's scary to admit it," Jane said, shaking her head. "You had what I wanted..."

"We were just a married couple like other married couples. We fought more than we liked. Lisa was drinking too much..."

"And you were worried about her. I know, we talked about it. She was worried about it. She hated that you were so scheduled. She desperately wanted you to surprise her with something spontaneous, like skipping a day of work to be with her. She wondered, occasionally, if a long marriage was something that worked more because of inertia than passion and love."

"Wow, you *were* close." They were quiet for a minute.

"Do you know what tonight is?"

Ed shook his head.

"Our anniversary. Bill remembered yesterday. I think his secretary reminded him, so he called me last night and asked me to fly down to Atlanta today to celebrate. He didn't even think to send flowers."

"Maybe he's just spontaneous?"

Jane laughed bitterly. "I'm not Lisa, that's not my thing. Bill goes through the motions to keep up appearances. What was clear to me from Lisa was even when things weren't clicking, you were always in love. That's what made me jealous."

"I know you're right, but it's different when you live it. We knew we were in love, but we both wondered, sometimes, if love was really enough."

"You only wonder that when you are in love. You know love is enough when you're not."

Ed took a long swig of his beer.

Jane cleared her throat. "I probably shouldn't have said anything. I just thought it would be worse if you found out later that Lisa and I were friends..."

"I'm glad you told me," Ed interrupted. "She talked about Jane from OSU all the time. She was so excited when you went to that conference in DC and roomed together. She talked about walking around the National Mall together in the evenings and seeing all the history. It made her happy that you were willing to stay the weekend after the conference, so she could see the Smithsonian. She'd wanted to go to DC for the longest time. I went with the girls when they were in school, and she couldn't get off work."

"Oh my God," Jane exclaimed. "You were a chaperone dad! How cute. Did the moms flirt with you?"

Ed grinned sheepishly. "No, I kept them at arm's length. I refused to go down to the bar after lights out."

"You really do the right thing, don't you? I'm glad you agreed to have a beer with me."

"Probably shouldn't have. I don't want to start any rumors."

"Too late for that," Jane said. "I'll be telling everyone tomorrow."

"I can't let my other customers know. Soon they'll all be plying me with alcohol, and I'll turn into a raging drunk."

"Lisa once said you were a failure at being a drunk. I never understood what she meant by that?"

Ed grinned and shook his head. "I used to drink a lot when I was younger. I come from a long line of alcoholics on my dad's side, going back generations. My dad quit drinking when I was a kid, broke the cycle. When Lisa and I were young, I drank a lot. Way too much."

"Wow. Should I take my beer back?"

"No," Ed said. "I was never an alcoholic; I was just using alcohol to deal with stress. I learned better ways to deal with stress over the years."

"Like what?"

"Lisa would have told you I became a sex addict instead..."

"She bragged about how often you guys got it on. Said that week in DC was the longest she gone without sex in years."

The fire had burned down to a pile of coals, glowing red in the night but with no open flame. "I should go," Ed said. "Thank you for the beer."

"Thank you for the company," Jane said with a smile. "It's been nice to talk with someone. Please send me the quote for the barn as soon as you get it. I'd like to make a final decision right away."

Ed walked to his truck in the dark. After he climbed in the truck, he could see Jane sitting by the fire. She'd taken the flannel shirt off and draped it over her lap. She was holding another beer, still dripping water from the ice bucket and lifted it in Ed's direction in a salute. She looked incredibly sexy and lonely at the same time. He hesitated, wanting nothing more than to go back to the fire and sit with her and talk. *My God she was wonderful.* He could feel that ache at the back of his throat, a kind of physical guilt, that he felt when he did something he knew was wrong.

Ed sat there, frozen, unable to leave. It was a shock to realize he was attracted to Jane. *Go back and have another beer.* He dropped his keys on the seat, but did not open his door, Lisa and Rebecca both in his mind. Who would he be betraying? He grabbed his keys and started the truck and then turned around, not turning on his headlights until he was facing away. As he rolled down the drive towards the road, he studied her in the rearview mirror. She was watching him and raised the beer again as he pulled out of the drive.

His cell vibrated as soon as he was on the road. Ed let it roll over to the truck's Bluetooth and hit the button on the steering wheel to pick up.

"Ed Gideon," he said. "How can I help you?"

"Oh, there you are," Rebecca said. "I've been trying you all night." There was a sharpness to her tone that made him wish he had let the call go to voicemail.

"Sorry," Ed said, his voice hollow.

"I was worried something had happened to you," Rebecca said. "I called and called, and you never answered."

"I had dinner with the girls and then a meeting with a client." *Why am I explaining this to you?*

"Wow, that must have been some meeting," Rebecca said. "It's after ten. Did you sell a big job? I didn't know you had an appointment tonight."

"No, it was last minute. It was just an initial meeting, so I can put together a quote. It's for that couple I'm doing the big addition for, in Upper Arlington. They wanted me to look at their barn, see if we can convert it into a party barn."

"In Upper Arlington?"

He did not like the sense of challenge in her question, as if he were lying. "Yes, in Upper Arlington," he said. He took a deep breath, tapping his thumbs against the steering wheel to calm down. "Anyway, I just finished up. I was literally pulling out of the driveway when you called. I should have texted to let you know I was working." He hadn't even thought of texting her when he was with Jane. *With Jane?* That was the wrong way of thinking about it. He was just working on a quote for her.

"I don't understand why someone would expect you to work so late," Rebecca said. "It's just rude."

"Bob Evans is open until ten, isn't it?" Ed asked.

"That's different," Rebecca said. "We have posted hours and multiple shifts. It's just rude for someone to keep you so late."

"Not when they might spend a couple of hundred thousand with my company," Ed said, irritated. *If he wanted to have a beer with a client, with an old friend of Lisa's, for God's sake, then he was going to have a beer.*

Ed took another deep breath, the ache in his throat and chest still there. Just because Jane was lonely did not mean he was doing anything wrong. *Didn't he get to pick his own friends?*

"I just don't like it when I can't get in touch with you, and I have no idea where you are," Rebecca said. "It reminds me of Greg lying about where he was." She paused, and then continued in a rush. "I'm not saying you're like Greg; I know you're not, but I can't help feeling insecure."

"I'm sorry," he said, his irritation disappearing when he realized this was about her ex. "It's a big add-on to an already big job, and I didn't pay attention to the time.

"I missed you," he added. "The girls want to meet you. They were very emphatic at dinner."

"Sandy moves home this week?"

"Next. Thursday or Friday."

"Maybe I should meet them. And you should meet Greg and Lily."

The idea of meeting her kids suddenly made Ed feel hemmed in. "Yeah, I'd like that," he said, "but we agreed not to rush it for a reason. Let's talk about it this weekend." He pulled onto the ramp for 315 North, accelerating quickly, as if he were trying to get away from something. Ed hated feeling like he was lying to her about something, but what could he say about Jane?

"Tell me about your day," he asked.

CHAPTER TEN

Andie sat on the edge of her hospital bed, her feet not touching the floor. She had been awake for a couple of hours, and she needed to piss. Again. She had pressed the call button earlier and some bitch had brought her a bedpan. Did they think she was a fucking invalid? She did not want to use a bedpan. She was going to use the fucking toilet.

And she was fucking hungry. Not for the jello and broth they had been feeding her, or the slop they brought this morning. Who the fuck eats oatmeal? She needed real food. She could not remember the last time she had really eaten. She knew she had been drifting in and out of sleep for the last couple of days, waking up when they fed her, or when Little Miss Sunshine tortured her by bending her legs so fucking hard it felt like she was going to tear them off, but today was the first day she had not fallen right back asleep. The whiteboard on the wall had her name on it, but said it was Friday, June 4th. Were they trying to fuck with her mind? She knew it was barely May.

She needed to get out of here. Little Miss Sunshine was a chipper little bitch that Andie wanted to punch in the face. No one was that happy. The rest of them seemed like interchangeable bitches full of fake concern but not worth a damn. Andie shook her head, scooting another inch closer to the edge of the bed. She hated everyone in this place. She wanted to tell them to go to hell, but so far *fuck* was the only thing she could say. One of the nurses had told her that was normal.

Fuck normal. Andie did not have time to lie in the fucking hospital like a fucking quad. She needed to find out what had happened to Bobbi but could not ask. Another nurse, a bitch like you'd expect, had said Bobbi had visited almost every day since the accident. Didn't they fucking know why she was here? The accident part was getting found. If she ever figured out who found her, she was going to teach them a lesson they would never fucking forget.

Little Miss Sunshine came bounding into the room, a broad grin on her face, followed by a tall dour nurse straight from the Addams Family. "Whoa," Miss Sunshine said. "Don't get ahead of yourself! I said we'd go for a walk today, but that IV has to come out first."

Andie shook her head and scooted closer to the edge of the bed, so her feet were just an inch above the floor. She slid forward awkwardly, feeling her hospital gown opening in the back, and slipped from the bed. Miss Sunshine jumped forward to catch her. Andie grinned when her feet hit the floor, standing eye-to-eye with the nurse for a second, the pain shooting from her feet up her legs like lightning bolts, and then her knees buckled, and she pitched forward. Miss Sunshine caught her with an 'ooof' and they both went down, the IV tearing at Andie's hand as she hit the floor.

"She's going to be a problem," the dour nurse said. She stood in the doorway, making no effort to help.

Andie lay still for a second, her hand bleeding from the IV and everything God had given her on display. Miss Sunshine was staring up at her and laughing. Andie felt an immediate surge of anger, deepening her dislike of the young woman. She put her head down to hide her tears. *What the fuck is wrong with me?* She rolled to her left to get off the little nurse, the tile floor cold under her naked ass.

"I like your willfulness," Miss Sunshine said as she got her laughter under control. She sat up and offered Andie her hand. "I'm Dee. I'm your physical therapist. I'm going to say that every time I meet with you until you can tell me who I am and why I'm here. Okay?"

"Yes bitch," Andie said, but nothing came out, so she simply nodded.

Dee turned to the dour nurse. "Do you want to help?" The nurse sighed but came across the room. Together they got Andie up and on the bed. The nurse shook her head when she looked at the IV. The fall had almost ripped it out. She slipped the needle out and bandaged the back of Andie's hand. Dee came back up to the edge of the bed.

"That was quite an adventure," she said. "Was that a balance issue or were your legs unable to support your weight?"

Andie thought for a minute and shrugged.

"Do you know why you're here?"

Andie nodded. Who the fuck did they think they were dealing with?

"You were in a coma for a few weeks," Dee said.

Andie shook her head and pointed at the whiteboard.

"Time can seem a little messed up at first," Dee said. "Once you get your head around the calendar, you'll be okay." She smiled, but Andie didn't feel reassured.

"I know you're having trouble talking. It's called Aphasia and is quite common with folks who have strokes or other kinds of brain damage. I'm here to assess the physical impact, so we're going to see what works and what doesn't, physically, like walking, and we'll start rehab on those things. Does that make sense?"

Fuck this, Andie thought. She needed to go to the bathroom, and she wanted to see Bobbi. The rest of this bullshit could wait. She struggled to tell the young woman before her what she needed, finally spitting out the word, "Pee."

The Addams Family nurse, who had retreated almost to the door, grabbed the bedpan.

"No," Andie said, too forcefully, but the word came out immediately and clearly.

Dee pulled a long cloth strap from around her shoulders. It was several inches wide and about eight feet long. "This is a gait belt," she said. "It lets me support you while you walk, so your legs don't do all the work. Or we can use a wheelchair..."

Andie shook her head. *No.*

Dee grinned and nodded. She slipped the belt around Andie's waist and knotted it once, holding it with both hands at the knot. "Put your hands on my shoulders," she said, "and be sure to tell me if you're going to fall."

Andie scooted to the edge of the bed again, grabbing Dee's shoulders, the gait belt snug around her waist. She had a moment of fear when she slid to the floor, feeling like she was falling, but the belt and her hands on Dee's shoulders gave her just enough support that when her feet hit the floor she didn't topple over. Her legs were bent awkwardly, almost like they were stuck at the knees. Her left was worse than her right. Andie looked down at the floor. Her left foot was turned on its side, so her foot wasn't flat on the floor. Instead, she was walking on the outside edge of it, from the little toe to the heel. It felt like she was standing on razors. She bit her lip to keep from crying.

The walk to the bathroom was agonizing. Andie's right leg could support her weight despite the awkward bend of the knee, but her left leg was useless, never getting more than a half inch above the floor, her toes dragging on the ground with each step. Andie's left knee buckled each time she tried to put weight on it, nails in her foot, knee and thigh. She would have fallen without Dee and the gait belt holding her up.

Once inside the bathroom, Andie struggled to turn around for the toilet. Dee helped maneuver her, while Andie used a grab bar to keep weight off her left leg. Dee had to pull Andie's gown up so she could sit on the toilet. Andie sat down hard, her legs giving out, her pee spraying everywhere as she came down, soaking the back of her legs.

"Fuck!" Andie muttered, shaking her head in disgust, tears rolling down her face.

"Hey, that wasn't so bad, for your first walk in a month," Dee said with a grin. "You haven't had a shower in weeks, so now is a good a time as any. Let me take that gown and get a clean one."

When Andie was finished on the toilet, Dee transferred her to a white plastic shower chair on wheels and rolled her the two feet into the shower area. She pointed out the shampoo and soap, got the water going and pulled the curtain.

"I'll be back to check on you in five minutes," Dee said.

Andie luxuriated under the hot water, letting it flow over her for several minutes. Her arms seemed as normal as her legs were fucked up. She washed her hair twice and scrubbed herself with the washcloth. She wanted to get rid of that fucking sick person smell, the scent she could never forget from Gram slowly fading away. That smell of a body dying. She washed herself again and again. Dee gave her at least ten minutes and she was thankful for each one.

• • •

Ed pulled into Jane's drive at six-thirty Monday morning, to look the site over before the city inspector stopped by to sign off on the footer. The house was dark, except for a single light upstairs. The birds chattered madly as he climbed from the truck, the grass wet with dew. The sun was peeking through the treetops on the east end of the yard, the golden-pink light illuminating the work clearly.

The excavator had dug the footer for the addition, eighteen inches wide and thirty inches deep, outside the existing patio. Iron rebar had been laid throughout. Ed adjusted a couple of pieces, but everything looked good. He was sure the work would pass inspection and he could get the concrete footer poured today.

Ed heard the kitchen door open and glanced up. Jane, hair still wet from the shower, was standing in the doorway in a tightly belted white silk robe, holding two steaming coffee mugs.

"Hello, stranger," she said. "I saw you pull in from the bathroom. Would you like a cup of coffee?"

Ed nodded. She stepped down onto the patio, the robe parting slightly as she moved, showing her tanned legs and bare feet. Her breasts and nipples were evident under the silky material of her robe. "Cream and sweetener, right?"

Ed nodded and stepped over the footer, to take a coffee mug from her hand.

"Bill's not back yet?" he asked, feeling like a schoolboy checking on a rival. He turned partly away, studying the footer.

"He's on the coast for another week, pursuing a contract with one of the big studios. Sony or someone. And he gets more time with the kids."

"He does that kind of work?"

"No, but he's eager to get involved. I think he's looking for a deal for his company, you know, his golden parachute."

Ed took a sip of the coffee. "Bill doesn't seem the type to retire," he said.

"He won't," Jane said. "He'll start something new, to compete with what he's already built."

Jane settled down into one of the two plastic Adirondack chairs on the patio. Ed glanced at her out of the corner of his eye, trying not to stare. She patted the chair next to her. "Sit with me for a minute."

He sat. She crossed her legs and the bottom of her robe opened, showing off her bare feet, calves, and the lower part of her thighs. She had runner's legs, long and lean. Ed looked away, too aware of how beautiful she was. He felt himself reacting to her, that little twitch in his groin that said *I still rule your life* and he blushed. He felt like he was cheating on Rebecca just by sitting next to Jane.

He searched his mind for something to say, that nervous teenage feeling back, like just before he had asked Rebecca out.

"How much longer do I get to keep my patio?" Jane asked. "I love having coffee here in the morning."

"Just through the weekend," Ed said. "This afternoon we'll pour concrete and that has to cure. Thursday we'll lay the block foundation. Next Monday or Tuesday we will drop gravel inside the foundation for the crawlspace."

"That's too bad," Jane said. "There's a chance of rain this week, so I might not get to enjoy my coffee outside." Jane turned in her chair towards Ed, reaching out with her right hand to touch his left forearm. "Can I ask a personal question?" she asked.

Ed nodded, her touch an electric shock.

"I really loved Lisa," she said, "and I've been worried about you ever since she died. She had this—premonition is too strong a word because she wasn't thinking about the short term—but we talked about what would happen to our spouses if we died. I told her Bill would bring another woman to the funeral, and she... well, she worried that you would be one of those men who spent the rest of your life alone, in love with a memory and wrapped up in your work. You're not going to let that happen, are you?"

Ed was quiet for a moment. "Lisa actually said that to me more than once. It's hard, after twenty-five years, more actually, when you count the years we were dating, to think you'd ever be interested in someone else. But I started dating someone recently..."

"Really?" Jane interrupted.

Ed nodded. "It's just been a few weeks. She's divorced, two kids, and very nice."

"Her kids are friends with your girls?"

"Oh, no," Ed said. "Her kids are still small."

"Is she young?"

Ed was suddenly embarrassed. "Thirty-one."

"She must be very pretty and sexy," Jane said.

Ed nodded, feeling like he needed to explain. He told her briefly about how he met Rebecca.

"Lisa would be glad to know you're not alone."

"It's really too early to say," Ed said. "I'd forgotten how uncomfortable it can be while you're figuring out a new relationship. Everything means too much, you know? The other day Rebecca said she wasn't sure if we were a couple or just fu... buddies."

"You've been alone for a long time, Ed," Jane said. "You don't have to explain to me. I understand what it's like to be lonely."

Ed wanted nothing more than to take her in his arms and end her loneliness. There was something about her that captivated him, and he wanted to take her by the hand and go inside and make love to her. He knew that she would say yes. And he wanted her to say yes. He glanced at her out of the corner of his eye. She was staring off into the distance, towards the river. He finished his coffee and looked for somewhere to put the empty mug, finally setting it on the patio next to his chair. He stood up. She was staring at him, her brown eyes steady and intense.

"I'd better go," Ed said.

Jane nodded. She stood, her robe looser than before. Ed could see the tops of her full breasts under the robe. "I hope you'll stop by again for coffee and help me close down my patio."

"I'd like that," he said, his heart pounding, thrilled by the unspoken invitation.

Ed climbed into his truck, too agitated to go into the office. He hit a Starbucks drive-thru for more coffee and ended up at Highbanks Metro Park, walking along the Olentangy river, trying to calm the chaos in his heart. The occasional flirtations he had while married had been wonderful strokes to his ego, but he had never wanted to risk his marriage for an hour with another woman.

Would Lisa be in this situation if the tables were reversed? He knew she had had her own flirtations. The last had developed about the same time as her friendship with Jane and her work on the regional emergency response council. Lisa had been distracted, tense, a bit angry at him, complaining about feeling unloved.

Wasn't that why he had agreed to go dancing on their anniversary, to make a claim for Lisa?

Ed's cell phone buzzed once in his pocket. He felt an immediate surge of guilt, sure it was Rebecca sending him a flirty text. How could he even be thinking about Jane when he had Rebecca? He felt a strange mix of relief and disappointment that it was not her.

Staying late aft schl 4 proj. Can't go to hospital.

Bobbi had been avoiding her mom since Andie came out of the coma. The anxious young woman who sat for hours at Andie's side had been replaced with a surly teenager who didn't seem to care.

CHAPTER ELEVEN

The clouds were low and threatening and the morning birds were still. The silence just intensified Ed's sense of foreboding as he climbed into his truck. It was Friday and two weeks had passed since Andie Love had been moved to OSU. Two weeks of Rebecca on edge, irritated about everything. Last night, she had told him to go fuck himself after he asked her if she had ever dated two men at once, which he blurted out after she asked him how often women flirted with him on sales calls. Later, she had apologized in tears, once again blaming her ex for her insecurity. Ed had been happy to let her take the blame for the terrible call, but his own guilt exploded when a text came from Jane as Ed was getting ready for bed. *Don't forget to stop by for coffee tomorrow.* His heart had jumped when he saw it. *Sure,* he had responded.

The air was thick with little patches of mist dotting the road from the house to the freeway. Ed had to turn on his wipers as the air got wetter and wetter, spitting moisture like driving through a humidifier. The rain started, big drops that splattered heavily on his windshield, easing the stiffness in his neck and slowing his pounding heart. He was still on the outerbelt when the downpour hit, the rain sudden and blinding. Ed slowed to a crawl, knowing he did not have to decide between Jane and Rebecca this morning.

The exit to 315 South came quicker than Ed wanted. He took the exit, heading towards Jane's house, even though the excuse of coffee on the patio was washed away by the rain. Traffic was light so early in the morning, and the heavy rain made it lighter, so it was six-twenty when he pulled into her drive. The house was dark, no lights on in either the kitchen or Jane's bedroom. The hurt he felt, realizing Jane was not waiting for him, was immediate and deep, the rejection complete. Ed drove forward slowly, following the circle drive towards the barn and back towards Riverside Drive. He was surprised to see the large barn door was open, slid back on its track perhaps a foot, a dim light burning inside.

His heart started pounding again, the tightness in his neck back. He parked and dashed to the barn, slipping through the opening. Jane was inside, seated on two stacked bales of hay that were covered by a blanket. A single incandescent bulb burned in an open tack room, casting a wan light in the cavernous space. A large, black umbrella was open under the bulb, the light reflecting off hundreds of tiny raindrops clinging to the cloth. The damp and gloom made it feel like October instead of June.

Jane looked miserable, wrapped in a heavy wool robe, rubber rain boots on her feet. She stood when Ed entered, walking quickly over to slide the door shut behind him. When she turned to look at him, he could tell she had been crying.

"I almost didn't come," he said.

"You shouldn't have," Jane said, reaching out cautiously to take one of his hands in hers. "Bill came home last night. He was drunk and sure he'd catch me cheating on him. Then he professed his undying love for me and passed out on our bed. He's still there, dead to the world."

"I'm sorry," Ed said. "Rebecca and I fought last night too. I don't know what I was thinking..."

"I can't live like this," Jane said.

"You shouldn't have to." He could see she was struggling not to cry again.

"You're a good man, Ed. I don't know what I thought might happen, but whatever it was, it was wrong. Go live a beautiful life with Rebecca. She's young enough you could even have another baby. Grow old together."

Ed squeezed her hand, wishing there were something he could say or do to make things better. The kiss seemed to catch them both by surprise;

suddenly she was in his arms, her mouth so warm against his, their bodies pressed tightly together. His hands were caressing her through the thick robe, and he knew she could feel his erection pressing against her thigh. When her robe came open, Ed was not surprised she was naked underneath. She undid his belt, button and zipper, and pulled him free. They made love against a post, her legs wrapped around his waist, rain boots laying empty on the floor, her words a babbling brook in his ear. He came first, she followed a second later.

They clung to each other, breathless, his hands under her ass, pressing her into the wide post, his lips gently caressing her neck, tasting the salt of her sweat. His heart still pounding, Ed felt a deep connection to this beautiful, troubled woman, a yearning to make her cares disappear. He pulled back to look into her dark, half-lidded eyes. She grinned and kissed him, and he felt himself twitch at the thought of belonging to her.

When they came apart, after kissing for several more minutes, Jane was pale. She stood right in front of him, barefoot, pulling up his pants and making him presentable. Finally, she looked up at him.

"I didn't mean for that to happen," she said, her tears starting again. "I wanted it, don't get me wrong, but you have to have your life."

"I wanted it too," Ed said. "I've been feeling guilty because I want you so much. I don't know what I'm going to do, but I don't regret what just happened."

"You're going to go marry Rebecca and have a life again, Ed."

"Jane, I ..."

"Whatever we might have had will just get torn apart when I leave Bill. You know how ugly he is. I won't allow him to destroy you as well as me. I knew I was making a mistake when I married Bill. Now get out there and inspect something, in case he rouses from his stupor long enough to see your truck." She cinched her robe.

"I don't know that Rebecca is the woman I want," Ed said.

"Yes, you do," Jane said. "You light up when you talk about her, the same as when you talk about your girls. She's already part of your family." She pushed Ed towards the door.

Ed got soaked walking the foundation, the small umbrella he kept in the truck no match for the heavy rain. He was confused, but not unhappy.

Ed drove to the office in silence, his mind wrapped around Jane and Rebecca. Jane had just said nothing could happen between them, that Rebecca was his future. He wanted that, but he wanted Jane, too. He could not get his mind around it. He parked behind the shop, angling into the two spaces he claimed as his own. Ed grabbed his cell phone from the cup holder, surprised to see a text message that must have come while he was in the barn with Jane.

I have to be out by noon. What time will u be here? Why didn't u come last night?

Ed groaned. H had been so caught up in his head about Jane and Rebecca that he'd totally forgotten that Sandy was moving home for the summer. Fuck.

• • •

"Get out from under there," Ed ordered Blackie, who had wriggled his way underneath the kitchen table, his nose on Sandy's feet. King, too big to crawl under the table, sat behind Sandy's chair, snuffing at her neck as they finished dinner.

"They must have really missed you," Bobbi said. "They don't do that with me."

Sandy nodded. "It's annoying," she said, "but I kind of love it too. It's nice to be home."

Ed scooted back from the table. "We can go to the hospital as soon as the dishes are done," he said to Bobbi.

"Naw, I'm good," Bobbi said. "I don't need to go."

"No, you really do. You haven't talked to your mom all week."

"Yeah, but it's Friday night. Don't you have a date with Rebecca?"

"We kind of left it open this weekend," Ed said, standing up to take his plate to the sink. After making love with Jane this morning he had been sure Rebecca would take one look at him and know, but he had been saved by Sandy's text and had canceled for the weekend.

"I don't need to see her today. You made me go Wednesday."

"You didn't go up and see her, did you?"

"She's busy with rehab," Bobbi said. "She doesn't want me there."

"We're not debating this. You need to go, if for no other reason than to tell me what's going on. Let's get the dishes done and then we're going."

"I can drive her," Sandy said. "I can drop Bobbi off and go spend time with Becca and Cathy."

"Becca's not on a date?" Ed asked.

"No, she'll be with...." Sandy stopped. "We talked earlier," she said. "She was just going to stay home tonight. Cathy, too."

"Okay," Ed said with a shrug. "You can take her." He started to clear the pots from the stove. Both girls were staring at him. "What?"

"Call Rebecca and tell her you're coming over," Sandy said. "That's why we're doing this, so you can go on your date."

Ed shook his head. "I'll just finish here."

Sandy took the frying pan and the quart pot from Ed's hands. "I haven't done the dishes in three months. I think I'm due. Please call her."

Ed felt stuck. Sandy was watching him over her shoulder as she rinsed the dishes in the sink. Ed pulled out his phone and dialed. Rebecca answered on the first ring.

"Turns out the girls have plans," Ed said, "so I'm free. Would you like me to come over?"

"Please, Ed," Rebecca said. "I've been thinking about last night a lot. We need to talk." She hung up without saying goodbye.

• • •

Sandy nosed her Camry into a parking space at the hospital. She loved her car and hated that it sat in the garage, unused, for most of the year.

"I thought you were going to drop me off?" Bobbi asked.

"I want to see her," Sandy said.

"Why?"

"I don't know. Dad never let us go to any of the hearings. You don't mind if I look at her? I won't go in the room or anything," Sandy said.

"I don't mind. I think you should go in and tell her who you are and then put a pillow over her head and save the world from her next fuck up."

"Harsh!"

"Yeah, I'm so pissed at her. Your mom got taken from you, but mine chose to leave. She did it when I was a kid, too, leaving me with Gram so she could get high and fuck around. Who the fuck does she think she is?"

"Maybe you should be the one with the pillow," Sandy said.

"Don't tempt me," Bobbi replied with a bitter grin.

The garage was a block from Dodd Hall. In less than five minutes, they were stepping off the elevator into a busy hall. Sandy stopped a few feet from the room Bobbi had pointed out. She felt like she could barely breath. She turned and looked over her shoulder. Bobbi was staring at her anxiously, but she gave Sandy a little nod.

Sandy took a deep breath and reached out for the wall. The tile was cool to the touch; solid when the rest of her world suddenly felt flimsy. She took another step forward and stopped again. She wanted to turn around and run away, to run home to Dad to apologize for even thinking about coming here. Sandy took another breath, closing her eyes for an instant to center herself, but finally gave up. She edged her head around the door jamb and glanced inside.

Andie Love was lying on her side, awkwardly curled up. All you could see was her blond hair and forehead, the closed eyes and tight mouth, and the lump of her body under the sheets. She could have been dead, for all Sandy could see of her. Something caught in the back of Sandy's throat and her vision blurred. The teen wiped her eyes quickly. She would not cry. She giggled nervously, remembering how she had promised herself she would not cry at Mom's funeral and ended up bawling her eyes out. *Who wants to look at the person who killed their mom?* Becca was right, she should just hate her from afar.

Sandy took a couple of deep breaths. She did not believe most people were evil, but how do you fuck up so badly that you kill someone? She had an overwhelming desire to grab Andie Love and shake her like a rag doll and scream 'How could you do this?' at the top of her lungs.

Fuck me, she thought. I'm a mess. The cool tile under her palm calmed her. That was real, solid like Dad, steady and dependable. She took one last look at the woman in the hospital bed. She wished... wished what? That it had not happened?

Sandy turned around and left. She could see the questions in Bobbi's look, but she did not want to talk. "She's sleeping," she said as she walked by. "I'll be back by ten."

• • •

Bobbi thought Sandy was crying as she marched down the hall. She had not expected Sandy to be upset, and now felt stupid. Of course, Sandy was upset. Bobbi sighed. She had three hours to kill. She could go get a soda in the cafeteria, and call Pete. Maybe he would come down and sit with her.

A young woman in colorful scrubs came around the corner and smiled brightly. "You're Andie's daughter," she said excitedly, stopping next to Bobbi. Bobbi frowned in confusion, making the young woman laugh. "We met the day Andie came over from the main hospital. I'm Dee, the physical therapist on your mom's rehab team."

"Nice to meet you again," Bobbi said.

"I'm so glad you came. Your mom has been talking about seeing you for days."

"School's been really busy," Bobbi said, feeling her blush rise, "you know, with finals coming up and everything."

"Are you going in?"

"She's asleep. I don't want to wake her."

"Nonsense. She needs the engagement," Dee said. "She's probably awake anyhow. She spends a lot of quiet time, doesn't watch much TV."

"She hates TV," Bobbi said, "except for the news, or when she's high." Before Bobbi realized what was happening, Dee had maneuvered her into the room and next to her mom's bed.

"Look who I found in the hall," Dee said.

Andie lifted her head, her eyes narrowing when she saw Bobbi. She smiled but did not look happy. It reminded Bobbi of the first parent-teacher conference of each school year, when Andie met her teachers and tried to size up how much trouble they were going to be. Andie smiled because it was expected, not because she meant it.

Andie struggled to turn onto her back. She pushed awkwardly at a button on the bed rail and the head of the bed slowly raised. When it was about a quarter-elevated, Andie repositioned, pushing herself up into a sitting position. Every movement was labored and uncertain.

"Babe," Andie barked out when she was sitting up. Her voice was deeper than Bobbi expected, as if she were forcing the words out.

"Andie's having some speech issues," Dee said. "Don't be afraid if she slurs her words."

"Like she's drunk?" Bobbi asked.

Dee shook her head. "Not really," she said, explaining aphasia. "I'll leave you two alone, so you can talk." Dee gave Bobbi a brilliant smile and a gentle squeeze on the arm before disappearing.

"Hi," Bobbi said, wishing she had convinced Sandy to drop her off somewhere else.

"Sit."

Bobbi sat in the chair against the wall. The chair's ugly green pleather covering and stark wooden arms screamed institutional.

"Here," Andie said, slapping the bed.

Bobbi sighed but scooted the chair up to the bed. She had been sitting next to her mom for weeks, talking non-stop, and now she did not know what to say. She sat down again, but before she could lean back, Andie grabbed her hand and held it tightly. Andie had the same insane look about her that she had when she was drinking. Bobbi hated it.

"Friend?" Andie asked, her blue eyes boring into Bobbi.

Bobbi frowned. "No, I never met her before. She was the physical therapist."

"Not Dee," Andie said. Bobbi could hear the exasperation in her mother's voice. It was the first thing her mom had said that sounded normal. "Other girl, tall one. Friend?"

"Sandy?" Bobbi had not realized her mom had seen Sandy looking in from the hallway. "She brought me."

"She friend?"

"Not really," Bobbi said with a shrug. "We had the same art teacher last year, but she goes to college now. She was coming down here to visit her sister, so she offered to bring me."

"School?"

"Just two days next week for finals. We had to make up seven snow days."

"How doing?"

"Why the fuck are you asking? You don't fucking care." Bobbi jerked her hand free, startled by her own anger.

"Not true," Andie croaked. She reached for Bobbi's hand again. Bobbi let her take it, but it just made her feel more irritated.

"You wouldn't have done it if you cared about me," Bobbi said, her voice rising. "We finally had a life together and you threw it away."

"Fuck," Andie said. She shook her head and tried to smile, but it looked more like a painful wince. She drew in a deep breath, and then a second. "I didn't..."

"Killing yourself isn't throwing it away?" Bobbi could feel her control slipping away. She was shouting now but did not care. "You hated me so much that you wanted me to find you? How the fuck could you do that to me? Why didn't you just kill me too?"

"Thought about it..."

"That's enough visit time today." Dee scurried into the room, pulling Bobbi's hand free of Andie's. "I could hear the two of you shouting all the way down the hall." She turned to Bobbi. "Go wait for me in the hall."

Bobbi did as she was told. She stood in the hall, fighting the urge to cry, her heart pounding wildly. Her chest was so tight she thought she might be having a heart attack. Bobbi wiped her face with the inside of her arm, wiping the tears away before they could spill over. She tried to calm her breathing, and the pressure she was feeling in her chest slowly relaxed. She could hear Dee lecturing Andie inside the room. Bobbi could not make out what Dee was saying, but from her tone she was giving Andie hell. Bobbi grinned. It was about time someone told her mom off.

Bobbi took in another deep breath. She should have known that she could not count on her mom. Andie might as well have died six weeks ago. She sure as fuck could not live with her. Ed would send her away soon, probably next week when school ended. Where was she going to go?

"Come on, kiddo," Dee said, as she came out of the room. She wrapped her arm around Bobbi's shoulder. "Go sit in the lobby. I need to check on something, but I'll be right there. I want to talk with you."

Bobbi took the stairs down to the first floor and sat in the deserted lobby. Dee joined her a few minutes later, sitting next to her on the little couch.

"I should have seen that coming," she said as she settled in. "We probably need someone in there with you for the first meeting. We have some counselors..."

"No," Bobbi said, shaking her head. "I won't visit her again."

"Okay," Dee said. "We'll see. I called your dad to come get you..."

"You mean Ed? He's not my dad." Bobbi suddenly stopped. "You called him? How? He's on a date."

"His cell phone number is in the file as the emergency contact," Dee said. "I'm sorry, I thought he was your dad."

"I'm Black, how could he be my dad?"

Dee shrugged. "Well, a boyfriend of Andie's. Anyway, he's on his way down to pick you up."

"No!" Bobbi shook her head. "Why didn't he just call Sandy? She's my ride."

"He said nothing about that," Dee said. "He just said, 'I'll be there right away' and hung up. Maybe he could come with you the next time you visit and act as a buffer while you and Andie reconnect."

Bobbi turned part way towards Dee. "You don't know what happened, do you?" She told Dee what Andie had done.

"Oh my God," Dee said when Bobbi finished telling her about the wreck.

Bobbi laughed. It was freeing, a way to let out all the pain and anger that was coiled inside of her. "Yeah. So, he can't talk with her."

"Okay. We'll find someone else."

"What about you?" Bobbi asked, although she did not want to reconnect. "You seem to like her."

"I'm not trained to do that kind of work," Dee said. "I work with people's bodies, but I'm not so good with their emotions. And I do like Andie. She's a fighter. I like attitude and it's clear she has that."

"You don't mind that she killed someone?"

Dee shrugged. "It's not that simple. I can't judge people and then provide them the best possible care. Lots of people I've helped are here because of something they did, usually something horrible, like driving drunk, or stupid like jumping a bicycle off the roof of their house, and a couple, like Andie, killed someone. I don't know of anyone, though, who did it on purpose."

"But didn't she, climbing into her truck after drinking so much?"

"I'm not saying she isn't responsible," Dee said. "I'm saying she didn't go out looking for someone to kill. What happened in there?"

"I didn't realize how pissed I was. All this time I've just been praying she'd recover and now that she has, I just want to tell her to fuck off."

"I have moments like that with my mom and she's done none of the stuff Andie has, so I wouldn't be too hard on yourself. It's okay to be mad if you don't stay mad forever. She's still your mom."

"But she tried to kill herself. How could she just abandon me like that?"

"Like I said, I'm not a head doctor. I wish I could help, but I can't."

"Don't most people keep trying until they die?" Bobbi took a deep breath to fight the panic that was swirling around her heart.

"Some people try again and again," Dee said, "but not most people. One of the greatest risk factors for suicide is having attempted it before, and about 20% of people who kill themselves have attempted suicide more than once. But only seven percent of people who try to kill themselves and fail try a second time."

"I thought you weren't a head doctor?"

Dee laughed. "I took a class on suicide prevention when I was in college. I had an uncle who killed himself before I was born, and I wanted to understand why."

"Did it help?"

"It helped me, but I made the mistake of telling my mom. Just made her angry. She thought I was reopening old wounds, so I quit talking about it when I went home."

"Will we be weird when we become moms?"

"Do you know a mom who isn't?" Dee said. "I think the pregnancy hormones do something to your brain."

"Does that worry you? That you'll change when you become a mom?"

Dee nodded seriously. "Terrifies me, but not so much I don't want kids at some point."

"I don't know," Bobbi said. "I look at my mom and I'm afraid I'm too much like her."

"You've got a long way to go before you need to think about having kids," Dee said. "I'm thirty and I don't have kids yet."

"I'm sorry I've kept you so late," Bobbi said.

"It's my late night. Are you okay? I'm going to take off."

Bobbi nodded. "Thanks."

"I'm going to make a note on Andie's chart to have her counselor set up an appointment with the two of you for next week, okay?"

"Okay." Bobbi watched Dee disappear down the lobby corridor, knowing she wouldn't go to the appointment.

• • •

Ed drove to Rebecca's apartment as slowly as he could, his stomach roiling and spinning. It was a few minutes past two, her shift at Bob Evans finished, and he was supposed to take her to lunch. Last night he had been saved by the call from the hospital. What could save him today?

He had stood in front of her door last night, unable to knock, the stench of his infidelity wafting off him as if he were a dead animal by the side of the road, despite the fact he had scrubbed Jane's scent away in the shower before he came over. It hadn't worked of course, because Jane's scent was part of him now, marking his skin and hair and being, her taste not just on his lips but in his soul.

Rebecca had opened the door, wearing an oversized t-shirt that made it clear she was wearing nothing else, a hesitant smile on her face, just as his phone had rung. A few seconds later, Ed had agreed to go get Bobbi. Rebecca had wilted in front of him as he explained why he had to run, but he had been able to breathe again.

Now he was headed back, no more resolved on what to do than he had been last night. Yesterday morning had been a one-time indiscretion, except that Jane captivated him. Jane had a quality Rebecca could never possess right now: the confidence of a woman who had survived her thirties and most of her forties and knew who she was, who had gotten her head above water, who could complete herself. Rebecca was in the early part of her journey of self-discovery. Although Jane and Lisa had found themselves, Rebecca would not get there for another ten or fifteen years. Did Ed want to be part of that journey again?

Ed shook his head. The problem was not Rebecca's maturity, it was his. He had never been the kind of prick to think about dating two women at the same time. He hated the thought of hurting Rebecca by telling her what he had done, but he did not see another way.

He hated even more that he desperately wanted to stay quiet.

Rebecca was getting out of her car as he pulled into her parking lot. She smiled, hesitantly, when she saw him, her green eyes large in her face. She was so beautiful. Ed's heart raced at the sight of her, and he knew he could not let her go. She waited by her car as he parked, a smile on her face. "Come on in," she said. "I need to shower before we go eat."

Ed wanted to find an excuse to stay outside, where it was safe. Rebecca must have seen something on his face because she gave him a dirty grin, shaking her head. "I need to eat before we get up to that kind of fun," she said. "You wait in the living room."

Ed followed her inside. Rebecca ducked into the kitchen to open the fridge, pulling out two cans of Kroger's diet cola. She handed one to Ed as she brushed past him and then headed for the stairs. Ed followed her, his heart pounding. His Dad's AA token lay heavy on his chest, burning into him.

"Look," he said, "there's something I have to tell you..."

Rebecca stopped on the second step, her hand searching behind her back for the jumper's zipper and looked at him over her shoulder. "Ed, do you love me?"

"I, uh..."

"See, I don't know if I love you, either. I think I might, but I need more time to know for sure. You need more time, too. So, we're good. Really, we are." She turned and went upstairs.

"I'd like to believe that," Ed said, following her. He expected to feel relief at her words, but all he felt was his guilt, that overwhelming ache in his neck and chest that made him want to cry. He did not know if he hated what he had done more than what he was doing now. Which was the real sin?

"Pardon the mess," Rebecca said as they entered her bedroom. She kicked off her shoes. The small room, dominated by the queen bed and matching dresser, was becoming familiar to Ed. The bed was unmade today, a cotton nightgown pooled on top of the sheets.

"I was rushing to get to work," she said apologetically.

"You should see my bedroom," Ed said, but they both knew his room was much neater than this one.

"I'd like that," Rebecca said shyly. "Is that an invitation?" She turned away from him and lifted her ponytail. "Could you get my zipper?"

He stepped behind her and unzipped the jumper down to her waist, revealing the back of her bra through the thin material of her blouse. Rebecca shrugged her uniform from her shoulders, letting it fall to the floor. Her lacy black panties peeked out under the edge of her blouse. She turned and gave Ed a flirty look over her shoulder, wiggling her ass at him. "Like what you see, big boy?"

Ed nodded, unable to speak. She was so beautiful. She gave him a peck on the cheek and walked into the bathroom, unbuttoning her blouse as she went. She dropped it on the floor.

"Listen..." he said, his heart pounding. *Just shut up.*

"I know what you want," Rebecca said, looking at him through the open door, her bra in her hands. She stared at him, daring him to look away from her eyes to her naked breasts, an amused smile on her face.

"You know?" His heart skipped a beat.

"Ed, we all have secrets, half-truths, things we're afraid to admit because we're ashamed of them. As you know from our call the other night, I have my own secrets. I don't need to trade with you."

"I'm not trying to get you to tell me anything."

"It doesn't work that way, Ed. We've been on edge all week, irritable and avoiding each other. If you're done with me, just tell me you're done. Don't use a secret to break up with me."

"I don't want to break up with you."

"Good." She gave him that brilliant smile and turned away. Ed nodded, relief flooding over him. She was saving them from his best intentions. An image of Jane came to mind, in her barn, naked under her open robe, the tip of her tongue caught between her teeth as she zipped him up, and his heart sank. He had loved the way Jane had put him to order after they had made love as much as he had loved the sex.

"Look, this isn't..." he stopped, unable to continue.

"Okay, Ed, we'll do it your way," Rebecca said, back in the doorway, a sad smile on her face. "The other night you asked how many lovers I've had since Greg. You should have asked how many I had while I was married."

"No," Ed said. "You're not listening to me."

"You listen. You wanted the list of all the men I've fucked so you can feel better about whatever you did." Her voice dropped, and the look of shame on her face was an arrow to Ed's gut.

"After I found out Greg was cheating on me the first time, I went a little crazy. I was hurt by what he'd done, but even more hurt by the idea I wasn't enough for him. That I wasn't pretty enough, or sexy enough, or maybe I was too inhibited and wouldn't do things in bed that he wanted, or whatever. He never told me why he cheated, so I just had this emptiness inside me. Why wasn't I enough?"

"Rebecca," Ed said, taking a step forward, but she raised her hand and stopped him from moving closer.

"I needed to feel attractive and desirable, and wanted Greg to be jealous of me again. How screwed up was that, wanting my husband to be super jealous and angry again? I told myself that at least then I had known he loved me. Anyway, I fucked around and made sure he found out. Guys I met at the gym. There were three guys, over a year. Four technically, but I didn't sleep with one of them...

"Rebecca..."

"I thought that if Greg knew other men thought I was sexy he'd want me more. He'd been so jealous before, but it didn't work. He had already decided he was through with me. I realize now that he had never loved me, not really. I felt so abandoned when I understood. He didn't even get angry when he found out about the last affair. He said I was a terrible mother, to fuck around when I had kids. I reminded him of his affair. He told me to shut up because his situation was different. He was in love. That's when he told me he'd gotten his little bitch pregnant, and he wanted a divorce."

"Stop."

"You wanted this," Rebecca said. The blush had spread from her face to her breasts. "When he told me he'd gotten her pregnant, I broke down. I told you that Greg pushed me, but what I didn't tell you was that I slapped him first, twice. Punched him, really. I gave him a black eye..."

"Do what?" Ed asked, shocked.

"I gave him a black eye. I was so angry that he would do this to our kids. To me. What kind of man does that? That's when he pushed me, to get away from me. He threatened to call the police on me, to have me arrested and take the kids away."

"My God," Ed said.

"I begged him not to. Told him I'd do anything he wanted. He could have his little bitch and her baby, and I wouldn't complain, he just couldn't take my kids away. We fucked, right there in the hall, and afterward he told me he was leaving anyway. That my hitting him proved I was unstable. I must have cried for an hour, laying on the floor. I only pulled myself together when the kids woke from their nap.

"Greg held that over me for months, even after I moved out. He'd tell me he was still thinking about filing charges against me. I was afraid every day he was going to take the kids away. It took me months to realize he didn't want them full time."

"I don't know what to say..."

"I'm not done," Rebecca said, sitting down on the closed toilet, pulling her knees up and wrapping her arms around them as if she were cold. "I was desperate to be loved after that, and I did things I'm not proud of. I mean after the divorce, now. Guys would ask me out, guys that I knew couldn't be good for me or the kids, but I wanted so desperately to be loved that I would do whatever they wanted. Things I would have never considered when I was married. I kept thinking maybe that was why I lost Greg, because I was a prude or something. One time..."

Ed stepped forward and took Rebecca by the hand. "I don't need you to tell me this," he said. "It doesn't change the way I feel about you." He pulled her gently to her feet and wrapped his arms around her, pulling her tight against his chest. She was stiff in his arms for at least a minute, but then she softened and let her head rest against him, her tears wet on his neck. He hadn't understood what her divorce had cost her. His confession didn't seem important any longer.

Rebecca pulled her head back, looking up at him. "You wanted to say something?"

Ed froze. He couldn't stay quiet now, not after everything she had revealed. "Well," he began, "I... huh..."

"I don't know how Lisa handled it," Rebecca interrupted. "Not for twenty-five years."

"Handled what?"

Rebecca laughed, but it was sad, not joyful. "When you fucked your clients."

"I never cheated on Lisa," Ed said, sad that this statement, so true for Lisa, was a lie for Rebecca. "Not once. That's not who I am."

"But you were married."

"Hell, yes, I was married. And I never cheated."

"But we're not married."

"Does that make a difference?"

She stared at him, clearly trying to find the right words to express herself. She started twice, stopping each time before she said anything, and then shrugged. "I deserve to be happy," she said. "You make me happy. So, unless you want to break up with me, I'm done with this conversation."

"I don't want to break up with you." *Or Jane.*

He leaned in to give her a kiss, the faint scent of maple syrup surrounding them. They made love on the unmade bed, Rebecca on top, whispering his name, over and over, her voice breathy in his ear. Afterward, she pulled him into the shower, and he soaped her back, his hands playing with her ass until she turned on him and they kissed so long the water turned cold. It was time for an early dinner.

CHAPTER TWELVE

Andie stared at the lifeless construction site outside her window, the orange metal cranes disappearing into the dark, oppressive clouds. *Fuck.* Andie hated the idea it might rain again–it had rained every day for the past week—almost as much as she hated the breakfast tray an aide had left with her. Lunch and dinner were okay, but they could not make a decent breakfast to save your life; it was always powered scrambled eggs or institutional oatmeal or soggy French toast. Andie shoveled some of the scrambled eggs onto a piece of limp toast and took a bite, chewing mechanically. It was like eating cardboard.

It felt like she'd been here for an eternity, endless rounds of PT with Dee, absolutely useless speech therapy, and then the idiot shrink Ambrowicz. In between staring at her tits, he asked the most fucking stupid questions you could imagine. Ambrowicz's face was so bland and safe that Andie wondered if he'd ever had a beer, let alone gone a three-day drunk.

"You said killing yourself was just being 'realistic.' What does that mean?" Ambrowicz had asked in their last session.

Andie had stared at him, knowing she didn't have the words. How could she describe the wonder of getting so high she couldn't remember who she had fucked, but could still feel every touch, could see every cock, could lay in her stupor and revel in each second of what had happened, totally sated, feeling the need slowly building back up? She had never had the vocabulary, even before her speech got fucked up, to describe the ruin of her own soul. She had tried, at AA meetings, but had seen the blank looks on the faces of the people at the meeting. If addicts didn't understand her, how was it possible that someone normal would? When a dog has rabies, you put it down. You have no choice.

Andie took a sip of her coffee and wrinkled her face in disgust. Lukewarm and bitter. What the fuck was wrong with these people? Breakfast was not her problem, though. What was she going to do about Bobbi? Bobbi hadn't been back since their shouting match a week ago.

Bobbi was beautiful, and unaware. Not just pretty, Bobbi had this glow, this thing from inside, a sense of herself, or a spirit—Andie couldn't describe it—that made you stand up and notice her. Boys were going to be all over her soon if they weren't already. They were going to want her because she was pretty and the ones who were empty inside were going to want her for that glow, that spirit. Like vampires, they would want to consume her, thinking she could sustain them. Without help, Bobbi would have no defense against them. They would be the ones showing her attention and she would end up seventeen and pregnant. Or if she got on the pill, they would use her up until she hated herself and wanted to die, all the while thinking she was having a great time.

Andie pushed the eggs away. She wondered if booze had lost its taste, too. Isn't this like being dead? If nothing has aroma or taste, if music has no beat, and even the sun on your skin is cold, what's the point?

Everyone thought Andie tried to kill herself because of the anniversary of the fucking wreck. How was killing herself going to make that better? She had killed someone. Big fucking deal. Killing someone was meaningless compared to living in world that meant nothing if she was not high. That need burned brighter in her today than it had the morning after the accident.

The wreck. Call it murder if you like, but not an accident. The hunger to get high had grown more and more insistent until it had threatened to consume her. Andie had been in her bedroom, awake at four in the morning, thinking about the stash of pills in her drawer. She got up, searching her drawer in the dark to find the baggie, and had brought it back to bed with her. She wished she had some vodka to chase the pills down–just two of them–for the perfect high. In the morning, once Bobbie left for school, she could walk over to Kroger for a bottle. Maybe tequila would be better than vodka. She did not really care, as long as it was not gin. Gin might as well be formaldehyde, but if gin were all she could buy… She had giggled at the idea, and then cried. If she got high again, she would never come down.

She thought about flushing the pills down the toilet, but that would not keep her from the liquor store at Kroger. In that moment, dying had seemed like the only true solution. She had just wanted to save her soul.

Andie sighed and looked out at the clouds loitering above the construction site. She hated the weekend. No PT today or tomorrow. Not even any speech therapy or a visit from the creepy shrink, Ambrowicz. She hated the staff, but Dee was growing on her. A ball of energy, and cute as a button. Mean as fucking badger, too. Dee pushed Andie much harder than Andie would have pushed herself, but Andie would not let little Miss Sunshine win.

Andie closed her eyes, biting her lip to keep from crying. Not thinking about what would happen to Bobbi once she was dead was proof that two years of sobriety and AA meetings had done nothing to change her fucked up approach to life. She did not even know where Bobbi was staying. Bobbi had looked clean, well fed, had said she was going to school, so she was not living on the streets, but who had taken her in?

"You didn't like the eggs?" The aide was back, picking up the tray of half-eaten food.

Andie gave her the biggest smile she could muster. "No. Taste like horse shit." They were all worthless here, every fucking one of them, except maybe Dee.

• • •

Sandy stared at the ceiling of her room, then back at her laptop. She turned it off, bored with Facebook. Having Bobbi in the house was weird. She remembered when she was seven or eight begging her parents for a little sister, not understanding the mechanics of it, or the odds of a brother instead of a sister. Sandy had been disappointed for months after her mom had told her there would be no baby.

Could it be that Bobbi was supposed to be that kid? That would suck.

She liked Bobbi, but Becca was going to shoot somebody if Bobbi were to stick around much longer. "You'd better not be friends with her," Becca had said when Sandy was leaving after her last visit.

Why shouldn't I be? Becca did not get to make the rules forever. Maybe it was time for Sandy to play older sister for a while. She stood up from her desk and headed downstairs. Bobbi was lying on her bed listening to music, Blackie curled up next to her.

"Wanna get some dinner?" Sandy asked.

"I don't have any money."

"No, I got it. Is Donato's okay?"

"Sure."

Donato's Pizza was in a little strip mall about fifteen minutes from the house. The girls ordered at the counter, a medium sausage with onions and green peppers and an order of cheesy garlic bread and two sodas. Bobbi winced when it came out to almost twenty dollars, but Sandy waved away her concern.

"I told you, I've got a job. I got it." She went and sat in a booth by the front windows, right in front of her car.

Bobbi slid in opposite her. "Is your sister still pissed about me being here?"

Sandy grinned and nodded. "Becca's afraid Dad will ask you to stay forever."

"I can't do that. Ed's done so much for me."

Sandy felt relieved to hear Bobbi say she could not stay.

"What was your mom like?" Bobbi asked. "No one ever talks about her."

"It's still too hard, I think."

"Oh, I'm sorry. You don't have to..."

"No, it's okay. Becca and I talk about her all the time. Not with Dad, though. He still seems lost without her. That's why we're so glad he found Rebecca.

"Now about Mom. She was happier than Dad, well... more flexible. More spontaneous. Dad is very even keeled, and Mom was a lot more emotional. If you pissed her off, she'd give it to you good. I never wanted her mad. And she had lots of friends. He doesn't have very many at all. I even wondered if she was having an affair a couple of times."

"Really?"

Sandy nodded. "She'd get really close to people and her job had weird hours..."

"So does Ed's..."

"Yeah, but could you ever imagine him cheating? And I'm not saying she did or anything. She was just too close with people sometimes."

"My mom would kill someone if they cheated."

"I'm sure Mom would have too."

"No, I mean it. She stabbed a guy once 'cause he cheated on her."

"Do what?"

"It was just a butter knife in his arm, barely broke the skin. I think he laughed. He never called the police. It was weird, because she slept around all the time, even turned tricks."

"No way."

"Yep. She would do anything to get high. She told me once Gram had been the same way, but I never believed her. Gram was the only good thing in my life growing up."

They ate silently for a few minutes. "Do you really think your mom cheated?" Bobbi asked.

"No," Sandy said, shaking her head. "She loved him too much. She just got too close to people. It made me uncomfortable sometimes to see her hug someone or kiss them."

"Your dad didn't care she had all these guy friends?"

"She got close to men and women. That's why I wish she were here right now. I think she'd understand about Becca and Cathy being together better than Dad will. She'd help him... Fuck."

"Becca is gay?"

Sandy stared at Bobbi for several seconds and then shrugged. "You can't tell Dad. If you do..."

"Why would I do that?" Bobbi asked, shaking her head. "It's none of my business."

"I just want Becca to be able to tell him when she's ready."

"Then maybe you should move out," Bobbi said. "You're a blabbermouth."

Sandy grinned. "I know. She needs to come out soon, so I don't screw everything up. What would your mom do if you were gay?"

"She wouldn't give a fuck one way or the other."

"That's pretty cool. Most parents would freak out."

"Well, my mom's a freak, so it doesn't matter. She never cared about stuff like that. She always said that people were too self-righteous, and she didn't want to be that way."

"Maybe you should go see her again."

"Yeah, I've been thinking about it. Dee said I need someone with me to be a buffer so we both behave."

"Okay." Sandy said. "I'll go with you. We can go right now."

"No," Bobbi said, shaking her head. "She'd think I was attacking her. I can't take you."

"You don't have to tell her who I am," Sandy said. "I'm just the girl you're staying with."

"I don't know."

"Who could be a buffer?"

"They have a counselor working with her. That's who I thought it would be."

"Okay. What do you want to do tonight?"

"You really mean it? You'll go with me right now? Why?"

"I hated your mom for a long time. I don't understand why she is alive, and my mom is dead. I thought God was fucked up. I hated you when I heard about you staying with Dad. But then I met you and you are so not hateable."

"Thank you, I guess."

Sandy laughed. "Yeah, I know. My point is, I think I need to know her to decide if I hate her. If she's not someone I can hate, well, that might be okay. And maybe not. But I feel like I should meet her."

"Okay."

"Really?"

"I gotta go back. Might as well go now."

Twenty-five minutes later, Sandy was pulling into the same garage she had parked in the week before. When she got out of the car, she could feel her heart racing.

The Dodd Hall lobby was deserted when the girls entered. They took the elevator to the second floor. A group of young men, one of them using a wheelchair, were clustered around a coffee table covered in fast food bags, playing cards. The men were laughing loudly and looked both girls up and down when they stepped off the elevator. The guy in the wheelchair whistled and Sandy flipped him the bird. The guy slumped in his chair, clutching his chest as if he had been shot, making Sandy shake her head and grin. A chorus of laughter followed them down the hall.

Bobbi stopped outside the door to her mom's room. "Are you sure?" she asked quietly, looking over her shoulder at Sandy, her blue eyes piercing. Sandy nodded. Her heart was pounding in her chest, and she felt a little dizzy. She was embarrassed to feel so nervous. She wished she could be calm, like her dad, or determined like Becca, instead of always feeling out of place. Bobbi walked into the room, Sandy following a step behind.

Andie looked up, an oversized paperback in her hands. She grinned when she saw Bobbi and set the book on the bed. Sandy could not get over how normal Andie looked. She was small and pale but did not look like someone who had almost died. Or who had killed someone.

"Hi," Bobbi said. Sandy gave a little wave.

"You... back," Andie said.

"Yeah," Bobbi said quietly. "You couldn't have thought I was never coming back."

"Don't know," Andie said with a shrug. "Stubborn."

"Me? What about you?"

"Who?" Andie asked, pointing at Sandy.

"I'm Sandy." Sandy was surprised her own voice worked. She had not thought Bobbi looked anything like her mom, but seeing them side-by-side, she could see Andie in Bobbi's face, especially in her nose and mouth, and in those amazing blue eyes.

"Sandy brought me. I'm staying at her house."

"Friends... from... school?" Andie spoke slowly, as if she were picking each word from a list and saying it separately. Sandy wondered how she and Bobbi could have even had an argument.

"Kind of," Sandy said. "I go to OSU now. I'm home for the summer."

"But... let Bobbi stay?"

"My da... yes," Sandy said, catching herself.

Andie turned to look at Bobbi. "Nice. Why?"

"Maybe so I didn't end up down in the county foster care center," Bobbi said. "They let me come see you in the hospital."

"You don't..."

"Which I did every day while you were in a coma, for hours at a time. Ask around."

"Hey," Sandy interjected, panic rising in her chest. "You guys aren't supposed to fight, remember?"

"Fuck." Andie stirred uncomfortably. She looked at the girls like she wanted to say something, but then picked up the oversized paperback. "Puzzles help brain. Help with words. Couldn't talk right. Now just some words. I don't have."

"The puzzles help?" Sandy asked. Bobbi didn't say a word, glaring at her mom.

"What they say. Just... piss me off. Not patient." She held the puzzle book open. The two puzzles on the opposing pages had just a few words circled. "Speech... doctor expects whole fucking thing done... by Monday. Ain't gonna happen." She dropped the book back on the bed.

"Why did you do it?"

Sandy looked at Bobbi, shocked she had asked the question. *Why the hell did you drive drunk and kill Mom?* Her stomach lurched like going over a hill too fast in a car and she squeezed her eyes shut. She was not sure she wanted to hear what Andie had to say.

"Don't know," Andie said. "You clean apartment? Keep clean?"

"Answer my question. Why would you try to kill yourself? Why would you do that to me?"

Sandy snapped her eyes open. They were not talking about her mom. Bobbi's dusky skin was flushing, but Andie was not excited at all.

"Fucked up," Andie said, shrugging. "Wasn't thinking..."

"Are you going to do it again? Try to kill yourself?"

"No," Andie began, then faltered. She suddenly looked fragile. "I don't know. It's hard."

"Don't screw it up next time," Bobbi said. "I won't stay around to watch."

"Hey guys," Sandy said, feeling more helpless than ever. "We're not here to argue."

Andie smiled at Sandy. "Name again?"

"Sandy. Bobbi and I had the same art teacher last year. Now I go to OSU."

"That so? Rich, huh?"

"Mom!" Bobbi interrupted.

Andie looked at Bobbi. "Just asking. Moved out when pregnant. Never finished high school. Had to work."

"Sandy pays for a lot," Bobbi said. "I'm going to work with her this summer, so I can start saving for college."

"Sorry," Andie said sarcastically, raising her hands in mock surrender. "Small talk." She looked at Sandy. "Bobbi call you?"

"I'm sorry?"

"How Bobbi... with family? Called you?"

"No," Sandy said. "I was at school." She wondered again if coming here was a mistake.

"Her dad was at the hospital the night you overdosed," Bobbi said.

"Why call 911? Note said not call."

Sandy was shocked by the hostility in Andie's voice. She reminded Sandy of a cornered animal, at turns docile and aggressive.

"You don't get to make that decision, Mom."

"How? Broke lock?"

"That's what you're worried about? You almost died, and you're worried I broke a fucking lock?"

"Have to pay..."

"I didn't break the goddamn lock, Mom. I used a dime to unlock the door. I did it all the time."

"Snooping?"

"Fuck, yeah. I checked to see if you were drinking or getting high all the time. I never trusted you. If you were a normal mom your stupid fucking plan would have worked. Fuck you." Bobbi turned and left, giving Sandy a shake of her head.

Andie looked a Sandy and grinned. "Wow, awkward."

Sandy nodded, unsure if she should stay or go. She studied the woman in front of her. Andie looked lost again, like she was on the verge of breaking into tears. Did she even know what she was doing? Sandy knew she should leave. *You killed my mom.* God did not really expect us to forgive. How could he?

"She cares about you," Sandy said, struggling to get the words out. "Dad said she spent every day after school with you. She'd hold your hand and talk with you for hours. And she was the one who figured out you weren't brain dead and got you moved back to the hospital."

"She did?"

"That's what Dad said. You would squeeze her hand while she was talking with you. Bobbi was sure you were responding to what she was saying. Well, I better go."

"Tell her love her, please?"

"Sure." Sandy turned to leave.

"Stop," Andie commanded, the word coming out as a sharp bark. She smiled apologetically and shrugged her shoulders when Sandy turned around. "Thank you."

"For what?"

"Being friend. Bobbi's friend."

Sandy nodded, thinking about what the small woman had just said. "Yeah," she said finally. "I guess we are friends."

CHAPTER THIRTEEN

Jane Sanderson smiled broadly when Ed walked into the cafeteria at the hospital and waved him over. He had not seen her since they had made love in the barn, more than a week ago. She was wearing a brown dress with a matching jacket that accentuated her narrow hips. A rush of desire, shame and guilt hit him like a punch in the gut, making it hard to breathe. He walked slowly across the cafeteria, trying not to stare, wondering how he had never noticed that she was so beautiful when he was pitching the addition.

"Hello, stranger," Jane said when he reached her table. She sat, and after a second, he did as well, putting the folder with the plans for the barn on the table. "Would you like some coffee?"

Ed shook his head.

"How is your girlfriend? Rebecca, right?"

"She's good. We're good," he said awkwardly. "You and Bill?"

"We're done. He's living at a hotel downtown."

Ed's heart gave a little flip. "I'm sorry to hear that..." he let the thought drift away, uncertain if it were true.

"My marriage had been dying for years, but I shouldn't have involved you. I just needed.... I don't know. I needed to be wanted, if just for a few minutes. To feel beautiful..."

"You are beautiful. Incredibly beautiful..."

"But I'm not thirty-something."

"Thank God."

"Thank you for saying that." Jane blushed and held out her hand for the folder. When Ed gave it to her, she opened the folder and turned to the last page of the contract, pulling a pen from her purse.

"Stop," Ed said.

Jane looked up, startled, her brown eyes contracting warily.

"You haven't read the contract."

"Oh, I trust you."

Ed reached across the table and pulled the contract away. "If we're going to be this awkward together, then forget it," he said. "I can't guarantee a quality job if my client won't talk with me."

Jane blushed again, Ed unsure if she was embarrassed or irritated. "I'm just trying to spare you..."

"Spare me what?" he interrupted.

"Embarrassment. Regret."

"I don't regret what we did, nor am I embarrassed by it. Surprised? Hell, yes. Did I risk hurting someone I care about? Yes, but the truth is I care about you too. If I weren't dating Rebecca, I'd be asking you out right now." Now you know the truth, he thought, his heart pounding like he had just run a marathon.

Jane smiled nervously and held her hand out for the contract. "What did you come up with?"

Ed opened the folder and spent the next fifteen minutes walking her through the quote.

"What the hell," Jane said. "Let's do it."

"You don't have to do this job right now," Ed said. "It's a good job for next summer, or even a couple years from now."

"I don't want to inconvenience you."

"It's not an inconvenience, plus I'd get to see you again all next summer."

Jane blushed. "Now who is leading on whom?"

"Sorry."

"Look, about last week..." Jane closed her eyes briefly and then shook her head. "I'm embarrassed. I was lonely, and Bill forgetting our anniversary again? I just went a little crazy."

"It's okay," Ed said. "It helps to understand I was a way to lash out at Bill."

"No!" Jane said, fiercely. "Don't think for a minute that what happened was about Bill. I felt an attraction to you the first time I saw you. I never expected to, and it embarrasses me to admit it. I shouldn't be attracted to my best friend's husband, even if...even if she's gone."

"I worry that I've made you a promise I can't keep."

"No," Jane said, a sad smile on her face. "I understand there was no promise. Bill and Rebecca make that impossible. I'm still glad we stole that moment. It will live with me forever. But you don't owe me anything more."

Ed nodded. "I have to be honest with you," he said. "Part of me wishes it wasn't over, but..."

"But you're in love with Rebecca," Jane interrupted. "I know you are. It's a good thing, Ed. I want you to be happy." She signed the contract quickly and slid the papers back to him.

He did not know how to tell Jane that he was in love with her as well.

"You do owe me one thing," she said.

"What?"

"Your friendship. I need you to be my friend."

• • •

Olive Garden was packed for a Wednesday evening, staff scurrying from table to table and a long wait in the lobby. Ed and Sandy were meeting Becca for dinner, at Becca's request.

"There's Becca and Cathy," Sandy said, heading out to the parking lot. Ed was surprised that Becca had brought Cathy. He wished he had known, however, and brought Bobbi as well. The girls drifted inside by the time the hostess called their party.

Becca and Cathy were sitting on one side of the table, Ed and Sandy on the other. "Hey, Sands," Cathy said after the waiter finished taking their order. "We're thinking about getting tickets to see Pink in Cleveland. Tickets go on sale next Tuesday. I can get a third ticket and you can pay me back."

"Sure," Sandy said. The girls began an animated conversation about their favorite music that continued through dinner. Ed listened distractedly; he didn't know half the bands they were talking about. He assumed the girls had asked him to dinner to ask about when they would meet Rebecca, and he was trying to find a nice way to say not soon.

When everyone had finished eating, Ed pushed his plate away and looked across the table at Becca. "What did you want to talk about?" he asked, steeling himself.

Becca, blushing, looked at Cathy, who gave her a nudge with her elbow. Becca grinned nervously at Sandy and Ed and then brought her left hand up from under the table. "I'm getting married," she said, lifting her hand so Ed could see the small diamond solitaire on her ring finger. "No," she said, blushing again, "*we're* getting married."

Sandy squealed with delight.

Ed stared at Becca, not comprehending.

"But you're not dating anyone," he finally said, more question than statement because obviously she was, even if he had not met him.

"Yeah, we've been dating for two years," Becca said. She and Cathy were holding hands on top of the table. "We're getting married."

Ed looked at Cathy. She was beaming, her smile as big as a house, a faint blush on her cheeks as well. He had not known she was dating anyone either.

"Are you picking the same day? Like a double wedding?"

Sandy started laughing, her hand on his forearm.

"No, Dad," Becca said, blushing more deeply. She held up Cathy's left hand to show off the matching solitaire Cathy was wearing. "We're getting married. Cathy and me."

"Do what?"

"We're getting married," Becca repeated, her smile disappearing. "We love each other, and we want to be married."

They loved each other? Ed shook his head. Becca had been dating boys since he and Lisa had allowed her to date, back when she was fifteen. Always boys. He looked at the two young women sitting across from him, fingers entwined, the twin solitaires gleaming under the lights, their arms touching so casually in a way that was not casual at all and he did not understand.

How had he missed this?

"Say something," Becca said, her voice dripping with hurt.

"Are you gay?" Ed asked, ashamed that was what spilled out of his mouth, ashamed of the edge of anger in his voice, ashamed of the way Becca wilted in front of him. The anger, at least, was something he could understand. He hadn't been paying for her to go to school for *this*.

"I knew you wouldn't understand," Becca said, tears falling.

"No, I don't understand. You never said a word. How could you surprise me like this, with no warning?"

"Do you think this is easy?" Becca said. "You're nicer to the people you sell your stupid kitchens to than you are to your family. I knew you'd be smug and superior."

"What did you expect me to say? Hallelujah? You don't have the right..."

Becca stood up, pulling Cathy to her feet. "I don't have the right?" she asked him. "The right to what? Breathe? This is no different. I hate you." She turned and walked out of the restaurant, Cathy in tow.

"Wow, Dad," Sandy said. "You really fucked that up." She followed her sister outside.

Ed sat, stunned. He should get up and follow Becca, apologize before she left the parking lot, but he could not move. And he had to pay the bill. By the time he paid, she and Cathy would be gone. He was fucking up but did not know what to do.

Ed drove home in a frosty silence. Sandy jumped out of the truck as soon as he stopped and was in her car and gone before he got to the door to let the dogs out. He went out into the yard and headed towards the barn, even though it was too dark to mow. He sat in the dimly lit barn, Lisa's absence threatening to swallow him up forever. Lisa would have known what to do.

His cell phone buzzed at that moment.

"Ed Gideon," he said absently.

"Dinner must have been a disaster," Rebecca said. "You sound awful."

"Yeah."

"Tell me."

Ed went through the evening, trying to understand it as he explained it to Rebecca. *Where had he gone wrong?*

"It's probably just a phase," Rebecca said. "She'll get over it and they'll break up."

"You don't know Becca," Ed said. "She doesn't go through phases. She didn't just decide on the spur of the moment to get married. What should I do?"

"Tell her everything is okay," Rebecca said. "Tell her you'll pay for the wedding."

"You approve?"

"No, I don't approve," Rebecca said. "How could you think that? It's obviously wrong."

"I don't understand."

"I'm saying that when this all comes crashing down you want to be there to help. Apologize and tell her you'll pay for the wedding, but you won't. Once she realizes she's making a mistake, or she falls in love with a guy, she'll need you. Make sure she knows you're on her side."

"I don't see Becca doing that," Ed said. "Tell me why you think she's not really...."

"Becca's at a very vulnerable point in her life," Rebecca said. "She lost her mom, she's getting closer to graduation, she's looking for security. It's easy to manipulate someone like that. Like me with Greg. This girl, Cathy, obviously saw how low Becca was and how easy it would be to make her fall in love and that was what she did."

"But why would she do that? I've known Cathy since they were both freshmen. I didn't know she was gay, but I wouldn't have cared if I had known. Why would she do something like this?"

"Becca's beautiful and smart. Who wouldn't be attracted to her? Evil people do evil things."

"Cathy is not evil," Ed said. "She's a good kid."

"But clearly confused," Rebecca said. "She must have just wanted someone to love so badly that she went after the closest person, who was Becca. Don't you think you would have seen some warning sign if Becca were gay?"

"That's what I've been trying to think about," Ed said after a minute. "This is where I miss Lisa; she'd tell me what I hadn't noticed. Becca dated in high school, not a ton, but she did date boys. When she was in elementary school, she had crushes on her teachers..."

"Oh my God," Rebecca interrupted. "I had crushes on my teachers. That doesn't mean anything. I told my mom I wanted to marry Mrs. Wilson when I was in kindergarten."

"What did she do?"

"She told me Mrs. Wilson was already married, so I couldn't. I cried. It was very cute."

"What do I do?"

"You lie. Give her the space to figure out this isn't what she wants. Send her on a study abroad program or something where they'll be apart for a couple of months and let nature take its course. Whatever you do, don't give her a reason to dig in her heels and fight you."

"You're serious? I should lie to her and pretend everything is fine?"

"It's just a white lie. When I first split from Greg, I told the kids it was temporary, even though I knew it wasn't. It gave them time to adjust. I lied to Greg about working and looking for an apartment. I even lied about wanting to get a divorce, so he'd stop his affair."

"How'd that work out?" Ed asked.

"That's not a great example," Rebecca said, ignoring his tone. "Nothing was going to make Greg behave. Think about it this way. Greg junior told me he wants to play football. I said yes, but let's start with soccer. I will never let him play football, but it's not worth a big argument, at least not now. And I think he'll fall in love with soccer. Becca is smart and pretty. When the right guy comes along, she'll realize her mistake."

"I don't believe in lying. And I don't think she's mistaken."

"You don't want her to be gay, do you? It's your job to protect her. So, yes, you lie and help her see the mistake she is making. It *is* a mistake."

"I don't know," Ed said. "I'll think about it. I've got to go."

"I love you," Rebecca said.

"You too," Ed said, absently. He thumbed off his phone, staring at it in the gloomy barn. The conversation with Rebecca left him feeling even more unsettled than just watching Becca storm out of the restaurant. Rebecca had sounded sincere, and he knew she was only trying to help, but he did not believe in lying to anyone, let alone his kids. Had he and Lisa ever lied to the girls on purpose? To this day, he insisted Santa Claus existed. But they had never lied to the girls about anything major. And they did not lie to each other to avoid a tough conversation.

Becca was not going through a phase; she was much too self-conscious to claim a lifetime partner on a whim. If she said she was gay, then Ed believed her. It just felt like one more thing, on top of Lisa dying and this business with Andie Love, which was crushing him. Couldn't something normal happen, just for once?

CHAPTER FOURTEEN

Dee stood next to the hospital bed, Andie's thick folder in her hand. In the six weeks Andie had been doing PT, she had graduated from needing a wheelchair to taking awkward steps in the therapy pool to using a walker to drag herself slowly down the hallway, but her left leg was still too tight to make straight on her own, bent awkwardly at the knee, her foot twisting onto the side. The right leg was less rigid, but not much stronger. She did not have the strength or balance to stand up or walk without support.

Dee's cell phone rang, a look of irritation flashing across her face as she set the file on Andie's bed and turned away to answer the call.

Andie glanced at the folder, feeling like a kid cheating on a test by reading her neighbor's work. She opened the folder, glancing at the information on the inside cover, and froze, slowly making sense of what she was seeing.

EMERGENCY CONTACT...... Ed Gideon.

"What the fuck!" Andie screamed. "You gave Bobbi to him?"

Dee spun around, her hand covering the phone, a puzzled look on her face.

"You knew, didn't you? Don't lie to me, you fucked cunt. You knew, and you let this happen. I should fucking kill you."

"I'll call you back," Dee said into the phone.

"You knew!" Andie shrieked again.

Dee stepped closer to the bed, raising her hands to her waist to show she was not a threat. "I didn't know until you had that big fight with Bobbi. I said she needed a buffer and suggested Ed. I thought he was her dad."

"He's not her fucking dad."

"Bobbi told me," Dee said. She sat on the edge on Andie's bed. "She was a lot nicer about it."

"And you didn't think it was a fucking problem?" Andie began slapping the bed frame over and over with her left hand. Dee reached out and took Andie's hand in her own. Andie pulled her hand away but let it rest on the bed.

"With Ed, Bobbi was in school every day and got to visit you. Everyone knows where she is."

"I want her out of his house right now." Andie took a couple of deep breaths, trying to calm herself. She needed to think.

"Where will she go?"

"I don't fucking care. She can't stay with him. It's not safe."

"He's not going to hurt her. In fact, he got you moved back to the hospital. He saved your life."

"Why the fuck would he do that?" Andie asked.

"I don't know."

"I don't want Bobbi around him. I'm calling Children's Services."

"Ed won't hurt her. You know that."

"I don't know shit."

"Look," Dee said. "Give me a couple of hours. I'll call an emergency team meeting and share your concerns. The team will consider all the options..."

"I don't want you to *consider* it. I want her out of there."

"I hear that," Dee said. "We can come up with a better solution than sending her to the county. Maybe someone here could take her in..."

"You?"

Dee shook her head. "Bobbi's a great kid, but I'm not ready to parent a teenager, not even for a few weeks. But that's what we're talking about, just until you can get home and then she's living with you again. I'll talk with our team about what we can do. I'll call a meeting right now."

"Really?"

"Yeah. Promise me a couple of hours, well, until tomorrow or Thursday, and I'll make sure everything is okay."

"Tomorrow. She can't stay with him any longer."

Dee nodded. "I'll do my best. So, we're okay with everything?"

"Yeah." Andie watched the younger woman walk out of the room. If Dee had offered to take Bobbi, Andie would have felt okay. She had given her the opportunity to do the right thing, but Dee had not. Andie grabbed the phone off her bedside stand and pressed 9 for an outside line.

• • •

"Did you talk to Becca?" Rebecca asked.

Ed was in his truck, on his way to a sales call. "I really don't want to talk about Becca today."

"Ed, I will not let you destroy your relationship with your daughter. I can't imagine what would happen if I wasn't here to fix things. Did you call her?"

"No. I was too busy."

"Ed, you need to get it together. It's been three weeks since she told you, and you haven't done a thing. You need to call Becca. Promise me you'll call her tonight."

"And lie to her?"

"If that's what it takes. This is her life, Ed. You have a responsibility as her parent to protect her."

"What if..."

"What if what?"

What if she's right? Ed shook his head. "Nothing." He didn't need to fight with Rebecca today. He would not tell Becca that everything was okay when it wasn't. He wished he understood why Becca and Cathy upset him. "What's on tap for you tonight?

"Lily's got dance class."

"Sounds like fun."

"Speaking of fun, let's have a cookout! I had hoped we'd do it on July 4th, but that didn't happen."

"Do what?"

"The big reveal! I'm ready for you to meet Greg junior and Lily."

"I hadn't thought about exactly how we'd introduce everyone."

"I know you haven't, that's why I'm suggesting a cookout," Rebecca continued. "I'll bring the kids and you bring the girls. I guess Bobbi would be there, but that's okay."

Ed sighed. He did not want to think about this right now. "I don't think Becca would come. She's too upset."

"That's why you have to call her and apologize, Ed. You need to make sure she comes. Then, I could talk with Becca. About this Cathy person. She'd be willing to hear from me. You said yourself she wants to meet me. I could just take her aside and say that I heard about what was going on and I..."

"No."

"No cookout?"

"A cookout is fine," Ed said. "Sometime. No conversation with Becca. I need to deal with that."

"I agree, but you don't seem to want to address it head on."

"I don't think lying is addressing it at all."

"Grow up, Ed. You may have had this perfect life, where you and Lisa never had to say or do anything you regretted, but most of us don't live that way. You don't want to lose Becca, and if you don't call her that's what's going to happen."

"But I won't lie to her."

"How is calling her and repeating that you're upset going to help? She already knows that. You'll just be pushing her away more. Don't make this harder than it has to be."

"I don't know."

"Of course, you don't. Sometimes I think you're ambivalent about love, period."

"That's ridiculous."

"I know you and Lisa had this great thing, but it's really difficult to sit outside that and realize you can never measure up..."

"I never said that..."

"Sometimes I don't think you even want me to measure up. You'd rather just live in your memories than deal with reality."

"That's not true."

"It's not?"

Ed did not say a word. *Jane wouldn't be like this*. She would not feel the need to prove something. Maybe he should drop by and see her soon. At least he knew he never had to tell Rebecca about Jane. Not since Rebecca believed in lying.

"You're letting life pass you by," Rebecca interrupted his thoughts. "Good night, Ed." The phone went dead, ending the discussion with a finality that spoke volumes about their relationship.

• • •

Ed was still irritated with Rebecca when he wrapped up his sales call. *Why didn't she mind her own business?* Becca was his problem to figure out; Rebecca needed to butt out.

He was about ten minutes from the Sanderson's, and he owed it to Jane to do a check on the job; he hadn't been out to her house since they had made love in the barn. He was avoiding her, even though their conversation two weeks ago had cleared up any awkwardness between them. He was sorry Jane's marriage was over, but happy she would no longer be under Bill's thumb. She deserved better.

An orderly mound of steel jacks lying next to the barn was the first thing Ed saw when he pulled onto Jane's property. The eastside of the barn needed to be raised three inches to repair the stone foundation. The addition was further along, completely framed and the exterior sheathing in place, with cutouts for the windows and doors.

A white SUV pulled up the drive and parked next to his truck. Jane got out, giving him a wave and a smile. She walked over to where Ed squatted by the addition.

"It's nice to see you back on the job," she said. "I wasn't sure you were ever going to be back."

"I wasn't either," he said with a grin.

"I've got to change and then you can explain to me where we are." She walked gingerly over the broken ground near the addition and then disappeared around the side of the house. Twenty minutes later she was back, in jeans and a t-shirt, her high heels replaced with canvas sneakers, a long neck beer bottle in her hand.

"So, Mr. Contractor," she said, pointing through the addition to the back of the house, "when do the walls come down?" She took a long swig from the bottle.

"No beer for me?" he asked.

Jane shook her head. "I didn't want to be accused of trying to tempt my contractor into special pricing or anything."

Ed laughed. "I started out in sales," he said. "Everything's already at a special price." He held his hand out, asking for the beer.

Jane shook her head slowly and took another swig. Then she stepped forward and gave him the bottle. Ed took it, feeling the coolness of the glass in his hand. He kept his eyes on Jane as he raised the bottle to his mouth, acutely aware of the intimacy of his lips covering the bottle's mouth, where hers had been. He took a swallow and handed it back to her, his eyes never leaving her face. She blushed under his frank appraisal.

Jane drained the bottle and walked away, never saying a word. A few minutes later she was back, carrying a small bucket packed with four open bottles of beer sitting in crushed ice. She set the bucket on a framed window cutout and handed a water-beaded bottle to Ed.

"Thanks," he said.

"What happens next?" she asked, taking a bottle for herself.

"I'm bringing in a dumpster tomorrow," Ed said.

"How big?" Jane asked with a frown.

"Big enough. I don't want a debris pile to build up. When we tear off the back of the house, we're going to create a pretty big mess."

"Okay." She took another drink of her beer and leaned against the new wall, looking at him sideways. "You started in sales?"

Ed nodded. "I thought I was going to be an architect when I went to college. I took it slow, lots of calculus and physics, but my first summer, I got a job working for a builder. I drew up building plans and learned sales. When Lisa and I got married, and I dropped out, I had a career."

"Why be an architect?"

"I liked the idea of building things. Did you always want to be a doctor?"

Jane laughed. "I wanted to be a poet, but God and the world conspired against me. I was always good at math and science, tops in my class. No one could believe I would waste myself on poetry. My folks, my teachers, even our minister, everyone assumed I'd be a doctor. I felt like I was letting them down if I even took a poetry class."

"Do you write?"

Jane blushed. "I do. It's my hobby." Ed loved the way she flushed from her cheeks all the way down her neck.

They sat quietly for a moment, each sipping their beer. The sun was hanging behind the trees, casting the long light of evening that bathed everything gold. The glow softened everything it touched, haloing around Jane's head. When she smiled, tipping her beer bottle to the side as she drank, the smile lit up her eyes, transforming her entire face. Ed knew he needed to leave. He wanted to kiss her again, to hold her against him. She captivated him, and he wanted to discover everything he could about her.

Rebecca loomed behind him, a ghostly presence who, despite her youth and vitality, suddenly seemed fragile and in jeopardy. *What's wrong with me?* I have the most beautiful lover in the world. Why would I risk losing Rebecca to sit here and flirt with Jane?

He realized with a start that Jane had moved and was now standing directly in front of him, holding another beer bottle out to him. "Earth to Ed," she was saying, a cheeky grin on her face. Ed could feel his blush rising as he shook his head and took the beer. "Sorry," he said. "Got lost in my thoughts for a minute. What were you saying?"

"I was asking if you wanted some dinner."

"Let me text Sandy and Bobbi."

Jane nodded and ambled away to look at the jacks lying on the ground next to the barn, giving him a moment of privacy. His first text was to

Rebecca saying he was working late and would call her tomorrow. Then he sent a text to Sandy telling her to make something for dinner. She responded immediately: *Going out.* Ed was fine if she wanted to spend her money treating Bobbi to dinner. He felt relieved that the two of them were getting to be friends. He turned his phone to silent.

Jane was back when he finished. She linked arms with him and walked around to the front door. They ended up in the kitchen, Ed sitting on a tall stool at the island while Jane made oversized burgers.

"How do you do it?" he asked her, pointing to the huge burger on her plate. "You weigh nothing."

"One twenty-nine," she said with a grin. "I exercise like a son-of-a-bitch," she said. "An hour, first thing every morning, on the treadmill, or I go for a run. My body is more functional than my brain at six am, so a nice run is perfect." She took a big bite of the burger, wiping away a dribble of mustard that ran down her chin.

"Do you miss it?" he asked when she'd swallowed the bite.

"Miss what?"

"Writing."

"I compose while I run. Don't always get it written down later, but I can write a whole poem in my head over several days."

"And you just remember it?"

"Line by line. You do the same thing."

"Not on your life. I could never do that."

"You walked through this kitchen and envisioned something that Bill and I had never imagined. All you wrote down were the measurements, but I know you had a vision before you left."

They ate in silence for several minutes, finishing the burgers, washing down the meal with the last of the beer. Jane took the empty plates over to the sink and washed them, ignoring Ed, staring out at the framed addition outside the kitchen window. Without the lab coat and power suit she looked vulnerable and alone. She had kicked off her sneakers when she came in the house and was standing at the sink in her bare feet. The casualness of it seemed freeing, as if she could truly leave her work at the office when she left. Lisa could never do that, telling Ed story after story about what she was dealing with at work, sometimes squirreling herself away in their home office for hours to work on reports or calling staff to discuss challenges. He could not remember a time she'd been content to just wash the dishes and not be solving a problem at the same time.

Jane finished washing the plates and placed them on a drying rack. When she turned around, Ed was right behind her. He took her in his arms, pulling her close, kissing her. She returned the kiss eagerly, wrapping her arms around his neck and pressing her body against his. He had her pressed against the front of the sink, his hand on her waist. Her mouth opened for him, her tongue dancing with his. His hand slid down, three fingers inside the top of her jeans. He could feel silky panties against his fingers.

Jane put her hand on his chest and slowly pushed him away. She broke the kiss slowly, looking up into his eyes. "I didn't invite you in to seduce you," she said. "You don't have to..."

Ed shut her up with another kiss. After several minutes, she slipped sideways, away from the sink, and took him by the hand. He could feel her pulse beating in his palm, her heart racing. She led him silently through the house and up the stairs to her bedroom.

She undressed him as he stood by the bed. She unbuttoned his shirt, stopping to finger his necklace.

"What's this?" she asked, kissing him at the base of his neck.

"My Dad's forty-year AA token," Ed said. "When he died, it was the one thing I wanted. I wear it every day as a reminder of what you can accomplish with faith and a determination to do the right thing."

She slipped it over his head and kissed it, before setting it on her side table. They made love and then spooned naked in her bed, watching the moon rise through her bedroom window. It was after eleven when he left.

• • •

The joy Ed felt as he pulled out of Jane's driveway slowly dissipated during the drive home. Jane had eclipsed Rebecca so completely this evening that the only honest thing to do was to call it off with Rebecca, but he knew he would do nothing. He wanted them both.

What a bastard.

He rubbed the base of his neck, where it met his shoulder, with one hand. The ache was back, the physical manifestation of his tainted soul. He deserved to hurt, deserved to be alone, deserved any punishment God saw fit to impose. Ed sighed, finding himself back at the one unanswerable question left from Lisa's death. Had he deserved that?

The house was dark when he pulled into the drive. Sandy's car was gone. She and Bobbi must have gone to a late movie or something. At least he would not have to face them, would not have them see the guilt on his face and demand to know what he had done. The dogs were waiting impatiently by the back door, ready to go out. He waited on the deck while they did their business, Blackie looking over his shoulder at Ed the entire time. They followed him nervously around the kitchen as he set up the coffee for morning.

Ed almost missed the paper on the table. He set the empty coffee carafe on the table, so he could read the hand-written note. Written on Franklin County Children's Services letterhead, it said Bobbi was being sent down to the Children's Services facility in Groveport, and that he could call a case manager in the morning to discuss. Ed stared at the letter in disbelief, his chest feeling tighter and tighter. He crumpled the paper up and slammed his hand on the table, then swept the carafe to the floor, shattering it. The dogs scattered.

"Fuck!"

He stomped on a large piece of broken glass, smashing it into smaller bits under his shoe. If Andie Love were in this room, he knew he would kill her. Fuck, if he had a gun, he would go down there right now and just shoot the fucking bitch in the head and free Bobbi forever. *What the fuck was she thinking?*

Ed walked down the hall to Bobbi's room, but it was empty, her belongings gone. Two drawings taped on the wall, one of the dogs sitting near the barn, and a self-portrait that he had told her he liked the first time he'd seen it, were the only evidence she had never been there.

His guilt flooded back in, searing him, replacing the anger that had consumed him seconds ago. If he had been here, instead of fucking around, he could have.... What could he have done? Bribed someone? Called Maggie? If Andie Love figured out Bobbi was staying here and begged the county to investigate, he could not have done a thing. Had Bobbi called him? He pulled out his cell phone. Two missed calls were from her, one at 7:40 and the second at 7:52. He had been with Jane then, his phone turned to silent. He sucked in several deep breaths, almost burning the back of his throat, but not getting any air at all.

What kind of mother sends her kid to a facility? Ed went back to the kitchen and grabbed a broom to clean up the broken glass. Was Andie Love trying to fuck with his life, or was she just a drunk, still thinking and acting like an alcoholic? He touched his hand to his chest, feeling his dad's AA token under his shirt. Ed had been five when his dad quit drinking. Forty years of sobriety had not turned his dad into a rational man. The huge celebrations and sudden rages never disappeared completely, but booze was no longer to blame.

Ed dumped the remains of the carafe in the trash can, too exhausted to think, the glass tinkling lightly as it fell, too. Bobbi had never been his problem, and now Andie Love would be out of his life forever. His problem was Rebecca and Jane. Or maybe the fact that he did not have any fucking boundaries and was disgraceful.

He poured himself a scotch on the rocks and took the dogs outside. Still nervous from his outburst, they stayed just outside his reach. Staring up into the starry night he felt like he needed to pray. He was surprised; he had not really prayed since Lisa died, other than his daily gratitude list and rotary meetings where you were ordered to bow your head.

Was Lisa in heaven, watching over him, or was she just gone? It was all the same to him; she was not here. What was praying going to do? God would not change anything. God just was, all-being, an implacable force that governed creation. Prayer was for the supplicant, not for God.

Tonight, Ed wanted to pray. He needed understanding on how to love two women and not hurt them. He needed help for Bobbi. He needed to know what to do about Becca and Cathy. He needed to be free of the anger he felt towards Andie Love, a swirling tornado in the center of his being, threatening to swallow up all that he was. It would be so easy to disappear into hate, but he did not know if he could ever come back.

He spoke quietly, sharing two years of loneliness and pain and anger and hatred and sorrow and guilt, ignoring his tears, letting the pain free him from the weight of everything he had been holding. When he finished, King was sitting next to him, his big head in Ed's lap, whining softly. He nudged Ed's hand several times, until Ed got up and headed to bed, feeling as empty as a dried corn husk. His scotch sat on the table, untouched, dew gathering on the cool glass.

• • •

First thing Friday morning Ed called Maggie. He quickly explained the situation. "What can I do?"

Maggie sighed. "I'll need to talk with someone at the county to find out what happened and what order is in place governing the removal."

"They'll tell you that?"

"They will tell your attorney. I'll need a retainer making it official. Write me a check for twenty-five."

"Twenty-five hundred? Is that enough?"

Maggie laughed. "Twenty-five dollars. That's to make the relationship legal. If we end up going to court, I'll ask for more. Drop a check in the mail this morning. I'd like the postmark to be today."

Ed wrote the check immediately and asked Marjorie to take it directly to the post office. Then he sat at his desk, unable to focus, waiting to hear more. It was a little after twelve when Maggie called back.

"We don't have a lot of options here," she said. "The county's goal is always family reunification, and you're not Bobbi's family..."

"I can't do anything?"

"I didn't say that. I just said the deck is stacked against you."

"Bobbi wants to stay with me. Why can't she choose?"

"If this were a custody battle between her biological parents, yeah, that would work, but this isn't anything like that."

"I'll pay anything..."

"Ed, stop. You've got to slow down and think this through. That's my advice as your friend, and your attorney..."

"You'll help?"

"Of course, I'll help. But you can't get custody back."

"But Andie Love is a menace to society..."

"If you were anyone else, I'd be demanding an immediate custody hearing. Andie Love is the poster child for a neglectful parent, but *you* can't win. The county will never return her to your custody."

"What do I do?"

"Convince Andie Love to let Bobbi stay with you until she's released from the hospital."

"How am I supposed to do that?"

"I don't think you can, but we need to try. Once she shuts that down, then we have Bobbi go to court and sue for emancipation. That could take a year and there is no guarantee Bobbi would win."

"Christ."

"There is some good news. She's unrestricted, so you can visit and even take her out on day trips unsupervised..."

"I'll head down right now."

"Slow down. This is a process and it's not winner take all. She's going to be with the county for months, unless you convince Andie to change her mind, so give Bobbi a few days to adjust to her new home. Let Andie realize she can't see Bobbi in the current set up..."

"She can't?"

"Legally she can, but the county will not take Bobbi to visit her. You will. That's part of our leverage. She'll need you to see her own daughter."

"She'll hate that."

"But hopefully she'll realize you're not a threat. That's our plan."

• • •

The text came in a little after one. He was in his truck, stuck at a traffic light, waiting to pull onto the freeway. *Free for lunch?* Ed stared at it. Rebecca. He had no appointments this afternoon that he could use as an excuse to say no.

Ed sighed. He wanted to ignore it, to just pretend he had not seen it, but that was not right, not after being with Jane last night.

Thought you had to work?

Schedule messed up. 2 many ppl working lunch.

When?

Now. I'll bring lunch home with me.

See you in 30.

Ed put his phone down, hating himself. Now he felt like he was cheating on Jane. How did my life turn into an episode of *The Jerry Springer Show*? He knew he could not keep seeing both women, but he did not know which one he should let go. It was time to be honest with himself. He did not want to choose. Jane knew about Rebecca. Could Rebecca be okay with the status quo? Ed hated how much he hoped that was the case.

Which meant he needed to tell her.

When he parked next to her car, his dad's AA token was heavy on his chest. Is this what his dad felt like, before he quit drinking? Had Dad known his life was coming apart, and gone on, lying to everyone, hoping everything would not shatter into a million pieces?

I can't live a lie any longer.

He got out of the truck and knocked on her door. Rebecca opened it almost immediately, a wide smile on her face. She was wearing a heavy cotton bathrobe, cinched tightly around her waist. "I was changing," she said, blushing deeply. Ed loved the way she colored so easily. It reflected a kind of naiveté that was almost absent in the world today. She gave him a quick kiss on the lips, pushing the door closed behind him and throwing the deadbolt. "Lunch is in the other room," she said, scampering down the hall. She undid the robe as she went, letting it fall from her shoulders to the floor. She was wearing a garter belt and stockings, no panties, her ass cheeks swaying as she went. She pirouetted, hands over her head, giving Ed a glimpse of the sheer demi bra she was wearing, her full breasts captivating him.

He followed her into the little living room at the back of the apartment. A bottle of Champaign was icing on the coffee table. She sat down on the table, next to the bottle and glasses. "Bon appétit!" she said, a huge grin plastered on her face. Ed stared at her and any resolve he had to tell her the truth disappeared. He knelled before her on the floor, leaning in to kiss her left thigh. That ache was back in his throat, the one that meant he was doing something he should not do. He had lost his way and was unwilling to do anything to get back on track. He wanted Rebecca and he wanted Jane and he should be fighting to get Bobbi home and he hated himself.

• • •

The Children's Service facility in Groveport was red brick, a one-story administrative building, four two-story dormitories, and a small playground with a few scattered concrete picnic tables, the complex surrounded by a tall wire fence that reminded Ed of a prison. The only thing missing was razor wire around the top of the fence.

When he went inside Bobbi was already waiting for him, a nervous smile on her face. She gave him a big hug and they went outside to sit on a concrete picnic table and talk.

Ed reviewed the options he'd discussed with Maggie and the drawbacks to each of them.

"I want the emancipation thing," Bobbi said. "I'll be old enough to drive soon, so I can live on my own. I'm done with her."

"You've got two more years of school left and then you can go to college and get out. I think that's a smarter plan."

"Two years is forever."

"It sure feels that way but going to court could take as long."

"I'll never get away. I can't afford college on my own and she won't pay for it..."

"You leave that to me," Ed said. "I'll make sure you get to college."

"Why would you do that?"

"You're a great kid and I can afford to help. Do we have a plan?"

"You really mean it?"

"Yeah, but I have one condition."

"What?" Bobbi looked at him distrustfully.

"I want you to visit your mom again. Every day."

"No fucking way. Why would I do that?"

"Because she's the only mom you'll ever have. I only got involved so you could see her. That's still got to be part of the plan."

"Even if I wanted to, I can't get up there. It's too far away."

"I'll take you. When I'm busy, Sandy can come down."

"You'd really drive all the way down here?"

Ed nodded.

"But I don't want to see her. I hate her. She had no right to send me here."

"Technically, she did, or at least the county thinks she did."

"You wouldn't have sent me away. You always do the right thing."

"No, I don't," Ed said, thinking of Jane and Rebecca.

"Bullshit. You took me in to keep me out of here in the first place."

"And now we need your mom's consent."

"There is no way she'll ever change her mind," Bobbi said.

"She might not," Ed agreed. "No matter what she decides, she's not going away, so it makes sense to repair your relationship. I'll pick you up tomorrow and you can visit."

Bobbi stared at him. "You really mean it, don't you?"

"Yeah."

"Okay, I'll go, but not for her. I'll go because you think it's important. That's the only reason."

"Fair enough."

"But not tomorrow. I want her to have another day to think about what she did. You can pick me up on Wednesday. And tell Sandy I miss her."

CHAPTER FIFTEEN

Andie looked up from the puzzle book to see Bobbi standing in the doorway of her room. "What the fuck are you doing here?" she asked, unable to hide her delight. "You're supposed to be locked up."

"I'm allowed out until nine," Bobbi said, scowling.

"I'm glad you came to see me."

"Fuck you," Bobbi snapped. "I'm only here because I have to visit, so I can go to college. I hate you."

"You'll get over it," Andie said. "How did you get here?"

"How do you think?"

"I wouldn't have asked if I fucking knew..."

"Ed brought me. I didn't even want to come."

"He's not allowed to see you," Andie said.

'Well, you fucked that up, Mom," Bobbi said with a tight grin, "just like you fuck up everything."

Andie stared at her daughter for several seconds. "He's manipulating you," she said, finally. "Turning you against me."

Bobbi laughed. "You never gave a damn about me. Gram said I couldn't trust you. She said you'd never stay sober."

"That's not true," Andie snapped. "I've changed."

"Gram said the wreck was a shock to your system, but once the guilt wore off, you'd go back to your old ways. She said that's what happened when Betty died."

"She was talking about herself," Andie said. "She quit drinking when Betty killed herself, stopped bringing men around. That lasted a year, maybe fifteen months and then she fell off the wagon. She fell hard, too. Dad was already dead by then, in a botched robbery or something."

"Gram said Betty died in a car accident."

"She drove into a bridge abutment head-on. She killed herself."

"Why?"

"She was sixteen and pregnant. She told me she was scared. The man who got her pregnant was one of Dad's drinking buddies. He had four kids at home. Betty didn't know what to do."

"Gram said..."

"Gram was full of shit. I was fifteen when Betty died; sixteen when Gram started drinking again. She would get drunk and talk about how lonely she was, how she couldn't get a date because of me. She would tell me Betty killed herself to get away from me."

"Gram didn't drink..."

"She quit again, eventually. I think she knew you needed her, so she got sober and quit fucking around. You remember when she got so sick when you were in fifth grade? When you went from her house to foster care? That's when she quit drinking for good."

"Who was my father? Someone from your high school?"

"I was never sure who. I got drunk at a party and blacked out."

"He must have seen you at school. Didn't anyone say anything?"

"I quit the day I found out I was pregnant."

"You *really* never graduated high school?"

Andie nodded. "Got my GED when you started kindergarten."

"Why didn't you tell me any of this?"

"Why would I? Gram was good to you, and you needed her. She loved you, even if she couldn't love me."

"Damn."

"Yeah." Andie patted her bed and scooted over making a place for Bobbi to sit next to her.

Bobbi looked at her, incredulous, and laughed. "You think I believe any of that bullshit? That's what I expected to hear from you. Tear down a dead lady so you look better. Why don't you just own what you did?"

"What the fuck do you know about me?"

"I know you killed a woman and never even said you were sorry. She was a wife, and Becca and Sandy's...." Bobbi stopped, but it was too late.

"I know who the little bitch is," Andie snapped.

"You killed her mom, but you never apologized."

"What the fuck good is an apology?"

"Isn't that what your AA bullshit says you're supposed to do? Or is that just a game, too?"

"You can't understand."

"Try me."

Andie looked down, shaking her head. When she looked up, Bobbi could see tears in her eyes. "I can't atone for what I've done. To you, to them, to anyone who's life I've fucked up. Especially Ed. His wife should be alive, not me. I'm the one who deserves to be dead."

"Forget it," Bobbi said. "I have to go."

She left the room, walking slowly down the hall, blinded by her own tears. She had no hope now. Nothing was going to change. She should have just left Andie to die in the nursing home. It would have been less painful.

• • •

Ed was sitting in the lobby, working on client proposal on his laptop. "What's the matter?" he asked when he saw Bobbi wiping her tears away.

"She's going to do it again," Bobbi said.

"Do what?"

"She wants to die. I don't know if it will be right away, or in a few months, but she's going to try again. I can't be there to find her. I'm not coming back here. If she wants to kill herself, fuck her. I want to do the court thing; you know, divorce her. I have to be free of her."

"Slow down," Ed said. "We'll figure it out."

"I need to go to the bathroom." Bobbi turned and disappeared down the hall.

Ed closed his laptop and slid it into his satchel. He stood and shook his head, stretching to work out a sudden tightness in his chest and shoulders. He wanted to shake Andie Love until she got some sense in her head.

He headed after Bobbi but couldn't ignore the anger burning in his chest. He turned away from the restroom and walked quickly to Andie's room. Andie was in her bed, staring out the window. The tightness in his chest spread to his neck and jaw. *Walk away.* He knocked once on the door frame.

"You came back?" Andie asked, her voice pinched, turning away from the window. Her eyes, red from crying, widened when she saw Ed.

Ed stopped a few feet into the room.

"Get out." When Ed did not move, she grabbed the Nurse's call button. "I said get out. I'll call security."

"Do you think I'm going to hurt you?" Ed asked.

"Just get the fuck out."

Ed shrugged and turned around. Why had he thought they could have a rational conversation?

"And stay the fuck away from Bobbi."

Ed stopped in his tracks, started to leave, then stopped again. He turned around and walked to the side of the bed. Andie shrank away from him but did not push the call button.

"I won't," he said. "Bobbi needs someone in her life who won't abandon her."

"That's me," Andie growled. "I'm her fucking mother."

"No, you're not," Ed said, shaking his head in disgust. "You're just a selfish drunk, too wrapped up in your own drama to see what Bobbi needs, let alone care."

"I care."

"Bullshit. Bobbi said you're just going to try to kill yourself again."

"No fucking way," Andie said, her eyes darting to the side as if looking for an escape route. "She misunderstood. I told her I'm the one who should be dead."

"It's the same thing."

"No," Andie said. She closed her eyes for a second, taking two deep breaths. When she opened her eyes, she looked directly at Ed. "Bobbi thinks I need to apologize to you." She paused for a moment, and then continued, her voice emotionless. "Can you imagine emptier words from me than 'I'm sorry?' I *killed* your wife."

"Deal with it. Do penance somehow. Go talk to kids about the dangers of drunk driving, or put flowers on Lisa's grave, hell I don't care. Just don't take it out on Bobbi."

"I'm not."

"Isn't it ironic that you didn't spend a day in jail and Bobbi's locked up? No matter what they say, it really is a prison. The doors are locked all the time, and it's got this tall fence..."

"Fuck you. I didn't ask for the cops to fuck up. I was ready to go to prison. I told everyone I killed her. Every cop, my attorney, the fucking prosecutor. It's not my fault someone forgot to read me my Miranda rights. I didn't deserve them."

"The outcome is still the same, isn't it? You're free and Bobbi's locked up."

The room was quiet. A Code Blue message came over the loudspeaker for the main hospital. An orderly was pushing a cart down the hall, the rubber wheels of the cart squeaking in a way that made Ed want to punch someone.

"Why are you helping Bobbi?"

"My girls never had an opportunity to say goodbye to Lisa. I didn't want Bobbi to get sent to the county and not get a chance to say goodbye to you."

Andie paled and turned to look out the window. "Are you trying to take her away?" she asked when she turned back to Ed.

"Not if you act like a real mom," he said. "But if you keep up this bullshit, then yes, I will."

"I don't know what to do," Andie said, "to keep her safe."

"Let her come back and live with me. She likes it there. Once you get out, she moves home with you."

"I can't do that," Andie said. "I don't trust you. I don't trust anyone. I don't want her with Children's Services, but what the fuck am I supposed to do? How can I keep her safe?"

Someone laughed in the hall outside the room and Ed had a weird sense of being mocked. *What if she made sense?*

"You know, I woke up after the accident..."

"Woke up?"

"My soul woke up. I remember laughing after I hit your car..."

"Laughing?"

"It was so funny. Your car rolled over, six or seven times, but it went nowhere, just up and down. I swear I could see both of you inside, and you were laughing too. It was funny. Then I had to find my phone, I'd dropped it when I hit you, so I looked around and found it on the floor and when I looked up again, you were out of the car, on the ground, partway under it. I could see you perfectly because of the light from my truck. You were talking to your wife, whispering, while she died. You knew she was dying, but you didn't let her know. All she knew was that you loved her.

"Suddenly, I was sober, and I could think again. I knew what I'd done. If I'd had a gun in my glove box, I'd have shot myself on the spot. As fucked up as I'd been, I'd never killed anyone. That was too much, even for me. I knew I could never make things right for you, but for two years, I tried making them right for Bobbi, and then I fucked that up too. I don't know what to do."

"You start by letting her come home with me, until you're ready to go home."

Andie stared at him, and then shook her head. "No. Even if you don't mean to, you're going to take her away."

"Then we'll see you in court. Your choice." He went into the hall without looking back, sliding a step away from her door, and stopped with his back to the wall. He wanted to punch something. Or someone. His heart was pounding in his chest, the blood coursing through his body like a horse on a racetrack. He should not have spoken to her. He had given her a voice;

one he did not need in his head. It had been easier to ignore her, to think of her as an abstraction, as the monster who had taken Lisa from him. She had been a thing. Now she was a person; just a fucked up, scared woman. One who suffered as he and the girls suffered.

The urge to make her suffer more was so vast within him, a deep oil reserve that had been buried, but now was exposed. He could feel it forcing its way to the surface, demanding the light, the air, the all of his attention. She deserved to suffer, didn't she? She said she had laughed after she hit the car, laughed when it was spinning and flipping through the air, laughed when Lisa had been flung from the cocoon of his love to the pavement and crushed. Who the fuck deserves to live after that? He hoped she would kill herself. He would go out and buy her the pills right now. Ed shook his head. Pills would not work in a hospital. Someone would check on her and find her before she was dead. He needed a gun, but he could not just waltz in here with a shotgun. People would think he was trying to kill her himself. He did not want to do that. *Well, hardly.* He could go to Wal-Mart and buy a handgun. Was there still a three-day waiting period? Or did they have an immediate background check? That gun store on Cleveland Avenue, by Northern Lights Shopping Center, would be better. What was the name of it? He could not remember, but he knew right where it was. If he gave her a gun and some bullets would that be so bad?

How long would it take to get Bobbi out of the system after that? He should call Maggie and ask....

How fucking stupid am I? You don't ask an attorney about something like that.

Ed took a deep breath, and then a second. The pounding in his ears was dying down, his heart rate returning to normal. He was a fucking idiot, but then he already knew that.

He took another deep breath and closed his eyes, blocking out the hospital. Everything was quiet, except the sound of a child crying. He locked in on that sound, the frantic sobbing of a lost child, and let it clear his mind. Someone needed help. A kid had wandered away from whatever room her parents were visiting and got lost in the maze that was the hospital. Ed could deal with that. He flicked his eyes open, searching. It took him a few seconds to realize there was no child. Andie Love was crying. Sobbing, almost hysterically, unable to catch her breath. She sounded like Becca had the first time she spoke to him on the phone after the accident. The ache and loss in her voice had crushed him. That feeling that he had somehow caused her pain. He was to blame.

Ed could hear that same pain and sense of loss in Andie's sobbing. She understood that she had lost Bobbi, understood that Ed would take Bobbi away, understood that she had destroyed more lives than she had ever helped.

Ed never moved, his back to the wall, as Andie's crying slowly subsided. It never quite stopped, but it lost the manic edge of panic and despair. He needed to go find Bobbi and take her back to Groveport. He would call Maggie in the morning and get her started on emancipation.

Andie shuffled out of her room, using her walker, moving ponderously into the hall. She wore a short hospital gown tied tightly in the back and paper slippers, her pale bare legs bent sharply, walking hunched over the walker like an old woman. She shuffled forward, her face red from crying. She saw him leaning against the wall and stopped, almost falling, her face opening weirdly, like a woman seeing her lover for the first time after an extended period apart.

"I'm sorry," she said. "I didn't mean to destroy your life. I wish a train had been on that track because I'd be dead, and your family wouldn't even know. I..."

"It doesn't work that way," Ed said. "It is what it is."

"Take her," Andie said. "I'll just fuck her life up. Take her home. I'll call and tell them I was wrong. Just don't hurt her. Don't take out your hatred for me on Bobbi."

Her arms shook, and Ed realized they were holding her up more than her legs. She fell, spinning away from the walker towards the floor. Ed caught her as her strength gave out. She could not weigh ninety pounds he thought, as he guided her to the bed. She was sobbing again, one arm around his neck, her head against his chest. He set her on the bed, helped her pull the covers up over her spindly legs. She was wiping her face on her arm, trying to wipe the tears away.

"I'll call in the morning," she said after catching her breath. "You can come sit here and listen, so you know I'm not lying. I'll give you custody."

"You mean it?"

"Yes. Just promise to keep her away from me, make sure she's safe..."

"No," Ed said. Andie looked like she was going to shatter into a thousand pieces.

"You have to save her..."

"No," Ed said again. "You're her mother. I'll make my offer again: Bobbi stays at my house until you go home. Then she moves home with you."

"Why would you help me?" Her intense blue eyes searched his face.

Ed shrugged, Lisa suddenly hovering behind him. "It's what I have to do," he said finally.

"You are one fucking piece of work," Andie said. "I don't understand you at all."

Ed shook his head. "I'm not sure I do, either."

CHAPTER SIXTEEN

Andie's missing. The text came while Ed was measuring a kitchen on a remodel quote. As soon as he was in the truck, he called Sandy. "What do you mean she's missing?"

"Medicaid sent her to a nursing home on the south side called The Dell, but she isn't there. She told folks at Dodd Hall she couldn't afford the ambulance transfer, so she had someone pick her up. Bobbi's freaking out. She's sure her mom went somewhere to get drunk."

As bad as that was, Ed knew the alternative was worse: that she had already tried to kill herself again. "Where are you now?"

"Home."

"Make dinner. I'll be home shortly, and we'll figure out what to do."

Ed got on the outerbelt and made his way north. He tugged at the collar of his shirt as he drove, feeling like it was choking him, loosening his tie so he could breathe easier. How had he believed Andie could be trusted to do anything she agreed to?

On a whim, he drove to Bobbi's apartment. The door to the apartment was open, Andie Love slumped on the couch inside, her head in her hands. He wondered if she had already taken another overdose of pills. He flipped the light switch, but nothing happened.

"Power's out." Andie sounded like she was on the verge of tears. "They were going to send me too far away, and I couldn't do that. I got dropped off here."

"I didn't think about the utilities," Ed said. "I paid July rent, but I never thought about the electric or gas. Bobbi's worried sick about you. You should have called."

"Phone's disconnected."

The apartment was suffocating. It had to be one hundred degrees inside, and no air was moving even though the doors and windows were open. Ed could barely breath and he was standing in the doorway. "You can't stay here," Ed said.

"Where the fuck else do I go?"

Ed knew he should just walk away. She was not his responsibility. *Don't you dare,* Lisa intruded, her tone sharp as a knife. *Take care of this.* Ed sighed. Lisa could be a bitch at times. "Get in the truck."

Even with the running board, Andie could not lift her legs high enough to climb into the cab. "Let me help," Ed said, after five minutes of watching. Andie shook her head. He watched for another minute and then stepped forward. "Let me help," he repeated, too impatient to wait any longer. He caught her around the waist with his left arm, scooping up her legs with his right. He lifted her into the seat, a strong breeze blowing her hair into his face. He could see she was crying as he set her down on the seat. She buckled herself in angrily as he shut the door. He put the plastic bag with her clothes and her walker in the truck bed.

They rode home in silence. The sense of grief in the cab was overwhelming, like the ride home after Lisa's funeral. That feeling that something has been ripped from you too soon, that you will never again notice the beauty of a sunrise or the joy of a child's laughter. Grief was a lie that was all too true. It was and was not everything you felt in that moment, both permanent and fleeting.

What was Andie grieving? Her lost independence? Lisa? That Bobbi wanted to be in his life? Ed was still lost in his despair about Becca. He had not spoken to her since she ran from the restaurant five weeks ago. What was he going to say, that it was all okay? It was not, but he did not know why. And Lisa would not tell him what to do.

When he reached the house, both girls came out onto the porch. Bobbi rushed to the truck, pulling open Andie's door and hugging her, tears streaming down her face. Ed pulled the walker from the truck bed and then lifted Andie down from the cab. She did not cry this time, but awkwardly followed Bobbi into the house. The step to the porch took a few minutes. Ed waited impatiently, letting Bobbi help her. He carried her bag of clothes, following them down the hall to the guest room. Andie stood awkwardly in the center of the room, Bobbi draped around her neck and shoulders like they were best friends, Andie whispering into Bobbi's ear as Bobbi smiled and nodded. Ed dropped the plastic bag of clothes on the floor and backed out of the room.

It had been a mistake to bring Andie Love here. She had killed Lisa, and now she was in Lisa's home, celebrating. What had he been thinking? It was too hot in the room, too crowded with Bobbi and Andie and Sandy all talking at once. Too damn loud.

"I've got a sales call," Ed said, louder than he should have, everyone looking at him. "At the office. I'll be back later." He was lying, but he had to get out of there.

Ed pulled out of the drive knowing he was not headed to work. He could not go sit at his desk with this chaos swirling around his heart. He headed towards Upper Arlington, needing Jane. He could tell her what was in his head and heart. *Don't be stupid; she's your lover, not your confessor*. But he needed to hold her, to wrap his arms around her, to be loved by her.

Jane's driveway was empty when he pulled in. Ed's heart sank, the empty drive mirroring the emptiness of his life. He wanted her to be home so badly. He sat in the truck blinking away the tears that were threatening to spill over. He did not think he could deal with one more thing going wrong in his life. Maybe Lisa had been the lucky one, saved from all this pain by the peace of death.

Bullshit.

After climbing out of the truck, Ed walked around the back of the house to check out the progress made on the job. The new windows and French doors had been installed; their glass lightly covered with dust. Through the glass Ed could see that the opening into the kitchen had been cut and framed, a massive wood beam replacing the weight bearing wall. The kitchen was empty, the cabinets and counters removed, and drywall cut back to the studs in several places.

I'm fucking up, he though, letting the crap in my life impact work. This was the biggest job his company was doing this summer and he was not paying it the attention it deserved. He had not been this distracted after Lisa's death. Work was his foundation, giving a framework to his entire life.

He looked up when Jane's white Explorer rolled up the drive, stopping next to his truck. She climbed out of her SUV, wearing a white silk blouse and pleated gray skirt that fell just above her knees, a matching jacket thrown over her arm. Ed's heart jumped at the sight of her.

"Hello, stranger," she said as she picked her way across the torn-up yard. "I didn't know you were stopping over. Unfortunately, I'm all out of beer."

"I didn't come for the beer," Ed said.

"What did you come for?" she asked him with a flirty grin, stopping a foot away, her brown eyes shining in the late evening sun.

Ed stared, his body feeling too small to contain his joy. He wanted to shout that he had come for her, but he said nothing. He grabbed her hand and led her to the new French doors. He started to enter the lockbox code to get the key, but Jane had her keys in her hand and unlocked the door. She pulled him inside and then through the disarray of the kitchen, before giving him a deep kiss.

He took her by the hand and led her upstairs to her bedroom and then stripped her by the side of the bed. She stood silently, watching him, her brown eyes so big and deep he thought he would get lost in them. Then she grinned and pushed him onto the bed and undressed him. They made love slowly, kissing and touching and whispering, until they could not wait another minute.

After, they cuddled under the sheet, her head on his shoulder as the room slowly lost the evening light. He almost missed the tears on her cheek as the light faded.

"What's the matter?" he asked, his heart pounding again, the mood suddenly dangerous.

Jane looked at him, her face drained, her eyes still and dark. Finally, she spoke. "I feel like I've been lying to you," she said, looking away.

Ed felt like he had been hit with a hammer in the chest. He gently turned her head, so she was looking at him.

"Is this about you and Bill?" he asked, worried there would not be a divorce and that this beautiful woman could never be in his life.

Jane looked confused, frowning as she pondered his words. "No," she said slowly. "Bill and I are done. He decided it made more sense to negotiate with me than risk his empire in a messy, public divorce. We signed the dissolution papers this afternoon. That's not it."

"Wow, that was fast."

"We did all the negotiations two years ago. This has been a long time coming."

"Why didn't you go through with it back then?"

"My attorney suggested I put everything on hold. She thought I was too upset to make such an important decision. You know. After Lisa." Jane shook her head, unable to continue.

"The fact that you've been done with Bill for two years isn't a problem for me. It makes things better."

Jane shook her head again and wiped her eyes. "That's not it."

"Just say it."

"I don't know if I can say this right, and I don't even know if I should. It's water under the bridge..."

"But?"

"But I feel like I haven't been totally honest with you. If we're going to continue this," she said, waving her hand to encompass the bed, "I feel like I need to be honest."

"I want to continue," Ed said. "I just about burst to see you when you pulled in the drive. I have so much to share with you..."

"What about your girlfriend?"

"Rebecca and I are done. We haven't had that conversation yet, but I'm ready to break it off. You're too important to me."

"Don't," Jane said, looking away. "Not until you know the truth."

"What could be so bad?" Ed asked.

Jane scooted away from him, turning on her side so she was facing him. She pulled the sheet tight to her body, like a shield, covering her breasts. "Before the accident..."

"Yeah?"

"I was in love with Lisa."

"I know. You were best friends. Of course, you loved her."

"No," Jane said, with a soft shake of her head. "I was in love *with* Lisa."

"Do what?" Ed stared at her.

"My marriage was a sham, I was so alone, and Lisa was there for me. She made me realize not every relationship was toxic. The week we spent in Washington was one of the best weeks of my life."

The hammer was beating on Ed's chest, crushing with blow after blow. Lisa?

"Don't get me wrong," Jane said, a sad smile on her lips. "We didn't do anything. Neither of us was into girls, although if she had offered, I might have said yes. She just made me feel loved. I was jealous because she loved you so much there was no chance she'd ever leave you. I told her I was in love with her. She told me if you hadn't been in her life... who knows?

"Nothing happened. We were just closer. I felt safe with Lisa. I could be honest with her about my life. It looked so pretty on the outside and was so barren on the inside. I only went to Europe with Bill because Lisa encouraged me to go. She thought it might be romantic and give us an opportunity to reconnect. And if not, I'd know for sure it was time to leave him. So, I went, and discovered what I'd always known, that Bill would never prioritize me over his business or his other women.

"I didn't even get a chance to talk with Lisa about it. I came back and went to work, and she didn't show up for my first meeting of my first day back and I asked, and my world ended. Losing Lisa was so much worse than losing my marriage. She really was my lifeline. I went into a terrible depression. I could barely send a card. I couldn't think about what needed to happen in my own life.

"It took me two years to feel strong again and then I saw your truck in the drive and I couldn't move. I sat in the car for almost twenty minutes before I came inside. I thought my heart was going to break when I shook your hand. It brought back all my pain. And then later you told me about Andie Love and for a moment I hated you, but then I knew why Lisa loved you so much."

The room was deathly quiet. Ed could not think, could not escape the feeling of pressure in his chest, the pounding of blood in his ears. Was everything false?

"What am I to you?" he asked, surprised at the harshness of his tone. "A consolation prize?"

"No," Jane said, reaching out to touch his cheek. Ed twisted away, climbing from the bed. He dressed without a word, Jane watching, sobbing quietly, tears ruining her make-up. He was in his truck and on the way home in minutes, feeling as alone as he had after Lisa had died.

The lights were on in the guest room when Ed got home. He grabbed a beer from the fridge and went out into the back yard, King and Blackie trailing behind him. Ed walked away from the house, not wanting to sit on the deck where he might overhear Bobbi talking with her mom. He sat on a tree stump near the barn and took a swig of his beer.

Ed looked at the house and wondered how his life had fallen apart. He hated this place. He and Lisa had invested so much time and money and emotion into turning this place into a home and for what? You build a home for the people you love but they all leave you anyway. Becca and Sandy moved away. Lisa died. *Why hadn't she worn her seatbelt?* And then Rebecca had come into his life and given him hope and he had ruined it. He needed to break it off, to come clean that he was a judgmental prick who didn't deserve her. Now, Jane was gone, too.

How had he gone from alone to two girlfriends to no girlfriends? Ed took another long swig of his beer. He was greedy and dishonest and did not deserve to be with either of these incredible women who had wanted to be with him. He could not blame Jane for falling in love with Lisa. That was Lisa: loving, funny, compassionate, and a huge flirt. She would not have realized that Jane might have feelings for her. *Except that Jane had told her.*

Ed believed Jane that nothing sexual had happened, which hurt more than the idea of Lisa just fucking someone. Had she been getting something emotional from Jane that Ed had not been giving her? Lisa had always wanted more romance, more dancing, more nights of spontaneous fun. Ed had dreaded those arguments because he knew she was right, he did not do those things, but it made him feel like the things he did—phone calls, love notes, flirty texts, and surprise flowers—had never been enough. Had Lisa been in love with Jane because she had found someone who understood that part of her?

Ed looked at the house and imagined burning it to the ground. What had he been thinking, letting Andie Love come here? He had nothing left. His life had been ripped apart, wiped out like a trailer park in a tornado. King woofed once from the side of the barn and then he and Blackie raced away, chasing something in the dark. Ed wished he had their focus on the moment, when the only important thing was what was right in front of you.

Stars bloomed in the sky above him, and Venus, or maybe Mars, shone brightly above the tops of the trees. He craved that feeling of awe and insignificance he used to get when he and Lisa sat out here. They would talk about work and the kids, but as the night sky deepened and the stars came out, inevitably they would talk about their faith and sense of wonder and God in their lives. Today, God was an alien thing: the energy, the law even, behind all creation, but also the entropy, the disillusionment, the chaos of it all.

Ed missed that sense of wonder. It was like a hole in his chest, the place where his heart should have been. He missed the understanding that had come with it; that everything was bigger than he was, that God's blessings were bigger than his imagination, that life was more than the physical part that he saw and experienced. Tonight, the stars were uninspiring, cold and distant. Some were dead already, burned out or exploded into supernovae and no one even knew. Faith was just a fraud, a thin veneer that hid the extent of your pain and struggles.

Ed threw his empty beer bottle against the barn, grinning when he heard it shatter into pieces. He was too angry to walk inside to get another. He wanted to nurse that anger into true rage, let the power of it wash over him and burn away any regret he felt about his own behavior. He did not want to apologize to anyone or forgive them. What did it matter that he had slept with Jane while he was dating Rebecca? Or that he hated that Becca was in love with Cathy? And he sure as hell should not have cared if Bobbi spent three months in some fucking facility in Groveport. Why was it his responsibility to do the right thing for these people?

King came over and sat down next to Ed, right in front of him. The Doberman was so big that his head was level with Ed's, and he pushed his nose against Ed's cheek, snuffing softly. Ed pushed him away, eliciting a high-pitched whine. King circled the stump and came back, sitting next to Ed and dropping his head into Ed's lap. He pushed Ed again, hard enough to make Ed lean against the dog to keep from falling off the stump. King got up and spun, coming around so his head was down and his haunches up. Ed could see his stub of a tail quivering as he barked.

Ed closed his eyes, hoping the dog would disappear. It did not help.

Ed looked at the house. The light in Bobbi's room was off. A jerky motion in the dark caught his eye. Andie Love was walking unsteadily across the backyard, pushing her walker slowly in front of her. She was barefoot, wearing an oversized t-shirt as a night gown. She stopped when she was about ten feet away.

"Bobbi went to bed." She awkwardly turned the walker around, so she could use it as a chair. "Would you like some company?"

"No," Ed said.

"Well, that's too fucking bad because I've got to rest before I go back inside." She pulled the walker behind her, moving several steps closer to Ed and then sat down. "We don't have to talk if you don't want," she said.

"Good," Ed said. They sat quietly for a couple of minutes.

"Stars are pretty," Andie said. "I haven't seen so many since I was a kid. One place my parents went to party was out in the country. They'd have a big bonfire and eventually the adults would drift inside but us kids would stay out. The fire would burn down, and the sky would be amazing."

"You were a little astronomer?" Ed asked sarcastically.

"Not really," Andie said. "It was just safer to stay outside. If you went inside, you might notice that wasn't Daddy that Mommy was kissing. And when I was older.... But the stars were nice."

Ed did not respond.

"You can take me home tomorrow. I'll call in the morning and have the electricity turned back on."

"You've got money?"

"I've got two hundred and fifty-two dollars in my checking account. That will get me through the month."

"And then what?"

"I don't know. I'll figure something out."

"Okay."

Lisa was immediately in his mind, whispering furiously in his ear—*didn't I tell you?* Ed sighed. "You can't go home by yourself, you're not ready. You'll have to stay, for a little while, anyway. Until the PT says you're done."

"I can't..."

"You don't have any choice."

They sat in silence for a minute before she spoke again. "You know my attorney wrote something for me to read in court about how sorry I was. It was real pretty, but then I didn't say it."

Ed let the words cut through the fog that was surrounding him. This was more interesting than feeling sorry for himself. "I suppose you came out here to apologize now?"

"Fuck no," Andie said. "Why would you think that?"

"Do what?"

"I may be a lot of things," Andie said, "But I'm not a liar, not anymore. Do you think there are any words that I can say that would ever make what I did better? I'm not one of those people who can go to mass and confess or do my step work and make amends to someone and think that makes a difference. I killed your wife. I didn't mean to, so the fuck what? I should be in prison but I'm not. You tell me, how does saying I'm sorry make any of that better?"

"It doesn't," Ed said, staring at her. He wanted to get up and walk away, but he couldn't. It was like being stuck in the car as it rolled and rolled and rolled.

"My point..."

"But it says you know what you've done."

"Do you think I don't know what I've fucking done? Do you have any idea what it's like to watch a man hold his wife while she dies and know you did it? I think about her every day. How could God let this happen?"

"So, you feel sorry for yourself?"

Andie laughed. "Thank you," she said. "It's so easy to feel sorry for myself. I know I'm not the victim, Ed. You are. You and Lisa, and your girls and your friends and all the other people I've hurt over the years. Bobbi. She didn't ask for me for a mom. I've fucked up the lives of everyone I've encountered and then you take me in and give me a place to stay. It's so humbling."

"I shouldn't have..."

"I know."

"No, I'm serious. I didn't understand how difficult this would be, to have you here in this house. A few minutes ago, I was thinking about burning the house down, but the girls were inside."

"Rage is an emotion I understand. I tried to drown mine out with drugs and alcohol. I couldn't even see when I was blessed, like with Bobbi. I didn't quit hating my mom until I had to care for her as she was dying. I don't understand, but something about helping her and just holding her hand made a difference."

"Like Bobbi and you," Ed said.

Andie nodded. "Bobbi said more to me when I was in that coma than she had said her entire life. We talked tonight, without fighting, for the first time in a really long time."

"She can move her stuff into Becca's room tomorrow," Ed said. "Becca won't come home any time soon."

"No," Andie said. "We need to learn how to share space again. I just want to thank you for the opportunity." She stood up and turned around and pushed the walker back across the yard. Ed watched her go, each awkward step a revelation of strength he hadn't expected.

A crescent moon was rising in the east, the shadowed portion a faint promise of the full moon to come. Ed stared at it, wondering about the rounded shadows. Was his life like the waxing moon, growing toward fullness and light, or was it waning, headed toward blackness and oblivion? How do you even know?

He got up from the stump and walked to the barn. Little rivulets of beer led him to the place the bottle had hit. Ed bent down and picked up all the shards of glass he could find.

CHAPTER SEVENTEEN

Sandy was sitting at the kitchen table buttering a slice of toast, a cup of steaming coffee in front of her, when Andie came into the kitchen. Sandy watched the tiny woman move glacially across the kitchen, one step at a time, her body rocking from side-to-side with each step.

"Where's Bobbi?" Andie asked.

"She rode into work with Dad. She normally rides in with me, but I've got a sales call for a deck in Grove City this morning, so I'm not stopping by the showroom first."

"What's her job?"

"She took over my old position, ordering materials for the jobs."

"She can do that?"

"She's great. I'm way more ADD, so she's better than I was."

"Can I have some of that coffee?" Andie asked, stopping in front of the coffee maker.

"Sure," Sandy said. "The pot's almost full." After a second of watching Andie stare at the coffee maker Sandy shook her head, ashamed of her rudeness. "Do you need help?"

"No, I don't need any fucking help," Andie snapped. Then she turned her head to look at Sandy over her shoulder, a blush on her face. "Except Bobbi did everything yesterday. I don't know where anything is."

"Coffee cups are in the cabinet over the dishwasher, the second door to your left."

Andie rolled forward and reached up to open the cabinet door. "Fuck me," she said. The coffee cups were all on the second shelf, clearly beyond Andie's reach.

Sandy giggled and got up. "We'll have to rearrange the kitchen to make this work," she said, reaching over Andie to get down a coffee mug. "Would you like some toast for breakfast?"

"Sure."

Andie trudged from the counter to the table and sat down while Sandy brought her breakfast.

"I feel like I owe you an apology," Sandy said after a minute. Andie's head snapped up, a look of surprise on her face.

"What the fuck could you have to apologize for?"

"For the hospital," Sandy said. "I lied about who I was..."

Andie grinned. "I think I called you a lying little bitch when I found out who your dad was, but that was just me being an asshole. I never asked who your family was, and you never told me. I don't think that's a lie."

"I just didn't think you would have talked to me if you knew who I was," Sandy said, "and it was important to talk with you. I needed to find out who you were."

"Did you? Find out who I was?"

Sandy shrugged. "Not all of you, obviously. But I found out that you were more than just who I was imagining. It's kind of disorienting, to be sitting here having breakfast with you, but in some weird way it feels okay."

"I actually feel the same way," Andie said. "Disoriented, you know, about being here."

"I bet."

"You're a very brave girl, do you know that?"

"Me? Why would you think that?"

"You came to the hospital to help Bobbi and me. To help the woman who killed your mom. You took a big risk."

"Not really," Sandy said. "It's not like I asked you about what happened. I didn't give you a chance to say anything horrible."

"Do you want to know what happened?"

Sandy was quiet for a minute. "Someday, maybe, but not now. I'll ask when I'm ready."

"You really are brave."

"No," Sandy said, shaking her head, "Becca's brave."

"Why do you think that?" Andie asked before taking a sip of her coffee.

"She came out to Dad several weeks ago. It didn't go too well. He's still upset. I thought if we gave him a few weeks he'd get better, but he seems more agitated now than he did at first."

"He was surprised?"

"He had no idea. Dad doesn't pay attention to that kind of stuff."

"Did your mom?"

"Oh, yeah. I think Mom must have suspected long before I had a clue. She asked me a couple of times about what it was like in our high school for gay kids or if I'd feel bad if one of my friends were gay."

"Your mother never mentioned anything to Ed?"

"Apparently not," Sandy said. "And she never asked Becca directly."

"How is Becca doing?"

"She's really upset. He needs to figure it out soon. If he loses her, he loses me."

"Have you said this to him?"

Sandy shook her head again. "I'd just piss him off and make him dig in deeper. Mom was the only one who could just call him on something and get him to change his mind. Of course, he'd do anything for her. They were so head over heels as a couple that it was embarrassing."

Sandy looked down at her wristwatch. "Gotta go," she said. She left her dirty dishes on the table and headed out the back door.

• • •

Andie watched the physical therapist speed out of the drive, hating him. It was only Day Two and Travis had already given up on her, telling her there was no way PT was making a difference. He said she had to have surgery if she wanted to see any improvement. She turned to go inside, pushing the walker angrily in front of her. She hated needing a piece of equipment to do something as simple as walk.

Fuck, it hurt. Everything hurt. Was this her karma, to be here so Ed could watch her suffer? Andie wiped the tears from her face with her forearm. Fuck that.

She walked over to the fridge and pulled the door open and started rummaging through the shelves and drawers. She was going to have to make a shopping list, have Ed get some real food in the house. She found enough, between the fridge and the pantry that she could do a salad and pasta with sliced chicken in a mushroom sauce. *Thank God for Campbell's soup.* She sat at the kitchen table and wrote out a menu for the next ten days, putting down all the ingredients. She was a good cook, and she could do a lot better than what it looked like they had been eating.

She walked slowly through the house, the dogs trailing her nervously. They did not like the walker any more than she did. The house was clean, no dusting or vacuuming required. That left laundry, but she couldn't find a laundry room on the first floor.

The basement door was in the kitchen, next to the pantry. She flipped on the light switch and peered down a narrow set of steep stairs. She could see the basement floor was stone, not concrete. The steps were an inch or two deeper than normal. The washer and dryer were not visible from her spot at the top of the stairs, but she assumed they were down there. Andie pushed the walker right to the edge of the stairs and then lifted it in her left hand. She grabbed the handrail in her right.

Holding the walker in front of her she took a step forward, feeling with her left foot for the step. It was too far down. She pushed forward, feeling herself drop. Her foot hit the step and her left knee buckled underneath her, a stabbing pain shooting up her leg. She cried out, and pitched forward, dropping the walker as she grabbed the handrail with her left hand and caught herself, the walker crashing down the steps. Then she brought the right foot down, wincing as all the weight of her body rested on her left foot. On her second step, she switched to leading with her right foot. The pain was more bearable, but still intense. On the third step, her legs shaking violently, she sat down. She felt better immediately. Andie scooted down the steps on her ass, moving slowly but confidently down the stairs. She could see the laundry to her right.

Concrete has been poured over part of the stone floor, making a smooth surface for the laundry area. In addition to the washer and dryer, there was a laundry sink, a shelf for folding, an iron and ironing board, and even a wooden chair.

Andie snaked out her right leg and snagged the walker with her foot, pulling it back to the steps. She set it upright and used it to leverage herself up. She cursed the stone floor, hating how rough it was. Andie sat down heavily in the chair as soon as she reached it. Two overflowing baskets sat under separate laundry chutes. Andie did a load of Ed's dress shirts and slacks first, sitting back in the chair once it was in the wash. There was no way in hell she was going to go up the stairs until she was finished.

When Ed's clothes came out of the wash, she put in a load of Sandy's. Sandy was a good girl, and Andie hoped she would be a good influence on Bobbi. She could show Bobbi you do not have to be as fucked up as Andie was. She ironed Ed's shirts and pants when they came out of the dryer, hanging them on the clothes rack. Sandy's clothes were mostly t-shirts, jeans, socks and panties, so she folded those and put them in an empty basket.

Andie heard the dogs barking and wondered the time. She grabbed her walker and fought it over the cobblestones back to the stairs. She tried the reverse of what she had started to come down: left hand on the railing, right hand holding the walker. The steps were so far apart she only made it up two before she sank to her knees in tears, her legs shaking violently. She could hear someone come into the house. She was stuck, her legs curled underneath her, her left hand on the rail over her head, her right arm trailing with the walker dragging on the steps below. She was afraid if she let go the railing she would fall backward, but if she let go the walker it would clatter down the stairs, so she sat and waited for whoever had come home to get out of the kitchen.

She thought she heard girls' voices. She just needed to catch her breath to get another step or two done. When the basement door opened, it was Bobbi peering down, an alarmed look on her face.

"Ed," Bobbi called over her shoulder.

Andie shook her head in frustration. Why was he here? Didn't he work late most nights? A second later Ed was next to Bobbi, staring down at her. Andie shook her head at them. She could not let go of anything to wave them away.

Ed rushed down the steps. "What happened?" he asked as he reached her. He grabbed the walker from her hand and stood next to her. Andie grabbed the step above her. He carried the walker up the steps and gave it to Bobbi.

"What happened?" Ed demanded again as soon as he returned. Andie nodded towards the laundry area. "Did some laundry," she said.

"Why are you doing that?" Ed asked. "Bobbi can do whatever laundry you need."

"Not my laundry," Andie said. "I did your laundry. You and Sandy."

"Do what?"

"I did your laundry. Washed it and ironed it." Pushing off on the step with her right hand, she pulled herself slowly to her feet. She took another step, but her legs were shaking so badly she sank back down to her knees.

"Never do that again," Ed said. "I didn't bring you here to do chores."

"I'll do what I want," Andie said.

"Let me help you," Ed said.

"No." Andie turned her head away.

"I've got a sales call in thirty minutes," Ed said, "so we're not going to argue about this." He scooped her up in his arms. Andie thought about squirming away, but with her luck she would knock him off the steps and he would fall and die. She seethed with anger as he carried her up the steps. She was not a child. He carried her over to the kitchen table and set her down in a chair.

"You can't go down in the basement," Ed said.

"Fuck you."

"Seriously. You're not ready."

"I pull my own weight."

"I'm sure you do, but you're a guest in this house."

"I will pay you back for everything you've done for Bobbi and me," Andie said. "Every dime. I don't take charity."

"You can't pay me back," Ed said. "You owe this family too much. It can't be paid back, so you might as well stop trying."

Andie shook her head and looked away. She knew she was on the verge of tears, but she would not cry in front of this man. She saw the grocery list she had made earlier lying on the table. She grabbed it and gave it to Ed.

"We need some fucking groceries, so I can make dinners that are worth eating. Tonight's will be barely edible."

• • •

Sandy was rooting through the bottom of the fridge, looking for a Diet Coke. Andie Love was making dinner, sitting in front of the stove on her walker. Sandy hoped her dad would get home soon because dinner smelled great, and she was suddenly starving.

"Why the fuck did you do that?" Bobbi blurted out. "Are you trying to ruin everything?"

Sandy stood up, looking back and forth between them. Bobbi was sitting at the kitchen table, staring at Andie's back, anger coming off her in waves like heat off the blacktop on a summer day.

Andie turned and looked at her daughter over her shoulder. "What the fuck are you talking about?"

"This afternoon. Did you want him to rescue you? Do you like being picked up and carried up the steps?"

"I was just doing..."

"Do you think that you can be his little washerwoman and that makes everything okay? Or do you want to be his whore too?"

Oh my God, I've got to get out of here. Sandy closed the refrigerator quickly.

Bobbi turned to Sandy, a deep frown on her face. "Do you know what she did today?" she snapped.

Fuck. Too late. Sandy shook her head.

"She went down in the basement and couldn't get back up. She had to have Ed carry her up the stairs."

"Really?" Sandy tried to keep her voice as neutral as possible. She glanced at Andie. Andie had the same wrinkled brow and deep frown as Bobbi. They looked so alike in that moment, and yet so different with Bobbi's afro and dark skin, that Sandy almost laughed.

"She was doing the fucking laundry," Bobbi continued. "Who the fuck goes down the basement stairs with a walker to do the laundry?"

"Laundry is one of my chores when I'm home," Sandy said. "If you need anything washed, just let me know. I'm happy to do it."

"She wasn't doing her own laundry," Bobbi said. "She did yours and Ed's. Like she could make up for everything by washing some dirty clothes."

"You did my laundry?" Sandy asked, puzzled.

"Yes," Andie said.

Sandy felt a wave of gratitude and emotion well up in her chest. No one had done her laundry since her mom had died. Her vision blurred, and she shook her head, then wiped the tears away with her forearm. Andie was staring at her with an alarmed look on her face, so Sandy walked across the room and hugged her.

"Thank you," Sandy whispered to her, still crying, Andie as stiff as a post in her arms. After a second Andie relaxed and wrapped her arms around Sandy and held her. Sandy squeezed the older woman hard and then pulled away, embarrassed. She turned and looked at Bobbi.

"Quit being an asshole to your mom," she said. She started to leave the kitchen but saw her dad's pickup roll to a stop behind the house. He tapped the horn twice.

"Come on," Sandy said to Bobbi. "He's got groceries to bring in."

"Why are you defending her?" Bobbi asked under her breath as they left the house.

Sandy grabbed her by the arm. "Do you know what I'd give to have Mom back?" she asked. "I know you two have issues, but this is a gift. Don't fuck it up." She stalked away, leaving Bobbi staring after her.

• • •

The air was heavy and sticky, clouds gathering in the night sky, obscuring the stars. Ed thought it would rain tomorrow. The moon was a bright spot behind the clouds, casting an eerie pall over the night. It felt appropriate for his mood. Ed was sitting in the backyard, beer in one hand, cell phone in the other. He had come outside an hour ago to call Rebecca, but had been thinking about Jane instead, replaying the conversation from two days ago over and over. Jane telling him she had fallen in love with Lisa was a rude awakening. Those words had hit him like a punch in the face. Not because she had fallen in love with Lisa, but because Jane had always been *about* Lisa. He had found this talented, beautiful woman who had been deeply connected to Lisa. Jane was wonderful in her own right, but it was her connection to Lisa that he had been falling in love with, and that was not fair to Jane.

It was almost ten now, too late to call a woman who got up at four in the morning to go to work. Ed sighed. He deserved neither woman. He needed to call Rebecca and apologize and end it. That was the only thing to do, if he wanted to like himself, even a bit.

It had been a weird evening. Sandy and Bobbi were angry about something, snippy with each other all night, but oddly responsive to Andie. After the groceries were put away, she had told them to set the table, and they had. They washed the dishes together afterward, not speaking to each other. It felt like an echo of his family before Lisa had died, and Ed hated it.

The screen door slammed behind him. Ed turned and watched as Andie manhandled the walker across the deck. She scowled when she saw him watching her. Andie made it to the chair next to him and sank into it.

"Dinner was very good," Ed said.

"Thank you," Andie said. "And thank you for picking up the groceries. I like to cook."

"You don't have to cook or do laundry or any other chores. You're not our servant."

Andie sighed. After a minute, she spoke. "I don't know how to accept this gift you've given me. I can't repay it. It's as humbling and life changing as the accident was, and I don't know what to do about it."

"You can't do anything," Ed said, "so stop trying. It demeans what's being offered."

"I know cooking dinner doesn't equate with… what happened. A few years ago, I would have offered to fuck you as payment for what you've done for us," Andie said, her voice hesitant. "I was so fucked up I wouldn't even have asked. I'd have just crawled into your bed naked and considered everything even. Sex was just currency, and I was too."

Ed thought about how she had felt in his arms when he carried her up the stairs. So slight and warm and her heart beating hard enough he could feel it against his chest when he picked her up. He had a brief image of her naked and then shook his head. Was he crazy?

"Don't worry, I wouldn't disrespect the memory of your wife like that," Andie said, misreading the look on his face. "That's just how fucked up I used to be. I thought fucking someone took care of everything, so that's what I would have offered."

"You don't have to tell me any of this," Ed said.

"I do," Andie, replied, reaching over to put her hand on top of his. Ed pulled his hand away. He didn't want her touching him. He didn't want her here in his house, but he wasn't sure what to do to get her out. Maybe he could put her up in a motel?

"It was like I had a hole in my soul, this empty spot where truth and trust and love and honesty just got sucked away and all that was left was my true self. The me who didn't give a fuck about anyone else, not Bobbi, not Gram, certainly not you and your wife..."

"You're exaggerating," Ed said, feeling very uncomfortable.

"No," she said. "I'm saying I'm just trying to do my part."

"Okay, you can cook dinner."

They sat quietly for several minutes. Andie used the walker to leverage herself out of the chair. She started slowly walking back towards the house.

"Did the physical therapist come out today?" Ed called after her.

Andie looked back at him over her shoulder. "Yes."

"How was it?"

"Taxing. It hurt."

"Will he come every day?"

"He'll come five times a week until I'm better."

Ed watched her until she disappeared through the kitchen door.

• • •

Sunday dawned hot and sticky and never improved. The sky stayed that weird shade of Ohio gray, not truly overcast but not a bit of blue as far as the eye could see. Sandy took Bobbi to Easton to go shopping. Ed spent the day working on the yard, knowing he was getting a sunburn on the back of his neck and not caring, feeling like he deserved it. He did not know what Andie was doing, and he did not care.

He wanted to reach out to Rebecca, but he was not sure what to say. She had put him off this weekend, not that he objected. She was still angry he was not following her advice about Becca. Their phone calls had become sporadic. Even her texts seemed to convey a tone of disapproval.

He was cutting weeds in the culvert next to the road, absentmindedly running the trimmer through tall grass, sweat running down his face and neck. He thought about the last time they made love, and how wonderful it had been to cuddle after, and knew he was being a jerk. He had made her comments about lying to Becca a turning point, but why? And Jane was out of the picture, so there was no need for any awkward confession that put more distance between them.

Ed turned his trimmer off and set it on the ground and pulled his cell phone out of his pocket. He texted Rebecca, asking if they could talk later. He stared at his phone, hoping for an immediate response, but after a couple of minutes put it away and picked up the trimmer.

He felt better, knowing that reaching out to Rebecca was the right thing to do. He wondered if she had taken the kids to the pool in her complex. He would love to see her in a swimsuit. Maybe he should offer to take her on vacation somewhere, to give them a chance to rediscover each other.

An hour later the girls drove by him on the road, Sandy honking the horn and waving as she slowed to pull into their drive. Ed finished the yardwork after four. He showered before dinner and spent the evening reading the Sunday paper and watching the Reds game on TV. Rebecca never called.

CHAPTER EIGHTEEN

Ed spent Monday afternoon, August 2nd, dropping by job sites to see how things were going. Driving gave him plenty of time to think about how he had turned his life into a disaster. Six weeks had passed since Becca came out to him, and they still had not talked, not even a text. He needed to do something, or he risked losing her forever, but what? He did not know how to start a conversation about her being gay.

While he knew he and Jane were done, Rebecca was more complicated. He was desperate for the warmth of her body against his, the smell of her perfume lingering on her skin, and the desire of her kisses, but she had never responded to him yesterday.

Ed glanced at his cell phone in the cup holder in his console. He hit her speed dial number on his Bluetooth and waited, his heart pounding in his chest.

"Hey, it's me," Ed said when Rebecca answered her phone.

"Hi," Rebecca said, her voice flat. Ed could feel the gulf between them getting deeper by the second.

"I was hoping we could talk," he said.

"Were you? I'm not sure we have anything to talk about."

The phone went dead. Ed winced. What had he expected her to say?

His phone vibrated in the cup holder. He answered the Bluetooth absently.

"I'm sorry, Ed." Rebecca's voice wasn't flat now, but full of emotion. "I don't know what's happening to us..."

"Me neither," Ed said.

"I don't want things to end up like this. This kind of drifting away. I find myself questioning if this relationship is any good."

"I am too."

"You are?" The pain behind her question was knife sharp.

"Yeah," Ed said. "I worry that we're at very different places in our lives. Is there any chance I can see you?"

"Greg took the kids on vacation this week," Rebecca said. "Can you come by at six?"

"Okay. See you then," Ed said. He was gripping the steering wheel so hard it hurt, his entire body stiff and tight.

The afternoon plodded by with agonizing slowness, but Ed still found himself at Rebecca's apartment too soon, unsure of what he wanted from the relationship, knocking nervously on the door.

Rebecca opened the door, standing still in front of him. She looked like she had been crying. She was wearing a sleeveless blouse that hung below her waist, almost hiding her cutoff jeans. Her hair was pulled back in a ponytail. She looked young and vulnerable, and Ed hated himself even more. She stepped aside to let him in.

"How are you?" Ed asked, not moving.

"Fine," Rebecca said. Her voice was as flat as when they first spoke.

Ed stepped inside and stood awkwardly to the side while she shut the door. She slipped past him and walked down the short hall to the living room. She sat on the chair, curling her legs underneath her. Ed sat in the couch, catty corner from the chair, the coffee table from Wal-Mart serving as a shield between them.

Rebecca stared at him, her intensity making Ed uncomfortable. He struggled to find words, but before he could Rebecca spoke.

"What are we doing?" she asked.

Ed shrugged. "I wish I knew."

"Do you miss me?"

"Yes," Ed said. That was true. There was a hole where she had been in his life, an emptiness that left him sad and confused.

"I've missed you terribly," she said. "I don't want this."

"There are things you need to know," he finally said.

"I told you before, I don't want to know."

"I'm not a person who can keep secrets," Ed said, hating himself.

"Does it make you feel less guilty to tell me?" Rebecca asked.

"No," Ed said. "Telling you makes it worse."

"So, don't do it. Just let it go." Rebecca unbuttoned her blouse. Ed watched, fascinated, his cock growing hard in his pants as her blouse fell open to reveal the creamy skin of her full breasts. She shrugged out of it, her nipples fat and hard, and then stood and stepped around the coffee table and crawled onto Ed's lap. Her kissed were hard, angry. She undid his zipper, pulling him erect through his fly while he skinned her cutoffs down her legs. She straddled him, engulfing his being in the heat of her own, rocking up and down. His mouth was on her breasts, moving back and forth from one nipple to the other. Her hands were in his hair.

"Love me," she whispered as she rode him. "Please, please, please. Love me."

When they finished, she led Ed upstairs to her bedroom, a band of sunlight slicing through a gap in her curtains, making the room feel bright and cheery.

"I need you to hold me," she said as she undressed him. They climbed into her bed, under the sheet, Ed behind her, his arm thrown over her waist, and didn't move as the room slowly turned dark. An almost imperceptible shaking of her back against his chest was the only thing that revealed her tears. He could barely see her face reflected in the mirror above her dresser, the black holes of her eyes devouring him. "This isn't going to work, is it?" she finally asked, her voice cracking.

"No," Ed said, unable to deny it any longer.

"What did I do wrong?"

"You did nothing wrong," Ed said. "I'm not ready."

"You won't find another Lisa," Rebecca said. "If that's what you want, it won't happen."

"I know," he said. "It's not fair to you that I can't tell you what I want. You were such a wondrous surprise; I couldn't stop myself from loving you."

She moved forward an inch, so her back and ass were no longer nestled against him. "But you don't love me now?"

"No." Her body stiffened under his arm.

"Is she prettier than me?"

Ed was silent for a moment. "No," he finally said. "You are."

"What is it, then?"

"I don't know. I didn't mean for Jane to happen. She was a friend of Lisa's. We just had shared feelings about Lisa, I guess."

"She's older?"

"You mean my age? Yes, she's about my age."

"Do you hate me?" She stared at him in the mirror, her eyes never blinking.

"No, I don't hate you. Why would you think that?" Ed wanted to kiss the back of her neck, his heart breaking for her, but he didn't move.

"I think I hate you," she said. "You need to get out of my house."

Ed climbed awkwardly from her bed. She pulled the blanket up to cover her body as she watched him dress in the dimly lit room, the dying light from outside visible through the gap in her curtains.

"You're just like Greg and every other man I ever went out with," she said, no longer hiding her crying. "I thought you were going to be different. That you wanted me, not just my body. That you thought I was worth being loved."

Ed wanted to tell that he had loved her, but anything he said would be as hollow as an apology from Andie Love.

"This woman, Jane did you call her?" Rebecca asked, her voice tight. "Will you make a nice couple?"

"No," Ed said. "We broke it off."

"Good."

"I know. I don't deserve either of you." He hated himself for hurting her.

"I needed you to love me," she said as he left her room. "I loved you."

The sun hadn't set when he left her apartment, but the moon was already visible in the darkening sky, Mars, a single bright light in the sky, shining near it. Insects skittered in the glow of a streetlamp, scattering as a bat flittered into the light. The night air stuck to him, smothering. He wanted to go back inside and tell Rebecca he loved her and undo all the pain he had caused.

Ed struggled to breathe as he climbed into his truck; he was alone again. Lisa was irrevocably gone, made more dead by his failed relationships with Jane and Rebecca. The moon, shining sickly above him, couldn't be more barren than his life. Love was a lie, a failed promise that could never live up to the hype that surrounded it. It always ended, always in pain and loss. Why did we yearn for it, knowing it would destroy us?

Ed bit the inside of his lip, telling himself over and over that he would not cry. He thought about their first date, about how Rebecca had made his life so much brighter by spending that evening with him, and then the wonder of making love with her.

He headed to the office, the one safe space in his life. He spent several hours writing up quotes for recent sales calls he had made, and then reviewing other offers ready to go out. Anything to keep his mind off Rebecca, curled tightly on her bed, her eyes stabbing at him across the dark room. He had wanted her to understand, to let him off the hook gently. Why had he been surprised when she had revealed her pain and anger?

The house was dark when he finally went home, a little after one in the morning. Ed slept fitfully and was up and out of the house before anyone else was awake.

• • •

Ed was dying. His lungs were on fire, his knees ached, and the asshole kid was going to pass him again. He had been in a funk for the last two weeks, ever since he broke up with Rebecca. This morning, he had woken up at four thirty and knew he needed to get back on the track. He had not done his normal workout since the night John Smith had called and introduced him to Bobbi. Today he was punishing himself, running harder than he should after three and a half months off. The only sounds Ed could hear were steady crunch of the runner's feet as the kid caught up to him and his own labored breathing. The kid passed him as if Ed were walking, grunting an undecipherable greeting as he dashed past.

Ed didn't bother replying. He ran, letting the pain in his body wash away the pain in his heart. He could not separate the hurt he felt from the hurt he was causing. Everything felt wrong: Becca, Jane and Rebecca, Andie Love. And underneath it all Lisa. Nothing had been right in his life since Lisa had died.

Ed had not understood what he was doing when he brought Andie Love home. Her presence begged something of him, but he didn't know what. What did Lisa's death demand? The chuffing of his feet on the cinder block track seemed to chant '*Forgive. Forgive. Forgive. Forgive.*' But who did he need to forgive? Andie, for fucking up his life so violently, or Lisa for abandoning him?

Truthfully, he had been afraid he was losing Lisa in the months before the wreck. He had hoped their anniversary would set them on a new path. They went to Columbus because Lisa had wanted to go dancing. Dinner had been at Morton's downtown, and then they walked the three blocks to a new club Lisa had found. Ed laughed when the place turned out to be a jazz club, relieved there would be no dancing.

"Damn it," Lisa said, shaking her head in disappointment. "Let's just go home." She wiped away a tear that slipped down her cheek.

Ed shook his head. "Go clean up your make-up," he whispered. "We need some champagne. Twenty-five is a big deal." Lisa nodded, still unhappy, and headed to the Ladies room.

The young man who had taken their cover at the door stepped over. "Something wrong?"

"It's our anniversary," Ed said. "She wanted to go dancing, not realizing what this place was."

"I can get you one dance, if you want to stay. What are your names?"

"Ed and Lisa."

It was just after the champagne showed up that the bass player stepped up to the mic. "We've got an anniversary in the house, folks," he said, "and they need a dance. Please welcome Ed and Lisa!"

Lisa had stared at Ed, totally shocked. Once they made their way to the front of the stand, the bass player leaned down. "I hope this is okay," he said. The group then played a jazzed-up version of "Fly me to the Moon" while Ed and Lisa danced in front of a clapping, whistling crowd.

"Kiss her, man!" someone shouted, and Ed did, the night suddenly better than he had ever hoped. He did not think anyone in the club would forget the kiss soon.

But then Lisa balked at the hotel. It made little sense, she said, with Sandy at home, just forty minutes away, and a mortgage, and college tuition for two kids next year. They stayed long enough for Lisa to finish the champagne, but she had not been swayed about the hotel.

Ed's darkest fear clawed its way out of his gut. *Had she been so unhappy she wanted out?* That explained Lisa unbuckling her seatbelt. She had not cared anymore. She had abandoned him.

Ed let out a sob and stumbled off the track and onto the field. He sank to the ground, gasping for air, the field like concrete under his knees. He was drowning, dying for real. He bent over, the ground rough against his face, blind now, hoping his body could just lay here for months, eaten away by parasites and vermin, all that he really deserved. Ed let out a raw scream, spewing out two years of fear, two years of unspoken hurt that Lisa had done this to him by unbuckling her seatbelt. His rage exploded, and he pounded the field with his right hand, relishing the pain of it.

"Hey, dude, you okay?" It was the kid, standing at Ed's shoulder. Ed straightened up, nodding, waving him away, a look of surprise on the kid's face when he realized Ed was crying. The kid stumbled away like he had been slapped, back to the track, running a fast half lap and then disappearing into the parking lot.

Ed struggled to his feet, wiping his face with the back of his arm. He walked back to the track and started jogging again, slowly, trying to find his rhythm. He still had two laps to get to three miles. Each step forward was an effort, his breath coming in deep gasps that did not seem to draw any oxygen. He labored forward, moving now just to move.

What had he been doing at the time? Lisa would not have left if he had loved her enough. He knew he could withdraw easily enough. He was a slave to his schedule, almost obsessive compulsive about it. That was why it was so odd he had stopped running. He was driven to do things according to his schedule every day and he had gone three months without adhering to it. And taken in a fifteen-year-old who needed a safe harbor, and fallen in love with two women, and let the woman who killed his wife come live in his house, and fucked up his relationship with his daughter.

That was why he had a schedule in the first place, to keep shit like that from happening.

He thought about last night, when Andie had approached him after dinner. Ed had been sitting at the kitchen table drinking his second beer of the night while Andie busied herself cleaning the kitchen.

"Can I say something to you? About Becca?" she asked.

"No," Ed said, staring at her, but she seemed indifferent to his menace.

"Sandy thinks you're screwing up."

"Yeah," Ed said after a minute. "I guess I am."

"What are you going to do about it?"

"I don't know. I wish I could say it doesn't bother me, but that would be a lie."

"At least call her."

"And do what?"

"Tell her what you told me to tell Bobbi: that you love her. Tell her you know you're being an asshole and it's not her fault. Tell her Cathy is a wonderful girl and you're happy for them."

"I should give them my permission?"

"They don't need your fucking permission. Becca is going to get married to Cathy no matter what you do. Give them your blessing." Andie folded the dish towel on the counter and headed towards the room she shared with Bobbi.

Why the fuck had he even let her open her mouth? He did not need Andie's opinion on anything. He would do what he wanted, if he could just figure that out. He knew Cathy cared about the world, about fighting injustice, about being fair. When Lisa had died, he had been grateful Cathy was there to support Becca. Maybe he was just pissed because he had missed it all. What kind of father does not know who the fuck his daughter is dating?

Ed finished his last lap and bent over trying to catch his breath. He glanced at his wristwatch. Six twenty. He had just enough time to go home and catch a shower and get to the office by seven thirty. He walked back to his truck. He had a can of V-8 juice on the front seat. He shook it and popped the tab, taking a long swig. Ed started the truck and pulled out of the lot. He turned left towards the interstate rather than right towards the house. He needed to talk with Becca. Now was as good a time as any.

Ed drove to Becca's place slowly, out of breath, his heart never slowing after his run as it should have. Ever since John Smith had called and demanded he meet Bobbi, Ed had been caught in a raging flood, carried along by the torrent and barely able to keep his head above water. Going to see Becca felt like getting his feet on solid ground again, even if he didn't know how to make up for what he had said.

The sky was clear, and Ed felt his heart lift. August in central Ohio was hot, humid and gray, but this morning was clear with almost no humidity. He parked beside the brick row house, nosing his truck onto a patch of dead grass next to her car. Ed got out and walked around to the front of her apartment, smiling when he saw the pair of wicker chairs on her porch, the colors faded to a muted brown. The chairs had to be at least fifty years old, having passed from his grandparents to his parents and then to the deck at his house for a decade. Becca had begged for them when she moved here.

He settled into the chair furthest from the door, wishing he had stopped for coffee on his way down. He finally caught his breath, but his entire body ached. Ed looked at his watch. Seven fifteen. He had no clue what Becca's schedule was over the summer. He settled back in the chair, trying to ignore the sweet aroma from Buckeye Donuts next door. He could not imagine how Becca could live here and not eat donuts for breakfast every day. Ed closed his eyes and took in a deep breath. He wondered if he had time to run next door and grab coffee and a donut without missing Becca.

"What are you doing here?"

Ed snapped open his eyes. Becca was standing in the open door to the apartment, running shoes in hand, dressed in shorts and a t-shirt. Ed smiled. She had always been his child, not Lisa's.

"Hey," he said.

"Why are you here?"

"I thought we could grab breakfast and talk."

"I don't want to talk," she said. She stepped outside and pulled the door shut behind her, and then sat on the first step to put on her shoes.

"I get that," Ed said, "but I have some stuff I need to say."

"Like what?" Becca glared at him over her shoulder.

"An apology, to start," Ed said. "Why don't you grab Cathy, and we can go talk?"

"Cathy's still asleep," Becca snapped.

"Look," Ed said. "I know I hurt you. I'm sorry. I don't want things to get worse, so I'd like to talk."

"I have nothing to say," Becca said, standing up.

"Just listen to me then, if you don't want to talk."

"You're dressed for a run. You can come along."

"I did three miles this morning. I can barely walk."

Becca shook her head. "I bet."

"Hey, at least I made the effort. So, what about breakfast?"

Becca gave him a look and then shrugged. "Donuts, huh?" she asked, nodding towards High Street.

"Yeah."

They walked in silence to the store. Ed got an apple fritter and a large coffee. Becca picked out an apple and a small stick donut and coffee. They walked back to the porch and sat in the wicker chairs.

"I know I didn't say the right thing when you said you were getting married," Ed said. "I'm embarrassed by what I said."

"Good."

"I want you to know I love you."

"I know that Dad."

"I love Cathy, too. I can see how good she is for you. I'm glad you found her."

"You're okay with everything?"

"No," Ed said. "Someone told me to lie to you and say everything was okay, but I won't lie."

"Now you're going to get all evangelical on me and tell me I'm a sinner?"

Ed laughed. "No, I don't think you're a sinner. I don't think there is anything wrong with you or Cathy. You're in love."

"So, what's wrong?"

Ed took a bite of his fritter and shrugged. "I don't have a clue," he said.

"What does that mean for us?"

"Someone else told me I need to offer my blessing. I'll admit, I was shocked when you said you were marrying Cathy. I had no idea you were gay. I wish I could say it didn't bother me, but it did."

"Why?"

"I've got no idea. Just to be clear, it's not because of Cathy. I might have felt the same if you said you were marrying a guy. I didn't even know you were dating, so I was totally lost. I wish your mom had told me you were gay."

"She didn't know. We never talked about it."

"Oh, I'm guessing she suspected," Ed said. "I know she worried about you. That's something else I'm struggling with, that your mom didn't trust me enough to tell me what she thought."

"I was afraid what you and Mom would think..."

"We would just continue to love you, honey. Not perfectly, not without me saying stupid things, but we would love you."

"Can I tell you something?" Becca asked shyly.

Ed nodded.

"I can't always say stuff to Cathy," Becca said. "So, if I share something with you, you won't repeat it?"

"Of course not."

"Not even to Sandy? Or your girlfriend?"

"No."

"Sometimes I'm scared about getting married. I think about what it means, a whole life together, kids and all that, and I worry I'm not ready."

"I'd be worried if you weren't a little scared."

"You would?"

"I'd be afraid you weren't taking this seriously. What makes you the most scared?"

"Probably thinking about Mom and you."

Ed gave her a puzzled look. "The accident?"

"No," Becca said, shaking her head. "Because you and Mom had such a perfect marriage. I worry Cathy and I won't ever live up to that..."

Ed laughed. "Honey, your mom and I were anything but perfect. No relationship is perfect. We had our own challenges and there were a couple of times we thought about calling it quits."

"So, you think Cathy and I won't last?" Ed could hear irritation in her question, so he reached out and grabbed her hand and gave it a squeeze.

"I hadn't even considered that. I'm just saying being married is different than when you fall in love. There are pressures and stresses you don't think about in advance. Sometimes couples fall out of love."

"Did you and Mom?"

Ed considered the question. "Maybe. Maybe a couple of times. But we always fell in love again."

"What does that mean?"

"We had a good relationship, but it wasn't always even. Sometimes it was so easy it was a blessing from God. Other times it was hard. The worst times of all were when it wasn't either. When it felt like we weren't connected anymore. Like we weren't in love."

"What did you do?"

"We worked through it. We were committed to each other and to you guys, despite the times when both of us just wanted to chuck everything and run away. I'm sure that happens to most adults."

"So, what happens now?" Becca asked.

"You're going to plan a wedding. I'm going to pay for it. I do have two requests, however."

"What?"

"One, tell Cathy you're scared..."

"Why would I do that? She'll just think I don't really want to get married."

"You want to tell her because it sets a floor of honesty between you now that you want to maintain throughout your marriage. It also gives her permission to tell you what she's scared about, like maybe you don't really want to get married."

Becca was quiet for a minute, but then nodded. "Okay. What else?"

"I don't want the reception to be in New York."

"Dad, we can't get married in Ohio..."

"I know why the wedding has to be in New York, but I'd like the reception to be here in Columbus."

"Why?"

"So all your friends and family can celebrate with you. When you go to New York, lots of folks won't go with you. You could even repeat your vows here, so everyone can see what you and Cathy are claiming for each other."

"Do you mean it? You want to invite people?"

"Hell, yes. If you're getting married, we're having a party."

Becca sprang up from her chair and hugged her father. "Thank you," she whispered. She sat on his knees, wiping her eyes with the backs of her hand, laughing at her tears.

Ed glanced at his watch. "Look, I've got to go. Are we okay?"

"Yes," Becca said, smiling. "Can I tell Cathy..."

"Tell me what?" Cathy was standing in the open doorway, cup of orange juice in hand. Her disheveled blond bob made it clear she had just gotten up.

Becca jumped up and went back to the other wicker chair, perching on the edge. She patted the seat for Cathy to sit beside her.

"I came by to apologize for the way I acted," Ed said. "I'm sorry I..."

"You have nothing to apologize for, Mr. Gideon."

"Look," Ed interrupted. "You can call me Ed, or even Dad, but never Mr. Gideon. And I do have to apologize because I was wrong."

Cathy didn't move, looking back and forth between Ed and Becca.

"This is where you can say you accept," Ed said.

"I accept," Cathy said, a slight blush on her face.

"Dad wants us to have a second ceremony and the reception here in Columbus, so everyone can be with us."

"You do?" Cathy looked astonished.

"Yeah. I want to offer you my support, and make sure you both know I love you."

"Thank you, ... Ed."

"When do we get to meet Rebecca?" Becca asked. "I'd like to get to know her."

Ed shook his head. "We broke up."

"What happened?"

Ed looked down at his lap, feeling his face flush. "I wasn't ready to be in a relationship," he said.

"That's not what I expect to hear from you."

"Do what?"

"You always told me," Becca said, leaning forward in her chair and pointing at Ed, "that you have to fight for what's important. Don't just wait for something to happen but go out and make it happen. If you have feelings for her, you act on them. Don't let her get away because you're afraid you don't deserve her, or you feel guilty because she's so much younger than Mom."

"That's easy for you to say..."

"No, it's not." She got up and put her arm around Cathy's waist. "I almost blew it with Cathy because I was afraid to let the world know who I was. Promise me you won't let Rebecca get away because you're afraid to act."

Ed thought about his last time with Rebecca. It felt like months had passed since they'd broken up, but it was just a couple of weeks. She had desperately wanted to be loved before she said she hated him. Did she? Or was she just protecting herself?

"Promise me?"

Ed thought about his words carefully. He was still so confused about Rebecca and Jane and whatever had ever compelled him to get involved with two women at the same time. He didn't trust what he felt about either of them. "I promise I'll think about what you're saying," he said.

Ed stood up and gave Becca a hug and then Cathy. "I've got to go," he said.

"Don't forget your promise," Becca called after him as he headed down the steps.

"I'll think about it," Ed said. Could Rebecca want him back?

CHAPTER NINETEEN

Ed drove slowly past Jane's house, relieved her white Explorer wasn't in the drive. He was here to pick up the draw payment that was due with drywall but was too cowardly to stop by when Jane was home. He made a U-turn and pulled into her driveway.

The exterior of the two-story addition looked complete, matching the original house perfectly. Inside, the kitchen was drywalled and painted; cabinets had been hung and the island built, but no countertops or appliances were set.

Ed walked upstairs to see the new master bathroom. He stopped for a second outside Jane's bedroom, his eyes drawn to her big four-poster bed, stripped bare, as barren as a moonscape, the same as his wedding bed. Ed stared at the bed, blinking rapidly, the room blurring, the sounds of his crew downstairs in the kitchen suddenly miles away. A bead of sweat trickled down his neck. His heart slowed, the emptiness between each beat a lifetime. The void in his life was overwhelming. He would be alone until he died. The idea that he could find love again, after Lisa, had been a lie he had desperately wanted to believe. The empty bed made it clear, however, that love had abandoned him.

He gasped, sucking in a deep breath, and looked away from the bed, determined not to cry. An envelope lay on Jane's side table, the bedside lamp placed partially on top of it. Ed took a closer look and his heart jumped when he recognized his name in Jane's handwriting. He opened the envelope and found the draw check, but nothing else.

Ed left without talking with anyone. He didn't trust himself to have a conversation and not break down. He found himself on 315 headed towards the office, unable to get Jane's stripped bed out of his mind. The last time he had been in that room, he had been in a cocoon of bliss, sexually satiated, feeling a deep emotional connection with this stunning woman, and then Jane had flung him from her life, confessing her love for Lisa. If the accident had ended differently, if Lisa had lived and Ed had died, would Jane have gotten what she really wanted? Would she be divorcing Bill Sanderson to be with Lisa?

He could not blame Jane for falling in love with Lisa. He had fallen in love with Lisa the first time he saw her, signing him in for freshman orientation. Lisa had smiled at him, her eyes so lively and engaged, and he was lost, standing there for several seconds while she asked him for his name a second and then third time. He was embarrassed, but he looked at her name tag and wrote her name on his folder as soon as he left the table. When it turned out she lived in the same dormitory he did, Ed had taken that as proof that they were meant to be together.

He understood the twisted thinking that turned Jane's love for Lisa into an attraction to Ed. He had done the same thing, falling for Jane despite his burgeoning relationship with Rebecca. Rebecca had a freshness to her, smart and sexy as hell, which was like diving into a swimming pool, encapsulating him. Rebecca had resurrected him. Jane had...what did Jane have?

For the life of him, Ed couldn't figure it out. It must have been the connection to Lisa. He was finding Lisa in Jane, and she was finding Lisa in him. Which meant they had never really had a relationship at all. They had been caught up in something in their own heads, something with Lisa, and not with each other. *But it had felt so real.*

"Fuck," Ed said, unsure what he was cussing at. He hated the idea of being in the office surrounded by people, but he could not go home. Andie Love was there. He knew too much about her to hate her any longer, but he could not afford to like her.

He could go see Rebecca. She was at work, but if he walked in, she might take the afternoon off. He was sure she would take him back if he asked. He drove past the showroom and took the exit for Bob Evans. When he reached the top of the ramp, however, he turned the wrong way. Now was not the time to see Rebecca. He needed his mind clear, not troubled with thoughts of losing Jane and Lisa. He ended up at a hole-in the-wall dive, sitting on a stool at the bar, the Cleveland Indians on the TV behind the bar, a double scotch on the rocks in front of him. Ed took one sip of the scotch, the sharpness of the liquor clearing his mind. He pushed the glass away, dropped a ten on the bar and left.

• • •

Sandy honked as she pulled out of the drive, Bobbi waving madly from the passenger seat. They were going to a movie to celebrate Bobbi's sixteenth birthday. Ed waved back. On Monday, he was going to take Bobbi down to the BMV to get her learner's permit. He was paying for a driver's ed class and insurance. He had a mechanic come get her Gram's car and do a tune-up, making sure everything was in working condition.

Ed sighed and took another sip of his beer. A single star was the only thing visible in the dusky sky. It was a beautiful evening for late August, clear with no humidity and the temperature in the high seventies, but he still felt agitated. He should have gone with the girls to the movie.

The letter from Medicaid, that he had found on laying on the deck, was in his shirt pocket. Seeing it addressed to Andie had not stopped him from reading it. Medicaid had ended Andie's PT based on the recommendation of her physical therapist. The letter was more than a week old.

The screen door slammed as Andie came out of the house. A wave of irritation washed over him as she maneuvered her way from the porch to the deck.

Andie plopped into the chair next to him. "I hope you don't mind my company," she said.

Ed shook his head. "Enjoy," he said, standing up.

"Wait."

Ed sat.

"I can tell you're pissed about something. I'd rather deal with it than worry about it. What did I do?"

"What's up with your physical therapy?"

"Oh. Travis, the PT, put it on hold."

"When were you going to tell me?"

"I'm appealing. I know I'm getting better."

Ed pulled the letter from his pocket. "And when they say no?"

Andie shrugged. "Then I'm done here. That's what we agreed on at the beginning."

"Why didn't you tell me what was happening?"

"Bobbi's doing good here. I didn't want to disrupt her, but I can tell you're ready for us to go. We'll move out by the end of the week."

"I didn't ask you to move out."

"That was the deal, wasn't it? We could stay until I recovered. Well, this is as fuck recovered as I'm going to get. We'll move out."

"How are you going to pay for things?"

"I'll get my old job back."

"Where?"

"The Arby's by the apartment. I can walk there."

"You and Bobbi can live off what you earn?"

"It's not like we live in the fucking Taj Mahal. Neither of us eats much. We'll make it work. I'll move out of your fucking house by the end of next week."

She stood, grabbed her walker, and headed slowly towards the house. Ed thought she was crying. He grinned viciously. It was about time he fucked up her life for a change. Andie lifted her walker onto the porch. She moved more quickly, letting the screen door slam behind her. A few seconds later the light in her room came on, then the light in the bathroom down the hall.

Ed laughed, the perverse pleasure he was feeling at disrupting her life lifting his spirits. He should go inside and grab Andie's clothes and all her shit and throw it out in the yard, so the whole world could see he was a man again.

He was about to stand up when Lisa intruded on his fantasy. Ed could imagine the sharpness of her tone as she called him out. She would not yell, rather she would say something sarcastic and cutting, opening Ed's hypocrisies to the world, spilling them from his being as if she had knifed him in the gut.

You've never been the man you pretend to be.

Ed knew it was true. His life was all for show. That was why Jane had caught Lisa's attention, because Lisa had tired of living with an illusion. When he finished his beer, he went into the house. The kitchen was empty, but he felt Andie's residual hurt in the air. Ed glanced down the back hall. The door to the bathroom was open and the door to Andie's room was closed. He opened the fridge and grabbed another beer and headed back outside. He stopped on the porch, Lisa still challenging him. She would not let him off the hook. Now was the time to act like the man he wanted to be. Ed looked at the beer bottle in his hand and then went inside and put it back. He could make one thing right, no matter how he felt. He walked down the hall to Andie's room, knocked once and opened the door.

Andie was standing in front of the dresser, studying her reflection in the large mirror. She was naked, except for a bath towel wrapped in a turban around her hair. Naked, although petite, she didn't look like a child. Her back tapered to a narrow waist and her hips flared enough, making her all woman. Her ass cheeks were tight and well-toned, small under her hips, but sexy. Her breasts were full on her small frame and her mons was lightly covered in dirty blonde curls. Her legs were still bent tightly at the knees, and her left foot turned on its side, making her stance before the mirror awkward. She stared at Ed in the reflection, making no move to hide herself. She flushed slightly, her breath quickening, her blue eyes wide and frank. Ed could see the raw need on her face and felt his cock twitch in response.

"Sorry," Ed mumbled, not looking away.

"We'll be out in the morning."

What the fuck am I doing? Ed stepped out of the room, pulling the door closed behind him. He leaned against the wall, unable to move. How could he be attracted to her?

The door opened, Andie now in a cotton robe, pushing the walker in front of her. "I told you before there was a time in my life when I would have fucked you and thought we were even. But that's not what we want, Ed. You'll just hate both of us more, and that's not what I want for you. We'll be out in the morning."

"Don't leave," he said. "I'm not asking you to leave."

"Don't you fucking lie to me," Andie snapped.

"Do what?"

"Don't lie. You pretend everything is fine, but you can't hide how you feel. Your contempt for me is written all over your face."

Ed was stunned. After several seconds, unable to deny her words, he shrugged his shoulders. "I'm caught here. This is something I have to do, but I don't always want to."

"I don't want your fucking charity," Andie said. "I don't need you to save me. We'll leave in the morning." She started to close the door, but Ed stopped her.

"Having you here hurts," he said. "I'm learning things about myself that I don't like..."

"I'm not here for you, Ed," Andie said.

"Do what?"

"I'm not here so you can learn about yourself or feel good about how fucking charitable you are or put your demons to rest. That's not my responsibility. If that's what you want out of this, I'd just as soon fuck you and get it over with, rather than feel like I'm in debt to you."

"That's not what I'm saying," Ed snapped. "I'm trying to do the right thing here, but I'm not even sure what it is. I don't like the way I'm acting, or the thoughts that pop into my head."

"It's not my job to make you the man you want to be..."

"But I need it."

Andie turned away and walked awkwardly across the room, only one hand on her walker. She slipped the robe from her shoulders and let it fall to the floor as she reached the bed, revealing her naked back and ass. She turned, her breasts and pussy on display, and then sat on the edge of the bed, her legs splayed.

"Then just fuck me, like every other guy in my life. Use me. Make me what you want me to be. That's what men do."

Ed couldn't look away, his own anger and need swirling in his heart, the urge to hurt her flaring again. He crossed the room, grabbed her robe from the floor and thrust it at her. "That's not what I want," he said.

"What do you want?" Andie asked, her voice taut.

"I'm just saying I'm not kicking you out."

"I have to leave," she said, her intense blue eyes never leaving his face. She leveraged herself up, so she was standing in front of him, and pulled her robe back on. Ed towered over her. "It's wrong that I'm here. You know it."

"I have to learn to deal with..."

"Ed, this isn't about you," she said. "*I* need to leave."

"Why?"

"You may not fucking believe it, but I care about this family. I care about you and your girls, even the fucking dogs. Every second I'm here, I feel what I did to you. It was hard enough when I didn't know any of you. To be here with you and Sandy—not to mention the giant fucking portrait of Lisa in the living room–is more than I can bear. There's so much hurt here and it's all my fault."

"Sandy doesn't want you to leave," Ed said.

"No, she doesn't, but I'm going to have to move out some time," Andie said. "Now is as good as later."

"No," Ed said. "You don't have to move out. You or Bobbi. You should stay at least until she goes to college."

"Ed you're a nice man, but that's a fucking stupid idea. Even if I thought I could handle living here, I'd just be in the way. Maybe not immediately, but what about the next time you date someone? Just ignore the woman in the kitchen, she's my... my what?"

"I don't think I'll be dating for a long time," Ed said.

"Don't give up on love because you just broke up with someone. You'll meet the right woman."

"You could stay until you meet someone."

Andie laughed sadly. "Relationships are no good for me. I've always compromised myself to be loved and I can't do it any longer. I need to be strong enough on my own. I don't want to be in love, it never works out."

"You're lying," he said.

Andie glanced at him out of the corner of her eye. "Lying?"

"You're desperate to be loved. You're just afraid you're not worth it."

"And now the pot is calling the kettle black," she said.

"Yeah," Ed said. "You're right." He stood awkwardly in front of her for a minute. "Don't disrupt Bobbi right now. She's doing good at work. You should come on board. I'm sure I could..."

"No," Andie shook her head. "I'm not working for you. School starts in two weeks, and I want Bobbi back home a few days before that, so she can adjust to being home."

"Why not work for me?"

"I'm going to go back to school," Andie said. "Columbus State has an IT program. I could do that kind of work even if I never walk better. I can get my Associate degree in a year and a half. That's enough to get a job."

"Let me help," Ed said. "I can pay your tuition or..."

"I can get student loans, Ed. We're going to be okay; I promise."

"Really?"

"Yeah. Now promise me something."

What?"

"Promise me you won't give up on love. You deserve to be loved."

"Sure," Ed said, wishing it were true.

CHAPTER TWENTY

Ed parked in front of David's Bridal Salon, Sandy waiting impatiently for him on the sidewalk outside the store. They were meeting Becca to see the wedding dress.

Sandy immediately led him to the first display, just a few feet inside the double doors. An ivory wedding gown, with a beaded, sleeveless top over a billowing skirt, sparkled in the sunlight that streamed in through the big picture windows.

"This is it," Sandy said, giggling excitedly.

A tall blonde saleswoman with a tape measure around her neck approached. She wore a pair of reading glasses perched on the end of her nose, a silver chain circling her neck. Except for the tape measure, she was dressed very elegantly, but the big smile plastered on her face reminded Ed of a grandmother who had just finished baking cookies.

"Are we ready?" she asked Sandy.

"C'mon," Sandy said, grabbing Ed's hand and pulling him deeper into the store. Sandy led him to a padded bench near the rear of the store and sat down, pulling Ed down with her. There was a three-tier stage in front of them, surrounded by angled mirrors that would allow brides-to-be to inspect every inch of the dress they had tried on, but would also let everyone in the store see the gown.

Becca came out of the dressing room at the end of a short hallway, walking toward the stage, a shy smile on her face, wearing the gown from the window, Cathy trailing her in a similar gown. Cathy caught up to Becca, grabbing her hand.

Ed stared. He could not breathe. He had never imagined Becca in a wedding gown. She stood there beaming at him, happiness radiating off her in waves like light from the sun, haloed by a misty rainbow. Ed felt like a fool. He had almost driven Becca away, and for what? They deserved every moment of happiness they could tear from this world, and he needed to help them get it.

Lisa was there, he could feel her standing next to him, her hand on his shoulder and he knew she was smiling. She would have loved planning for the wedding as much as the ceremony itself, and for Ed to know that Lisa was somehow here just made the moment even more perfect. That sense of her was gone as quickly as he had felt it, but for the first time since her death he did not feel the chasm of her absence.

"Your daughter could be a model," the saleswoman said. Ed nodded. Becca was beautiful. "I mean it," the clerk said. "Look around."

Ed turned his head. The store had fallen quiet as shoppers stared at the two women in their wedding gowns. A mother and daughter walked closer, stopping near the stage.

"Do you like it, Daddy?" Becca asked. She twirled slowly in front of him.

Ed could not talk. He knew if he tried, he would just sob, so he simply nodded. He felt a hand on his shoulder again, heavier than before. It was the salesclerk. She gave him a hard squeeze.

"You're a lucky man," she whispered, and Ed knew she was right. He was blessed, and his blessing had always been in front of him. He got up from the bench and hugged Becca, and then Cathy, and then the two of them together.

He thought about how he must have sounded when Becca told him she was getting married, full of hate and anger. God had blessed him, and he had almost thrown the blessing away. How could he have been so self-indulgent?

"I owe you an apology," he said. "It's my job to make sure that you feel loved enough and safe enough that you can take big risks and know I'll always be here for you. I failed."

"No, you didn't," Becca said. "The truth is you won't always be here for us. I know that better than anyone. It was good for me to know I was going to do this whether or not you approved, because eventually I'm going to have to face the world alone..."

"Hey!" Cathy said, a grin on her face.

Becca wrapped her arm around Cathy's waist. "We're going to have to face the world alone at some time, Dad. Now we know we can."

"I'm still sorry."

"Good," Sandy said, wrapping her arms around him from behind. "Don't screw up when I get engaged."

• • •

Andie sat on the low stone wall outside the community center, waiting to be picked up from her AA meeting. She'd gone to a meeting every night for the last ten days, finding comfort in the hard truths that were shared again and again. Maybe if she had been this committed to her meetings before, she would have never tried to kill herself. Maybe.

There were too many fucking smokers at this meeting, so she was sitting apart, the laughter and drifting snatches of conversation driving home how alone she was.

A young woman, hardly older than Sandy, broke away from the group and started slowly in Andie's direction. She walked in starts and stops, looking around nervously, like she was ready to bolt in the opposite direction. Andie had seen her twice the last few days.

She stopped a few feet away. "I'm Lynn," she said. "You're Andie, right?"

Andie nodded. "Yeah."

"I'm Lynn," she repeated, looking at the ground as she rolled a pebble under her foot.

"You said that," Andie said, wondering if she had been this awkward when she had started. "What do you need?"

"I'm looking for a sponsor."

"Oh. There are some good folks at this meeting. Glenn is really sharp," Andie said, pointing to an overweight man sitting at a picnic table with the larger group. "My sponsor is Margaret. She's the Black woman on the steps. You should talk with her..."

"I did. She told me I should ask you."

"Fuck no."

"Why not?"

"I've only been sober a couple of years. I'm not ready to sponsor anyone. I'm not sure that I'll ever be ready."

"Margaret said you're really the only one."

"Well, she's wrong. I still want to drink and get high, every single fucking day. It eats at me. I'm not the right person."

"Look, I'm not even an alcoholic," Lynn said. She was twisting her hair around her fingers, looking even younger. "The meetings are okay, I guess, but I don't really want a sponsor. It's not like I'd be a bother. I'm not going to call you every day, or anything."

"Then why the fuck are you asking?"

"It's a condition of my parole," Lynn said, looking away. "I only got drunk a couple of times, but I have to go to AA, and that means I need a sponsor. Margaret said you're the only one."

"She shouldn't have. I can't do it."

"Why not?" Lynn looked like she was going to burst into tears. "If I don't get a sponsor, they'll send me back. Like I said, it's a condition of my parole."

"I killed someone when I was drunk," Andie finally said, expecting the young woman to recoil in disgust.

"I know," Lynn said. "That's why Margaret said you should be my sponsor."

"Margaret fucking told you that?"

Lynn nodded. "She said it wasn't hers to tell, but given the circumstances, she thought you'd be okay with it."

"What fucking circumstances?"

"I just got out of Marysville," Lynn said. "I served three years for vehicular manslaughter."

Andie sucked in her breath, shocked. "How old are you?"

"Twenty."

"Fuck."

"I killed my best friend. People said we looked like sisters. We were going to be roommates in college and marry identical twins, so our kids would look alike. We'd been to a party, and she got hammered. I knew she couldn't drive, so I told her I would drive us home. I didn't have a license, because I'd gotten a DUI a couple of months earlier, but we were only going three miles. I was careful, I didn't speed, I just missed a curve, and I rolled her car.

"We got thrown out of the car. I don't really know what happened. I looked in the car, but she wasn't there. It was so dark, and I couldn't find her in the dark. I sat down after a while and waited for morning."

"I'm sorry."

"Don't be. I really fucked up. I never thought to call for help. Isn't that crazy? I had my cell phone in my pocket the whole time, but I never called for help. I might have been able to save her if I'd just called for help."

Andie shook her head. What the fuck was Margaret thinking? She was supposed to help this kid? She couldn't even help herself.

"I'm not an alcoholic. I just have to show up and give your name to my parole officer. He might call you, making sure I'm coming to meetings, but other than that, I won't be any trouble."

Andie wondered if she was staring in the mirror and seeing herself years ago. Could someone have made a difference for her back then?

A horn honked in the parking lot. Andie looked up and waved. Bobbi was driving, Sandy in the passenger seat. They both waved back. Andie loved that Sandy and Bobbi were spending time together even though she and Bobbi had moved out.

"Is that your family?" Lynn asked. Andie nodded, her eyes misting, feeling ridiculous that she was so emotional over two girls in a car. Without thinking, she held out her hand for Lynn's cell phone. She put in her number and handed the phone back.

"If you want me to be your sponsor, you call me tomorrow, or it's no deal. And I'm not like Margaret. I'm a bitch, and I'll be a bitch to you. No half measures. We do this right, or we don't do it at all."

Lynn nodded. "That's what Margaret said I needed."

Andie shook her head in disgust, uncertain if she was more pissed at Margaret or herself. She grabbed her walker with one hand and pulled herself up and then walked slowly across the lawn towards the car. *What the fuck was Margaret thinking?*

• • •

Ed ran hard, his step light as he circled the track, his breathing heavy but regular. He'd run every morning for the last three weeks, finally back in control of his life. The more mornings he got up and came down to the school and tortured himself for forty minutes, the more normal his life became.

Bobbi and Andie had moved out. Sandy didn't go back to school until September 22nd, but she was on vacation in Florida for ten days with a group of friends from OSU, so Ed was living alone again, and hated it. He told himself that he liked not having to negotiate his schedule with anyone, but that was bullshit. He dreaded waking up alone every morning.

Ed missed Bobbi terribly. She had invited him to breakfast to say thank you; he was picking her up at nine and the clock couldn't move fast enough. Andie Love was another story. She was a sledgehammer, shattering the wall he had built around himself, forcing him to feel again.

He ran his last lap hard, the fastest of the morning, enjoying the ache in his lungs and side and legs. Once he finished, he walked another lap as a cool down, stretching as he walked. His mind kept drifting to a bid he was working on for a couple in Clintonville. They didn't think they had enough room on their cramped lot to do the addition they wanted, but Ed had the perfect solution. His plan tore down the unattached garage, common in so many Clintonville homes, to expand their backyard. He would then convert the existing carriage port to a garage, expand the master bedroom above the new garage, enough new space to add a master bath with a walk-in closet and a small private second story deck. He could do a traditional kitchen remodel as well as the next person, but jobs that challenged his creative side kept him in the business.

As he walked towards his truck, Ed smiled. Maybe all he had needed to get his life back on track was being true to himself. It felt like once he had come to terms that this was his life, that nothing was missing that he needed to replace, then everything had returned to normal. That was all he had ever wanted, wasn't it?

In an hour, he had showered and driven down to Andie's apartment. Bobbi walked out of the apartment as soon as Ed pulled up. She was wearing an embroidered jeans jacket Sandy had given her, her afro bobbing gently with each step. She smiled at Ed as she crossed the parking lot. She looked so different from the girl he had met back in May that Ed grinned. Maybe the summer had been worth it.

"Where are we headed?" Ed asked, once she climbed in the truck.

"Bob Evans."

His heart skipped a beat. "Are you sure?"

"It's the nicest place I can afford."

"That's not a problem," Ed said. "I can get it..."

"No! I said I wanted to take you out. This is my thank you. I'm paying. Bob Evans."

Ed nodded and pulled out of the narrow parking lot. They rode to the restaurant in silence.

"Why don't you go in and get a table? I need to check in at the office."

"Okay." Bobbi slipped out of the truck and headed into Bob Evans. Ed watched her, his heart pounding. When Bobbi had called and asked him to breakfast, he had not imagined they would come here. He had not been to Bob Evans since he and Rebecca had broken up.

Ed followed Bobbi into the restaurant once his heart slowed back to normal. Bobbi was waiting for him near the hostess stand. Ed scanned the restaurant for Rebecca but did not see her. Peggy, the brassy-haired older waitress, was waiting tables on the far side of the room. She glared at Ed when she saw him, and then scurried into the kitchen.

They were seated in about five minutes, Ed grateful he had not bumped into Rebecca. She had always worked Saturdays. Ed wondered if she was hiding in the back.

"I just wanted to thank you," Bobbi said after they had ordered. "I don't know what would have happened if you hadn't helped us. I can never repay you..."

"You are right now."

"Bob Evans isn't what I had in mind."

"That's not what I meant," Ed said. "I think we helped each other."

"Do you mean that?"

"Yes. How's it going with your mom?"

"Good, I guess. I mean she's Mom, it's not like she's rational, but I know she's trying. She signed up for Columbus State. She seems excited about it. She already went to orientation."

"Speaking of college, I'm serious about paying for you to go," Ed said. "Keep your grades up and..."

"Ed, I can't accept your money..."

"Yes, you can. I promised you that I'd pay for you to go to college."

"That's too much."

"No, it's not. And I expect you to work for me again next summer, and summers when you are home from college. Sandy will kill me if you don't come back."

They spent the rest of breakfast chatting. "I have to tell you something," Bobbi said after the waitress dropped off their check, her eyes so blue against her cinnamon skin. "I made you bring me here because I hoped you'd see Rebecca."

"Was this your idea or Sandy's?"

Bobbi flushed, but stared at Ed, her eyes unwavering. "Both, I guess. She tried to get you to bring her here for breakfast the day she left for Florida, but you wouldn't. She told me to drop it then, said you'd get mad, but I couldn't. You looked so happy when you were dating her, Ed. I want you to be happy. Please don't give up on her."

She looked so earnest that Ed couldn't get angry with her. Maybe the girls were right, and he should call Rebecca. He imagined her naked in bed, laughing, her skin so warm against his, and he was surrounded by her smell, her perfume underwritten by maple syrup. He should call.

Bobbi grabbed the check. "I hate to rush," she said, 'But I'm meeting some friends at the mall." Ed told her he'd meet her at the car and headed to the men's room.

Peggy was waiting for him when he came out.

"Rebecca doesn't work here anymore," she said, spitting out the words as if it hurt to speak to him.

"Do what?"

"She's gone. Jim took over a store on Broad Street and she went with him. Said she might meet someone nice there. Don't come back in here, you're not welcome."

Her words were like a knife to his heart, a deep thrust through his soul. Rebecca had left everyone she knew, the people she called her family, just to avoid seeing Ed again. He had done that. He had chased her away from the people she loved.

Ed drove Bobbi home in a daze. She was telling him about a new boy at her school, one she liked, but he was not listening. Once he dropped her off and left, he pulled into the parking lot of the strip mall down the road and sat, his breakfast heavy in his stomach.

The Bob Evans on Broad Street was the one closest to Rebecca's apartment. That had to be good, right? She could get to work in five minutes rather than thirty. And she liked Jim. She had said he really looked out for her during her divorce, so it had to be a good move.

His pulse was racing, the air conditioning in the truck doing nothing to cool him down. He thought he might throw up. Rebecca's absence was an echo of Lisa's, not so deep, but sharp. He had been lying to himself all this time, hoping she still loved him and would call and take him back.

Rebecca was like a desiccated flower, her vitality drained away needlessly by his greedy touch. He had never wanted to create the family she desired, he had just wanted someone, anyone, to love him. He was not worthy of being in love, not ever again.

Ed sighed and started the truck. At least he still had work.

CHAPTER TWENTY-ONE

"Got a minute? About the Sanderson job?" Tom Smith asked.

Ed sighed and set two aluminum pails in the bed of his truck, next to the scrub brush and soap. "Is there a problem?"

"We completed the final punch list on the addition," Tom said. He leaned casually against Ed's truck. "Everybody's happy."

Ed nodded. "Great."

"Final draw is ready."

Ed looked at the older man. "You didn't pick it up when you were there?"

Tom grinned and shook his head. "Nope. I don't handle money."

"Just take care of it, would you?"

Tom's grin faded. "Nope. We got processes, boss. Salesman always picks up the final draw. No exceptions."

Ed frowned. Tom only called him boss when he was giving a lecture. "Alright, I'll set something up."

"Mrs. Sanderson will be home this afternoon," Tom said. He nodded towards the bed of Ed's truck. "I said that would be impossible. I called Marjorie and set up an appointment for Monday, seven in the evening. It's on your calendar." Tom straightened up. At six-five, he towered over Ed. He put a big, meaty hand on Ed's shoulder. "We all miss her, Ed. Wish her Happy Birthday for us."

Ed nodded but said nothing. Tom ambled away, walking through the open garage door into the service bay. Ed stared after him. How do you get mad at the guy who remembers your late wife's birthday?

The cemetery was about a mile from home, on a slight rise, surrounding a defunct white clapboard church. When the wind blew hard enough, the bell in the tower would still ring. Lisa had loved walking the dogs up to the church, especially in the spring when the tulips bloomed. Ed pulled behind the church, following a narrow gravel track to the back corner of the cemetery.

Lisa's marker, and his empty plot, were in the middle of seven other graves, all crowded together under the massive limbs of a big oak tree. A cardinal flittered among the lower branches of the tree. Lisa had loved cardinals, calling out in delight whenever she saw a flash of red near her feeders. Ed wanted to take the bird as a sign, some signal from Lisa that she was still in his life. He got out of the truck once the cardinal flew on, reaching into the bed of the truck to grab the pails. He walked slowly back the way he had driven, to a small outbuilding behind the church. There was a spigot on the side of the building. Ed filled the pails with water and then walked back to the truck, stopping to pour cleaner into one pail and grab a scrub brush.

Ed scrubbed all eight marble stones, washing off the detritus of summer, saving Lisa's for last. He made three trips back to the spigot to fill the pails and rinse the stones clean. Lisa's marker, a swirled pink granite, was smaller than the other, older stones, jutting about ten inches above the ground. Ed knelt next to the stone, dipping his brush into the soapy water and began to scrub the face of the marker gently. He was careful not to read the name on her marker, but it did not matter. His fingers, sliding across the marble face as he rinsed the soap away, caught the cuts in the stone for the 'L,' the "S,' and the 'G.' Lisa Gideon. He glanced down at the stone, wishing for the anger that had buffered his previous visits, but he could not conjure it up. He did not hate Andie Love anymore. Had that been all that was left of his marriage? Ed came every year on Lisa's birthday to scrub the headstone, but that was all. The cemetery held none of Lisa's presence for him, except the terrible memory of watching her casket lowered into the ground. He hated coming here.

The house was quiet when he got home. He let the dogs out back and poured himself a scotch on the rocks and followed them outside. Blackie paused at the edge of the deck, looking back at Ed for direction, while King bumped against Ed's hip. "Go on," he said, waving them away, although he understood why they were unsettled. The house was empty again. Ed wondered if he should sell the place. After this summer he knew the house needed the energy of a family; it seemed selfish to keep it just for himself and the dogs. The girls would argue it was still their home, but wasn't that more nostalgia than truth?

The real reason he had never considered moving was the fear he would lose Lisa forever. As empty as the cemetery was, the house was full of her. Lisa was so present that Ed could call the place haunted, except she comforted him. This was the place she had been happiest. Maybe that was why she had refused the hotel – she would have rather made love here, in their bed, than in some antiseptic hotel.

Ed took a sip of the scotch and settled into his chair on the deck. Lisa would have sat next to him, her chair catching the late afternoon sun while his was already in the shade. He was not ready to sell, not yet. Lisa seemed happy with the thought. She was not ready to lose him, either.

The wind rustled among the leaves of the trees behind the house and the songbirds were trilling softly. The cicadas hummed in the fields underneath it all. The effect, however, was stillness. A moment when everything was in its proper place, and things were as they should be. Had that been the lesson of his summer, that things were as they should be?

No.

Ed took another, longer, swallow of the scotch. He could not let himself off the hook that easily. He had had the opportunity to change his life this summer and he screwed it up. His fear of being alone had made him greedy and selfish. Rebecca had deserved his faithfulness. He had used and hurt her. Jane had deserved his patience, that he not run away at the first obstacle, but also his self-control. He should never have made love to her while he was dating Rebecca.

Forgive yourself. That was Lisa, who knew the hurt he had caused, but who could still love him. *If you can forgive Andie Love, you can forgive yourself.*

The idea startled Ed. Had he forgiven Andie Love? Maybe. Perhaps it just helped to know Andie Love accepted responsibility for what she had done. Ed sighed. Was that what he had to do for Rebecca? Her pain had been palpable the night he had broken up with her, but he had not realized how devastated she was until he had been confronted by Peggy. He wished he could make it better.

Ed pulled his cell phone from his pocket and scrolled to his text messages. Her last message before they'd broken up had been a picture of the Princess cake she was going to get Lily for her birthday. Ed had responded, 'nice.' Jesus, he had been a coward. He took a deep breath, his head throbbing, his heart racing in his chest. Did he dare? Ed slowly tapped out a message, repeatedly correcting it, his fingers as big around as cucumbers.

I'm sorry for the hurt I caused you.

You deserve to be loved and I wish the best for you.

He stared at the words, his thumb hovering over the send button. Lisa's presence was gone, replaced by the ache in his neck and chest. Rebecca would appreciate his effort, wouldn't she? He could imagine her reading it, a slow smile forming on her lips as she took in the words, able, now, to release the hurt...

"Fuck," he muttered, and deleted the text. He set his phone on the table and drained his scotch. His pulse slowed, the ache in his chest receding.

Andie Love was right. Sometimes an apology was self-serving and meaningless. He wanted to tell himself that he had done the right thing. More than that, he wanted Rebecca to absolve him, but he did not deserve her forgiveness.

He slumped back in his chair, defeated and alone. Even Lisa was gone. He tried to conjure her up, wanting her love and acceptance, but she would not come. Maybe Lisa was right, and he needed to forgive himself. Not for what he had done, but for fighting what was. You can never beat the universe.

Ed watched the dogs nosing around the barn. They were happy. That was something, wasn't it?

• • •

A brilliant pillar of light sliced through the heavy clouds as Ed pulled into Jane's driveway. The late afternoon rain had broken and now, at seven, the day was beautiful. Ed pulled the truck around the top of the circle drive near the barn, so he was headed back toward Riverside Drive. He was nervous, and it irritated him. This was just a formality to pick up the check. There was no reason to feel nervous, except for Jane. Ed was uncomfortable about how they had ended their... fling? It had felt like more, but how could it have been?

Jane was waiting on the new stone patio. She was wearing a parchment-colored linen dress, belted at the waist, which captured her simple elegance perfectly. She raised her hand partway in greeting and smiled nervously. As he walked across the yard towards the patio, he could feel his heart hammering in his chest. Jane was so beautiful. Not just in a physical way. He immediately felt the connection he had had with her. Ed realized how much he had missed her and felt a deep pang of regret.

He had never admitted how badly Jane had hurt him, because that meant admitting how deeply he had loved her. She was the fulcrum between Lisa and Rebecca, while Rebecca had been the opposite, and therefore never possible. Jane had always been the dangerous one, the one who could capture his heart, made even more dangerous when she admitted being in love with Lisa. What had upset him so much? Of course, she had loved Lisa.

"Ed," Jane said.

"You look lovely," Ed said, frozen just off the patio.

"Thank you."

Ed just stared at her. He had thought he had moved past her, moved past the way his heart pounded when he saw her, moved past that longing to take her in his arms and hold her tight, moved past the need for her touch, but he had been lying to himself. She captivated him, just standing there. He had no right to hope she might consider taking him back. Dare he ask?

"You did a wonderful job on my house," William Sanderson said, coming out from the French doors that opened into the kitchen.

"Bill," Ed said, trying to cover the shock he felt. "I'm surprised to see you here."

"I like to know how my money's been spent," Sanderson said. He stopped next to Jane and put his arm around her waist. She laid her hand over his. Ed stared, feeling the blush on his face and the regret in his heart. Had he fucked it up that badly?

Sanderson held out a check to Ed. "Here's the final draw," he said. "I deducted money for fraternization, but everything else is there."

Ed gave him a puzzled look.

"I'm just shitting you," Sanderson said, grinning tightly. "I actually want to thank you for convincing me to spend the money and do this project right. I hate to think what a mess I would have gotten if I'd signed with Parkhurst. The patio alone makes this house so much more than it was and the addition—I can't tell what was original and where the new work starts. Just fabulous work. And you beat your deadline. You promised me you'd be done by the end of September and it's only the twenty-first."

"I'm delighted you're pleased," Ed said, looking at Jane. Why was Bill Sanderson touching Jane so intimately?

"The only thing Parkhurst would have gotten right is that he wouldn't have fucked my wife," Sanderson said.

The words hit Ed like a slap in the face. He stepped back, and then forward, clenching his hand into a fist, searching for words. Jane looked down, a deep blush blooming across her features.

Bill raised a hand to keep Ed from speaking. "I'll acknowledge that I'd given her cause, so I'm not blaming you. I'm just saying it ruins your character reference, so even though I love the quality of the work you've done here I'll be unwilling to recommend you to any of my colleagues or clients. In fact, I'll tell them to use someone else if it ever comes up. Probably even if it doesn't."

"Bill and I are going to get married again," Jane said quietly. "I told him everything."

"Take your fucking check," Sanderson said, holding it out to Ed.

Ed stepped forward, half expecting Sanderson to snatch the check away, but the older man didn't move. Ed took the check and started to leave. His whole being ached, inside and out, like it had just after Lisa died.

"Wait," Sanderson said.

Ed stopped, looking over his shoulder at the older man.

"There are questions about the barn," Sanderson said. "Jane has them. You need to answer them and then get the fuck off my property."

"Let me show you," Jane said. She stepped off the patio and headed toward the barn. Sanderson glared after her for a second and then went inside the house.

Ed watched Jane walking to the barn for several seconds before following. He was having difficulty breathing; it felt like a stake had been driven through his chest. Jane had disappeared inside the barn by the time he took a step. He knew he had no right to have feelings for her, but he could not believe that she had taken Sanderson back. It was his fault that she was going to spend the rest of her life with a man who had humiliated her just to put Ed in his place. He followed her to the barn.

She was waiting for him just inside the door. "I'm sorry," she said.

"You better find a new contractor to finish the barn," Ed said. "I'm pulling my guys out tomorrow."

"Please don't," Jane said. "I'm truly sorry. I didn't think he was going to be like that. You're almost done here."

"I don't care. My crews are finished. We will not step foot on this property again except to clean up. We'll be off site by noon tomorrow."

Jane pursed her lips in a failing bid to keep from crying.

"You should have told me he was going to be here."

"I didn't think he was going to act like that."

"Do what? Your husband is a bully, of course he was going to act like that."

"You're right," Jane said. She dabbed at the tears in her eyes with her bare hand. "You wouldn't have come if you'd known Bill was going to be here. I wanted to say goodbye."

"Write me a damn letter, like other people do," Ed said. "What happened here?"

"The day after we signed the dissolution agreement, Bill called me. He said he felt awful about what he'd done. He'd dropped his girlfriend. I told him I didn't care. He asked to meet and talk. I don't know why I agreed. It was the day after we... broke up? So, I met with him. For the first time, he was honest with me. He admitted what I suspected and some stuff I didn't. Said he was ready to change. I told him about you.

"Bill told me he didn't care, that I deserved some happiness and he'd earned my actions. Said he loved me and wanted to come home..."

"So, you took him back?"

"No, not immediately. I kept hoping you and I would talk, but we never did. He was calling me five and six times a day. Finally, he invited me to a party he was throwing for his clients. It was in the office, with a band and an open bar. He had been pestering me for weeks. I agreed just to get him to stop calling me, at least that's what I told myself. We drank too much and made love on his desk. He moved back in the next day."

"How did I miss all of this?"

"We were in the guest room down the hall. You never went in there. I left my notes in the master bedroom. I didn't want to hurt you." Ed could see the tears trickling down her face in the gloom of the barn. He realized this was all his fault, just like Rebecca had been. He had destroyed both women who tried to love him.

"I need to apologize," he said. "I'm sorry."

"Apologize? For what?"

"For running out on you when you said you'd been in love with Lisa. I don't know why I freaked out. I should have asked you to explain more of what you meant. I'm sorry I wasn't... good enough to just accept what you said."

Jane laughed. It was the saddest sound Ed could imagine. "Why do you think I told you? I felt so guilty, like I was leading you on. I knew you'd leave.

I needed to push you away. We'd gotten too close, and I wasn't sure if I was falling in love with you or with my memories of Lisa. You have nothing to apologize for."

"No," Ed said. "I do. I haven't been myself this summer. I broke all my own rules. I never should have let myself get so close to a client..."

"You're apologizing for making love with me?"

"Hell, no," Ed said fiercely. "I'll never apologize for that. Making love to you was the best thing I did this summer..."

"It was?" Jane asked, her eyes glistening.

"Of course, it was," Ed said. "It hurts me deeply that I let what you said about Lisa scare me away. I'm sorry I didn't have the courage to discover the truth."

"What truth?"

"That I was falling in love with you."

"I didn't want you to discover that, Ed. I pushed you away to make sure it never happened. I wasn't ready to have you say that to me. Bill and I had too much going on for me to reciprocate." She paused for a moment, her eyes alive in the gloom.

The rain started again, drumming on the rooftop in an irregular staccato beat that reminded Ed of a jazz trio. Of the jazz trio at the club where he and Lisa had danced the night she died. He turned his head and watched the downpour through the partially open barn door, the rain a heavy curtain separating them from Bill and the house. The downpour also brought back the memory of making love to Jane, here in the barn, while it poured outside. Both were moments that had changed his life forever.

"What ever happened with your houseguests?" Jane asked, drawing him back, her voice soft against the rain.

"Bobbi is back in school. Andie is going to Columbus State."

"They're still living with you?"

"No, they moved out a couple of weeks ago. Bobbi turned sixteen and got her driver's license. I think they'll be okay."

"You really helped Andie Love. I'm still amazed at that."

"Don't be. It wasn't as simple as it sounds."

"How so?"

"You develop a kind of intimacy when someone is living in your home for more than a few days. There were moments that felt normal, like we were all family. It was really weird, especially because there were also moments when I thought about burning down the house with Andie Love inside and just going to prison for the rest of my life."

Jane's eyes got big. "Really?"

Ed nodded. "It was much harder than I thought it was going to be. I couldn't ignore that she was there. It made me more aware than ever that Lisa was gone. The thing is, Andie's not a monster, she just did a horrible thing. She's never going to let herself forget it."

"Good."

"Yeah, but it holds her back. She deserves to be loved, just like you. It's hard to acknowledge that I really want the best for her."

"Your secret is safe with me. What about Rebecca?"

"We broke up."

"I'm sorry to hear that," Jane said, reaching out and putting her hand on Ed's arm. Her touch was like a shot of adrenaline, making his heart race even faster. "She seemed nice."

"She is nice," Ed said. "At some other time in my life it might have worked out, but I wasn't ready."

"Are you sure? You would light up when you mentioned her."

Ed smiled. "Yeah, I'm sure. And I was an idiot, talking with one lover about another. I deserve to be alone."

"We weren't lovers when you told me about her. You looking happy made me realize I really deserved to be happy as well. I'm sorry it didn't work out."

"Are you happy?"

"What?"

"Are you happy? With Bill?"

"He's changed, Ed. Not that you could tell tonight, but he really has. He spends more time with me and less with the business."

"But are you happy?"

Jane shrugged. "I'm not sure I know what happy is. I know I'm in a better place than I was at the start of the summer. Maybe that's happy."

"You deserve more than that," Ed said. "You deserve to be with a man who would never humiliate you to make a point, not for any reason."

"It's not that simple, Ed." She was quiet for a few seconds. "I don't want to be alone for the rest of my life. My time with you made me realize that. Bill needs me, and I need to be needed. I know it's not a perfect relationship, but something like what you and Lisa had doesn't happen for everyone. I'll be fine."

"That's not enough," Ed said. "You don't realize what an incredible woman you are. You deserve a man who is going to celebrate every moment he gets with you, and you'll never get that from Bill. He's incapable of making you the center of his life."

Jane shrugged. "Maybe, but..."

"Marry me," Ed said, his heart hammering in his chest. He knew the words were right before he realized he was thinking them.

"What?"

"Marry me. You'll never be happy with Bill, but you can be happy with me. I love you."

"You're serious?" Jane stared at him, her face suddenly pale, her eyes enormous.

"Hell, yes, I'm serious."

"You're really asking me to marry you? Knowing the man I've committed my life to is in my home, just a few feet away? You're asking me to let go of all this to be with you?"

Ed wondered if he was making a mistake, but then he knew he didn't care. What had Becca said to him about fighting for what he wanted?

"Yes," he said.

"How can I do that? We're planning our..."

"You're not married yet. Don't marry Bill, marry me."

"Why would I..."

"Because you love me. Because you loved Lisa. Because we're right for each other. I love you."

Jane stared at him, frozen. "You really are serious?"

"Hell, yes. I get that it'll be a mess. Bill will be an ass. He'll probably try to destroy me and my company. He's got enough money he might succeed, but I don't care. Marry me."

Jane took a step closer to Ed. "You're crazy, Ed. Bill will come after you with everything he has. I can't do that to you."

"You won't be doing it. You'll be my wife. Let's go down to the courthouse tomorrow and get a license and get married."

"What about the girls?"

"We can tell them after."

"No, I won't do that," Jane said, shaking her head and looking away.

"You won't?" Ed felt like she had knifed him in the heart, crushing his soul. She didn't love him?

She looked back at him, a slight smile on her face. "I won't tell your girls after we get married and have them hate me. They have to be there. All three of them."

Ed gave her a puzzled look.

"Becca, Sandy, and Bobbi."

"Four of them," he said, smiling back at her, his heart jumping.

"What?"

"Becca's engaged. Cathy's a lovely girl, and she's part of the family now."

Jane raised her eyebrows, but then grinned. "Okay. All four of them. Hell, even Andie Love, for all I care. Maybe it will help her move on with her life to see you happy."

"Do you mean it? You'll marry me?"

"Yes, I mean it," Jane said, a goofy-looking grin on her face. "I would love to spend the rest of my life with you."

Ed wrapped his arms around her, feeling the heat of her body against his in the cooling evening air. The kiss, so reminiscent of their first, lifted him clear of the gloom that had seemed to swallow up the light of day. Even in the barn, everything was crystal clear, almost glowing from within. He broke away to stare at her, wondering how God had blessed him so deeply, out of the blue, when only moments ago, he had felt abandoned and empty.

The blessing he had thrown away had come back to him, that was it. Jane had been offered once before and he had refused, and God, for whatever reason, had offered her again. Ed thought he might cry. Forgive me my willfulness, he thought, but of course God already had. And Jane had said yes.

"We need to tell Bill," Jane said.

"Fuck Bill," Ed said. "We can call him from the truck."

Jane took Ed by the hand and pointed out at the rain. "We're gonna get soaked."

"Yeah, we are."

They ran out of the barn into the downpour.

ABOUT THE AUTHOR

Jefferson was raised in rural Ohio, the second of four boys. The original free-range children, Jefferson and his brothers spent their time hunting and fishing and exploring the countryside around them and are still surprised they all survived into adulthood.

Jefferson currently serves as the Vice President of Enrollment Management and Marketing at Otterbein University, a private university in Westerville, Ohio. Previously, Jefferson taught college composition, worked as a telemarketer, a sales manager, a construction superintendent and a vice president of marketing. He and his wife Denise have three grown children.

NOTE FROM THE AUTHOR

Word-of-mouth is crucial for any author to succeed. If you enjoyed *Love*, please leave a review online—anywhere you are able. Even if it's just a sentence or two. It would make all the difference and would be very much appreciated.

Thanks!
Jefferson R. Blackburn-Smith

We hope you enjoyed reading this title from:

BLACK ROSE
writing™

www.blackrosewriting.com

Subscribe to our mailing list – *The Rosevine* – and receive **FREE** books, daily deals, and stay current with news about upcoming releases and our hottest authors.
Scan the QR code below to sign up.

Already a subscriber? Please accept a sincere thank you for being a fan of Black Rose Writing authors.

View other Black Rose Writing titles at www.blackrosewriting.com/books and use promo code **PRINT** to receive a **20% discount** when purchasing.

CPSIA information can be obtained
at www.ICGtesting.com
Printed in the USA
JSHW030733210623
43527JS00005B/23